Norman Waller is married with four children.

He has a smallholding in the Cotswolds that takes in rescue animals.

His previous book, *Flip of a Coin*, was published by Austin Macauley in 2016.

He has been a Samaritan for over twenty years.

Dedication

For
my children
James, Tina, George, Edward

Norman Waller

ANATOMY OF A SECRET

AUSTIN MACAULEY PUBLISHERS™

LONDON * CAMBRIDGE * NEW YORK * SHARJAH

ISBN 978-1-78823-601-0 (Paperback)
ISBN 978-1-78823-602-7 (Hardback)
ISBN 978-1-78823-603-4 (E-Book)

www.austinmacauley.com

First Published (2018)
Austin Macauley Publishers™ Ltd
25 Canada Square
Canary Wharf
London
E14 5LQ

Acknowledgements

My special thanks to Emma Evans
for her haunting book cover design

He'd gone now, and she lay quite still – feeling sick, hurting, utterly alone. She wasn't going to cry. She wanted to, but it did no good. There was only one person who could save her now and that was her father, but he was gone forever. So she would never be happy again.

Chapter One

The telephone rang. John put down his mug of coffee and smiled at his colleague.

'My turn, Linda,' he said. He walked into the booth, lowered himself into the chair and lifted the receiver.

'Samaritans – can I help you?'

There was silence, but John knew there was someone hanging on at the other end. He had been a volunteer for more than 12 years, and in that time, he had learnt to use that third ear which all volunteers developed and fine-tuned the longer they served. For a few moments, he listened to the silence, the phone pressed tightly to his ear, and then he spoke quietly, barely above a whisper.

'If you don't want to speak for a little while, that's fine. I've got plenty of time. I won't go away.'

The sound of a stifled breath, perhaps a whisper, drifted into his ear, and then silence again. He sensed the breath was delicate, weak and not that of a man, but more than that, he wouldn't speculate. Many years ago, at his training, it was impressed on him never to make assumptions as invariably they would be wrong. Listen to what the caller says and respond carefully to what you are told without jumping to conclusions. A misplaced word in response to a wrong assumption could be met with the phone going dead and the caller being lost.

'Sometimes the hardest part is knowing how to start and what to say.' His voice was gentle and slow, and after a moment, he heard a faint whisper. The sound seemed from a female voice, and young – but how young he couldn't tell. Over the years, he had spoken to hundreds of women in crisis. Often he didn't know their ages except they had ranged from teenage to those who were well past the age of retirement. The weeping of a woman through the loss of her elderly husband could sometimes be the same as a young woman broken in spirit because of being continually brutalised by her husband or partner.

'It's taken a lot of courage for you to call us so don't hang up. I can stay with you as long as you like, and you can speak to me only when you feel comfortable.' John sank back into his seat and listened intently for a response, but none came. Yet, his gut told him that whoever it was on the other end of the line, they were desperate to try and speak even though they were probably in turmoil. It was always tricky to try and encourage the caller to stay on the line, to relate a few words about the misery in their lives; but if you pushed too hard you could frighten them off. It was a fine line, and he had got it wrong on several occasions and lost the caller. He had always found it hard because he knew that sometimes he might have failed someone who had rung in desperate need. Other volunteers felt the same. Nothing was ever guaranteed. One of the most difficult parts of the job was not knowing what happened to the caller once the call had ended. Many of them would still be nursing their pain even though they may have found some comfort for a short while, as they talked to someone who seemed to care. Others, those who might have been suicidal, could still have crept away to find a dark and friendless space to end their life.

'Perhaps you can tell me if something has just happened, or has something unpleasant in your life been going on for some time?' John squeezed the phone in his hand. Had he pushed too hard? Would the caller be frightened off and hang up? He waited, but still no sound, and then he heard a faint weeping. He strained his ear to the phone. Was that the sound of a word being spoken? Surely, that was a young voice: very young – a child? Oh Christ, he didn't want that – the toughest of all calls.

'A year…' such a faint and timid whisper.

John didn't reply immediately. Better to keep things easy; relaxed. It was a good start – hopefully a real break-through – but he would let the caller choose if they wanted to say any more before he interrupted.

He heard the stifled weeping again and decided to gently press once more.

'A year is a long time.'

'Yes.' Just the faintest whisper again.

'My name is John. Do you want to tell me your name?' There was silence again, and John cursed himself for having put the question too soon.

'Bobby.'

He knew immediately this was the sound of a young girl's voice and, instinctively, he pressed into the phone, imagining in some strange way that he would be closer to her, giving her a sense of protection.

'Hallo, Bobby, I'm so glad you rang.' Again he allowed the silence to hang between them but felt that there was the glimmer of some genuine communication between them.

'How old are you, Bobby?'

Damn! That was too clumsy!

'Nine.' The voice was a little stronger now.

'Nine. You were very brave to ring us, Bobby.'

Across the room, Linda lifted her head and caught his eye. Instinctively, she knew this was going to be a tough call. Like most of the other volunteers, she found that the hardest calls – though not very frequent – were probably from children. She gave him a smile of encouragement, feeling for both him and the child at the other end of the line.

'You sound as if there's something really unhappy in your life.'

Again he was met with silence, except for some stifled weeping. Okay, he wasn't going to make assumptions, but he'd try and help her along and try and get to the target.

'Sometimes, it can be too difficult to say what's wrong, so I'll ask you a couple of questions, and you can answer just yes or no. Is that okay? I'll tell you firstly that everything you say will be confidential. We don't tell anyone. What you say to us on the phone will never be revealed to anyone else.' He waited a few moments and hoped that she would feel safe, for he knew that many callers had a terrible fear of being exposed and feared that what they were saying might get back to those from whom they most wished to keep it secret.

'Maybe you're being bullied at school.' He thought he heard the rhythm of her breathing change; maybe she was just taking a deep breath. Did that mean anything? Was his question getting close? He waited, but the silence dragged on. Would she hang up if he pressed her further? Damn it, he was desperate not to lose her. And yet, deep down, he had this sense that she was by his side and wasn't going to run. She wanted his help, his trust; she wanted to tell him of this dreadful misery in her life; someone who would listen to her pain and believe that what she said was true and not be punished for it. He put the mouthpiece even closer to him as if he was going to whisper in her ear; he had to be gentle; he could be making a dreadful mistake. 'Okay Bobby, let's try something else. Maybe someone has been hurting you… someone close perhaps…even someone at home.'

There was a long silence.

'Yes.' The sound was weak, but he felt the commitment in her voice.

'That was very brave of you to tell me. I'm going to ask you something else, but you don't have to answer if you don't want to. This thing that's being done to you, is it to do with touching your body in private places?'

He'd put it to her now, and there was no pulling back. Was his instinct right, and if it was, would that awful question send her reeling with more shattering pain? There was a long, dragged out silence, but he knew she was still there.

'Yes.'

In that single word, he felt the utter frailty, innocence and desperate despair of a broken child. And yet, perhaps, not completely broken. She was there, close, reaching out with a stifled scream for something, for someone to soothe her pain. John felt his eyes screw tightly shut, and his fingers squeezed on the phone as he huddled more closely over it. What could he say? What could he offer that wouldn't limp down the line and be no more than a useless sound, offering no comfort, no help. But he couldn't give help; not what most people would think of as help. It was not something they could do, no matter how much volunteers felt the urge to offer solutions for their callers' misery. It was not within their power, and there was no magic wand for removing their pain. All he could offer was some sense of compassion, a tiny finger of understanding, a simple feeling that someone cared.

'Who does these things to you, Bobby?' As soon as he'd asked the question, he feared it might be too much.

'Simon.' There was no hesitation and her voice was clearer now. Still frail, but she was in conversation.

'Simon. Who is Simon?'

'He's my...' She paused before going on. 'He married Mummy, but he's not my father.'

Christ, the poor kid was trapped. He must be her step-father. Linda caught his eye across the room and gave a nod to let him know that she had picked up the vibes and was there in any way to support.

'Have you tried telling your mum what happens?'

'She wouldn't listen. I said he kissed me...that he did more than that. She said it was normal because he loved me. She said I was making a fuss because he wasn't Daddy and that Simon was a good man and sends people to prison. She said that what I was telling her wasn't bad, and that I should be pleased because he loved me. But she didn't want to listen, and she didn't understand.'

John lowered the phone and stared at it as if it was a living thing that was relating what he was hearing. The muscles in his face grew taut, and his jaw clamped tight. He stared at the phone in anger, and then lifted it back to his ear.

'Men who do these things to children are put in prison.'

'It's my fault.'

'It's not your fault, Bobby. Never think that.'

'I don't want anyone to know. They'll all hate me. You won't tell anyone, will you?'

'Of course we won't. And people don't hate you.'

'They would do. I know they would. I would kill myself. I really would so I could be with Daddy.'

'We love you. Your mother loves you really... Surely she does.'

'I wish my daddy was here.'

'Where is your daddy?'

'He was killed. Another car ran into him when he was driving.'

John heard a door slam in the background.

'I gotta go!' The phone went dead.

'Bobby! Bobby!' He held the phone away from him. 'Shit! Shit! Bastard!' Anger, frustration, despair raced through every part of his body as he snapped the phone back into its cradle. Linda came over to him.

'What happened?'

'I dunno. Someone must have been coming. She scarpered like a frightened rabbit.'

****

Bobby heard the footsteps stop at the top of the stairs and then further steps coming up from behind. She pushed her phone under the pillow and pulled the duvet tightly round her. She caught the words of her mother's voice, 'Peep into Bobby's room, and see if she's all right, darling.'

'Will do, my love,' Simon's voice replied.

Bobby immediately tightened her jaw and sunk deeper into the duvet. A moment passed, and she heard the bottom of the door scuff across the carpet as it was slowly pushed open. A shaft of light from the landing lanced across the middle of her bed. She lay still and imagined Simon peering around the door. A moment later, she could just hear his footfall on the carpet as he moved towards her bed. Would he hear her heart pounding? Would he notice her tense breathing and know that she was faking sleep? Surely it was too dark for him to see her closed eyelids flicker as a giveaway that she was really wide awake. For a few moments, there was stillness, utter silence, and she heard and felt his hot breath hovering close to her. A hand gently pulled back the hair covering her cheek. She knew her lids would flutter but prayed it was too dark for him to guess she was awake.

'Good night, sweetheart. You were so lovely earlier on,' his voice was barely a whisper. She felt his lips touch her cheek and linger for a moment, but then he moved away, and the door closed behind him. She sank beneath the duvet and cried.

****

Linda came and stood close to John in the phone booth. 'Are you okay?'

'I hate those calls. When a kid's being abused. Step-father. Her own father was killed in a car crash. She's nine, for Christ's sake.'

'It sounds as if she was pleased to talk to you. You did what you could, John.'

He stood up and came out of the booth. He stared at her and shook his head wearily.

'I know we can't do more, but you always feel so bloody useless; especially with a child.'

Linda gently touched his arm and looked at him with a reassuring smile. 'Perhaps she'll call again. We'll warn the next volunteers on shift.'

John nodded in resignation that he had done what he was there to do. He could do no more. All their callers rang because they were suffering, and if they could give them nothing more than kind words, perhaps some encouragement to help them on their way, then so be it. That's all any of the volunteers could do.

They both sat down and stared at each other across the table. She knew what he was feeling, and he knew that she knew what he was feeling. It was the same for all the volunteers when they'd had a bad call. Of course, he'd have to ring in to his shift leader and off-load before their shift finished at midnight, but he was glad to have someone like Linda on this shift with him tonight. She'd been a volunteer for nearly as long as him and had become one of his best friends. Linda was about 39 and was married to Clive, who had a job connected with the railways. John had met him a few times but didn't know much else about him. Linda had talked to him about the marriage going through a sticky patch. Reading between the lines, he guessed that Clive was a bit of a bully and there were suspicions that he was not entirely loyal. It saddened him because Linda was such a lovely woman and deserved a good man. She managed a small florist shop in town and was always bringing in the odd bunch of flowers to brighten up the Centre.

Samaritans had become a big part in John's life. He'd been drawn to the idea of giving what little help he could to those who were scraping the bottom of the barrel. In a world where religions were in conflict with each other and at war within themselves, the Sams offered a simple philosophy of being non-judgemental. There was a profound sense of caring and support in the movement, not just for the callers but for each other. Because everything that was said to them by their callers was confidential and was the bedrock of the movement, it was necessary to have each other's support because they couldn't share anything that callers had told them with anyone outside the branch. The fact that callers knew that everything they said was confidential and anonymous meant they could feel able to reveal terrible things in their lives with a sense of relief that no one else would know, especially those who might be close to them or even involved in their particular misery.

When John was in his teens, he was fairly athletic and had played as a creditable wing-forward for his school rugby team and then for a local club after he had left school. After university, he had managed to build a small engineering company in which he employed a dozen staff. His life had changed dramatically when he met Charlotte, whom he married 15 years ago. He never believed that anyone as pretty as her could possibly have looked twice at him. He wasn't bad looking but was unlikely to immediately draw attention when he walked into a room. His dark hair was thick and unruly, and his nose was slightly bent from an injury whilst playing rugby, but it was only slight and many people didn't notice it. His mouth was wide and exposed a good set of teeth set in a firm jaw. He had an engaging smile. He was lucky enough to be able to eat anything without putting on weight, and he had always kept his body trim and fit by pounding the tarmac a couple of times a week. In any case, Charlotte fell for him, and they were married within six months of their first meeting. She had been a great support to him when he went through lean and difficult times setting up his business and neither of them had ever strayed. Charlotte would have made a good volunteer in the Samaritans but was content to support John, look after the home and bring up their nine-year-old daughter, Suzie. Many of her contemporaries thought it must be a dull existence, but she reckoned that was their problem, not hers.

Linda stood up. 'Come on, John. It's half past eleven. The new shift will be here in a minute. We'd better ring in and off-load. I'll turn off one of the lines and let you go first.'

'Okay. I won't be long'. He smiled and went to the phone in the other room. He'd unload, and when he left the building he'd leave all his calls behind.

****

Bobby suddenly woke and her body went rigid. She held her breath and listened, but all she could hear was the sound of the rain against the windows. Through the darkness, she could see from the little digital clock on her bedside table that it had gone midnight. Her thoughts drifted back to earlier in the evening, while her mother had gone out on her weekly visit to her friends, when Simon had come to her bedroom.

The more she tried to put out of her mind the thoughts of him and what he did, and made her do, the more they clung to her. The smell of his horrible flesh near her face nearly made her sick even before he pushed it into her mouth. His honeyed words and panting filled her with revulsion. Why did he have to do it, and then make her think it was best for her to keep it a secret? He'd told her what could happen if she ever tried to reveal what he did. As long as they both kept it secret, he could protect her.

She was just a child, and no one cared about what she thought or said. She knew his power and how everyone respected him and thought he was wonderful.

Nobody would believe anything she said against him and they would all turn against her.

She screwed up her eyes to force back tears as she thought about her father. Every time she pictured his face, his laughing smile, the way he used to hold out his arms as she ran to him, she thought her heart would break. Why couldn't Mummy understand how much she missed him? Why couldn't she understand how much Simon frightened her? Of course, he didn't love her; he only loved Mummy and Mummy wouldn't believe anything bad she said about Simon. Why did she always say it was just because she was missing Daddy and that

19

gradually she would realise how much Simon loved them and wanted to look after them? He was horrible, and she hated him, and he'd never be able to replace her daddy.

She turned on her side and curled up as if the position would give her some kind of protection. Thoughts of the phone call she had made earlier crept into her mind. She was glad she had made it. She had thought about it for weeks but couldn't find the courage. She had been terrified that it would all come out. That no one would believe her and that men would come and arrest her and send her to prison for telling lies. Mummy wouldn't help her. Daddy wasn't there. She would be all alone and would never be loved again.

She would find a way to kill herself. It would be better than the world staring at her and pointing the finger at her for being such a dreadful person. Everyone at school would laugh at her and despise her, and she would have nowhere to run to. The whole school had been given lectures by the headmistress about not talking to strangers. And there had been lots of talk about how some children had been abused by famous people in the past. But Simon was different. He was married to Mummy, who loved him, and she knew that anything she said about him would brand her as a liar.

She lay still, letting her thoughts swirl and drift in and out of her mind. The man on the phone had been kind and seemed to understand that she wasn't bad, and that it wasn't her fault which Simon had always said. But it must be her fault because she hadn't tried to stop him and run straight to her mother. After the first time Simon had done it, he had tried to be extra kind so that if she said anything nobody would believe her. They'd think she was a horrible little liar, and Mummy would believe everything Simon said because he was so convincing.

But the man on the phone – John was his name – had said that she should never think it was her fault; that it was Simon who was doing a bad thing. And he also promised that he would never tell anybody; that if she rang again and spoke to somebody else it wouldn't be any different. It would always be secret, and she could feel safe talking to them and telling them how she felt. They would believe her. Just like Daddy.

She suddenly felt a little better and sat up, now wide awake. She switched on the bedside lamp, got out of bed and went over to the chest of drawers where she kept some of her clothes. She opened the bottom drawer and slipped her hand to the bottom of the neatly folded clothes and pulled out a large notepad. She found a pencil and climbed back into bed. Inside the cover was her favourite photograph of her father. She turned over a few pages until she reached the page where she found her last entry. She thought for a moment and then began writing.

****

The voice of John Humphrys from the radio began to compete with the hiss of the kettle as it came to the boil. Charlotte poured the water into the teapot which she brought over to the table that was neatly laid out. In her eyes, the only way to eat any meal, even breakfast, was sitting down at the table. Sitting on the sofa and eating meals would happen in her household over her dead body. Radio in the kitchen was okay, mostly to catch the news as Charlotte had found she didn't have a lot of time for reading newspapers except to keep an interest in the economy and pass the occasional comment on the views of business gurus, a couple of which she had known at university. She was only 40 and wondered, sometimes, whether or not she might like to go back to work – perhaps part-time – when Suzie was older.

She sat down opposite John and stared at him as he delved into a sheaf of business papers next to him. He put a piece of toast into his mouth without looking up. She knew he'd been under quite a bit of pressure recently, having suddenly experienced difficulty getting money in from clients who were normally good payers. They were obviously having trouble too. He'd told her everything would be all right, but she guessed things were worse than what he'd let on and that's why he had become short-tempered and bloody-minded. At least, that was a recent pattern of his behaviour.

Charlotte was petite with short, fair hair. Although she loved the summer, she couldn't stay in hot sun for long periods because her skin was so pale, and she came out in freckles which was one of the things he found attractive about her. As a young teenager, she was good at gymnastics and was thought to have a big future in it, but she wasn't prepared to make the commitment. Instead, because she could run fast, she took up hockey and, for a couple of seasons, played for the county.

'It's half term next week. Will you have any time off, do you think?' said Charlotte and took a piece of toast for herself. John made no reply but continued to mumble to himself as he pondered the documents.

Charlotte looked skyward and silently counted to five. 'John!' Her voice cut across the table and startled him.

'Oh…err, sure. We'll fix up something.' His head dropped back to the documents, and she knew he was hardly aware of what he was saying.

'John! What did I just stay?'

John looked up and shook his head as if trying to refocus.

'Err…what?'

'For God's sake, John! Will you get your head out of that stuff and talk to me?'

John waved his arm dismissively, 'Oh, don't make such a fuss! This is important. I've got to sort it out.'

'Are you two quarrelling?'

They both looked up and saw Suzie standing in the doorway. John suddenly felt guilty.

He said, 'We're not quarrelling, Suzie. It was my fault. Come and have your breakfast. You'll be late for school.'

'You're always arguing over nothing,' Suzie moaned with a frown on her face as she sat at the table and reached for her glass of orange juice.

'We're just being silly. Take no notice.'

'I'll try and get home early tonight,' said John guiltily with raised eyebrows and a submissive smile at Charlotte.

'She's been invited to her friend's this evening. Her mother's collecting them both after school, but I'll meet her from school anyway. Just to see her mother,' said Charlotte.

'Good. See that you behave yourself, young lady,' John pointed at her with a twinkle in his eye.

'I've said I'll pick her up about eight this evening. They live in Shurdington.'

'Shurdington? I thought Becky lived in the Grove around the corner.'

'This is another friend,' said Suzie, 'They've got a Shetland pony called Pansy, and I've sat on her and ridden around the field.'

'She palled up with her a few weeks ago,' interrupted Charlotte. 'They only moved to the area recently, and she's new to the school. I often see her mother Pauline at the school, and I've met her husband too. He's an architect and is organising the new buildings at the school and the repairs to the clock tower. Pauline also told me that he's a magistrate. They're a lovely couple.'

John made a face. 'Oh! Better watch your Ps and Qs then, Suzie. Hurry up, I'll drop you off at school myself this morning.'

Suzie shoved a lump of toast in her mouth and jumped up. 'Coming. I'll get my bag,' she grinned as she rushed out the door.

****

Bobby stood and looked out of her bedroom window. She stared at the sky which was heaving with dark and swollen clouds. They reflected her mood. It was getting late, but she'd delay going down to have her breakfast as long as possible because Simon was still there. Then she heard her mother calling and knew she'd have to go down. But if she left her things in the bedroom, she could bolt her toast and have to come back and get ready before leaving. That would give her more time on her own without him. Better take her tie off too so that it looked as if she still had to get dressed. She scrambled her hair as a final touch and went down stairs. As soon as she entered the kitchen, Pauline stared at her, wide-eyed in surprise.

'For goodness sake, Bobby, look at the state of you. And where's your tie? It's getting late,' she gently scolded as she put a piece of toast on a plate where Bobby always sat.

'Morning, Bobby. How are you this morning?' said Simon quietly.

Bobby pretended not to hear and took a mouthful of toast.

'Bobby, Simon asked how you were. Please answer him,' pressed Pauline.

'I'm fine,' her voice was flat, and she stared in front of her.

'And...?' said Pauline and cocked her head on one side meaningfully.

'I'm fine, thank you,' Bobby mumbled through tight lips.

'Good,' Simon smiled and winked at Pauline as if to say, "everything is fine", and "don't push her", and then proceeded to crack the shell of his boiled egg. He loved boiled eggs and had one, sometimes two for breakfast most days. Simon was a good-looking man. At 52, his waist line had not increased dramatically, and he held his six feet frame like a guardsman. His white hair had a slight wave and gave him a distinguished appearance. When he entered the Bench to listen and pronounce judgement on members of society who had broken the law, he looked formidable.

Pauline said, 'Her friend Suzie is coming to tea after school today. I'll collect them both.'

'Ah yes, I've seen her. A pretty girl. I've spoken to her mother too when I've collected Bobby.'

'Yes. Her name is Charlotte. We should have her and her husband around one evening.'

'Good idea. Fix something up when you see her.'

'I will,' said Pauline and noticed that Bobby was frowning. 'Are you all right, Bobby?'

'I don't want any more. I'll go and get my things ready,' said Bobby, with a dead tone to her voice.

'Are you feeling all right, darling?'

'I'm fine.'

'Well, finish your toast. You'll have to hurry. It's getting late.'

Bobby devoured her toast in three or four mouthfuls. She stood up. 'Finished.'

'Go along, then. Go and get ready,' said Pauline in resignation. 'Give me a shout, and I'll see you in the car.'

Bobby nodded and started for the door.

'Say goodbye to Simon.'

Bobby didn't look at him but said 'Bye' and walked out.

Simon called after her. 'Bye, Bobby. Have a good day at school.' But there was no reply.

'I'm sorry, darling,' said Pauline with a sigh, 'I wish she'd show a little bit more...well, you know.'

'Don't you worry about it, my dear. I understand that it must be difficult for her. She loved her father, and it's natural for her to resent my trying to replace him. She'll come around eventually. She's a lovely child, and if I show her that I love her and want to be her friend, she'll get there,' said Simon, as he reached across the table to take Pauline's hand.

'You're so understanding and patient, Simon. I didn't realise I could meet someone so wonderful after Roger was killed, but you are the most wonderful thing that's happened to me and Bobby since then.'

Simon smiled with a shade of benevolence, 'I'm the lucky one to have found such a lovely woman with a charming daughter. You both are more than I deserve, and I shall love you both always.'

They both smiled at each other in silence which was broken by Bobby calling, 'I'm going out to the car.'

'I'd better go, darling,' said Pauline and came around the table to kiss him.

'I'm in court today, but I'll keep in touch. Bye.'

Pauline squeezed his hand and went out.

****

A couple of cars pulled up and parked on the road outside St Catherine's Primary School. The playground was still empty of children because it was only just around 3 pm, and lessons for the day had not finished. Two mothers got out of their cars and began to chat.

At the far end of the playground was a small workmen's hut, and a group of builders in their yellow safety helmets came out and walked towards the end of the school building which was constructed with a very tall clock tower. It was surrounded in scaffolding, and it was obvious that a great deal of rebuilding and restoration work was in progress. The clock tower was a well-known feature of the school building and, because it had been deemed unsafe, money had been raised from several sources, including parents of children at the school, to have the necessary repairs carried out. The clock was currently out of action, and much of the tower near to the top had been dismantled. Adjacent to the clock tower was a small, new classroom block being built, and the workmen dispersed to continue with the work on which they were working.

The two women heard the bells ringing from inside the school signifying that classes had ended and waited for the surge of children that would suddenly begin pouring out into the playground, either to make their own way home or be picked up by parents.

Charlotte had now arrived further down the road to collect Suzie and she sauntered past the other cars that were also arriving to pick up children. She spotted Pauline and made her way over to have a chat. She and Pauline had become friends through picking up their children from the school each day, and their children had struck up a friendship too.

'Hallo, Pauline. You're ahead of me today.' She looked across the playground to see if she could spot Suzie.

'Here on time, but I shall probably be the last away,' Pauline replied with a sigh and a smile. 'How are you, Charlie?'

'Oh I'm fine. Gearing up for half term next week.'

'I know the feeling. You must let Suzie come over if she wants to. They get on so well together.'

'That's so kind of you, Pauline. Bobby should come over to us. Suzie's already coming to you today for tea.'

'That's no problem. I'm so pleased that Bobby has found such a good friend. It's been a very difficult time for her since her father died.'

'Of course. It must have been very hard for you too Pauline. I'm so sorry for what happened.'

'It has been terrible, but I'm so lucky to have met Simon. I know it seems soon after I lost my husband, but he's been so wonderful, and he's incredibly patient with Bobby. I'm sure Roger, my husband, would be happy for us.'

'I'm happy for you too. And I think you are very brave.'

'Well, one has to get on with one's life. And as I say, Simon's been an absolute rock for me.'

'He's certainly making a huge contribution to the school with all these works going on,' said Charlotte as she turned and surveyed the clock tower.

'It'll be a great improvement when it's finished. And the school definitely needs the extra classrooms.'

Charlotte nodded and continued to stare at the clock tower with pleasure.

Many of the cars were soon beginning to draw away as the volume of children in the playground began to thin out. Some of the children – the usual stragglers – were hanging back and gossiping excitedly.

Back inside the school, the teachers were checking their classrooms and gathering up papers and books and occasionally putting class work into their bags to take home and mark.

In the locker room at the end of one of the corridors, Bobby stood quietly staring into her open locker. Her sad eyes were almost vacant in their expression. When she felt happy, her eyes were bright, and she was one of the prettiest girls in her class. When she smiled her whole face would light up. Her long blonde hair was usually in a single plait, but when it was loose, her long curls would bounce on her shoulders. But now the muscles in her face were tight, and she felt a kind of desolation and despair.

She wondered if Simon would be at home or at work or come to collect her as he did sometimes when he was free. Even if he wasn't around now and was going to come home late, she wondered if he'd come into her bedroom after she had gone to bed. Mummy was normally home on Tuesdays so she should be okay. If he was home during the evening, he would probably try and make a fuss of her which she hated him doing – and anyway, it would only be to impress Mummy. What she hated most was when they were just sitting around watching television or doing nothing in particular, she would suddenly look up and see him staring at her with that strange look on his face. He would usually smile then, and sometimes wink at her in a secret, knowing way. Oh, she hated it so much. She hated him and wished he could die in a crash the same way as Daddy had.

'You coming, Bobby?'

She jumped out of her trance at the sound of Suzie's voice.

'Oh yes. Sorry.'

Suzie came over to her, 'Are you all right?' She stared at Bobby anxiously.

Bobby fumbled to pull herself together. She'd had to do it enough times: to put on a brave face, a mask that hid what she was really feeling. She had worn that mask most of her life since Daddy had died and Simon had married Mummy. She'd manage. It was second nature to her now. 'Of course,' she replied with as much brightness she could manage. 'I was just sorting out stuff in my locker. I've got to take some of it home because it's half-term next week.'

'I've had to do the same. We're going to be the last out again. I expect they're waiting.'

Bobby shut her locker door and forced a smile at her friend. 'I'm ready,' she said and swung her bag over her shoulder and started for the door.

'Will your mum be collecting you or your dad?' Bobby went rigid and jerked her head around to Suzie, 'He's not my dad!' she spat out the words.

Suzie reeled back in shock. She swallowed, embarrassed for forgetting how sensitive Bobby was about Simon. 'Sorry. I didn't mean anything. I just didn't think.'

Bobby immediately regretted her outburst towards her fiend. She smiled and touched Suzie's arm, 'I didn't mean to shout. I'm sorry.'

They both smiled at each other, and there was a silence.

'I'll see you during half-term next week, won't I?' said Bobby with a worried look on her face.

'Of course you will. I'll come over if you like, and if your mum doesn't mind.'

'Mum says you can come any time.'

'Then I'll come when I can.'

'Promise?' Her voice was still anxious, almost with a sense of pleading.

'Of course I will. And I'm coming home with you now, aren't I?' Suzie smiled, and this time she touched Bobby's arm, 'You're my best friend. I can't wait to see your pony again.'

Bobby smiled back, nodded, and she felt slightly reassured.

'Come on, we'd better go. We're going to be the last. You know how ratty they get,' said Suzie and went through the door pulling Bobby with her.

Chapter Two

John pulled the car into the kerb and parked on the double yellow lines. He didn't expect to be long as Linda's florist was just across the road so it was worth the risk. He made his way across the street and went into the shop. It was empty except for Linda who was sorting different bouquets, and they both spotted each other immediately.

'Hallo, John. Lovely to see you,' she smiled at him and came over to greet him.

'You too. I love the smell in here.'

She leaned towards him with a twinkle in her eye. 'Fragrances for the gods, my boy. Is this social or are you buying?'

'I'm buying. A peace offering for Charlie. I've been a bit neglectful lately, apparently not spending enough time at home and forgetting meetings like going to the school on a "parents' meeting with the teachers" evening. I'm afraid I've also been giving a bit too much time to the Sams and Charlie's getting pissed off with it. She says I'm spending more time on them than being at home,' John lamented.

'Got to look after the sensible one in the family, John.'

'Hmmm. Thanks a bunch.'

'I've been doing a few extra shifts myself recently. It never worries Clive. The only thing he objects to me

32

doing is going to the prison. He thinks they should all be banged up with the key thrown away.'

'Oh well, it takes all sorts.'

Linda pulled a face, 'He thinks that when I go it's like me parading in front of a lot sex-starved thugs lusting to get hold of me.'

John chuckled and leaned towards her, 'Well, Linda, you are a very attractive woman and…'

'Oh stop it!' she said with a scoff. 'You men are all lechers. What about these flowers? What do you fancy?'

'I dunno. You choose. You're more likely to get it right than me.'

'Well, the roses are beautiful at the moment. Can't go wrong with those.'

'Done. How much?'

'This lot is £15 but I'm sure they'll last quite a long time.'

'Thanks, Linda. Wrap 'em up.' John took out the money from his wallet, placed it on the till and watched her wrap the flowers in pretty paper.

'By the way, I gather that that little girl Bobby has been on the phone again. Clare took the call,' said Linda casually.

'Really. Poor little thing.'

'Breaks your heart, I know.'

'She's a gutsy kid though. Must be awful for her to ring and tell us all the things she does. What a bastard her step-father is.'

'At least she does ring us. Apparently she's got a good little friend though, that's what she told Clare, so that's something. Her name's Suzie, I think, and goes to the same school.'

John felt a bolt drive through him, 'Suzie!? Really? What school's that?'

33

'Oh, I don't know. She didn't say, which is understandable. We don't even know whether she lives locally. She could be at the other end of the country, ringing the national number rather than the local one to the branch for all we know.'

'Yes, I suppose so,' said John thoughtfully and relaxed a little.

'Suzie's a pretty common name, and it doesn't matter what her name is anyway. It's not really relevant.'

'No, of course not.'

'She could well be a local though, otherwise it's unlikely that she would get through to our branch again,' Linda offered thoughtfully.

'Hmmm, that's a point,' said John, and he was in deep thought again.

'Doesn't make any difference. It's not for us to know who our callers are.'

'True. It's just that when the caller's a child it always makes you wonder. And to think her father's a policeman. Makes your blood boil.'

'I didn't know that.'

'Well she mentioned to me that he was responsible for putting bad people in prison. Must be a copper.'

'I don't think that can be right. I don't know what he does for a living, but I think Clare said that Bobby told her that she thought her step-father was a magistrate. That must be it.'

'Jesus!' John froze and his mind went into turmoil.

'What's the matter, John?' said Linda and stared at him.

'What a damn fool. I shouldn't have jumped to conclusions. She didn't say he was a policeman, I just assumed that,' he muttered shaking his head.

'Doesn't matter, does it?'

'No, no. I gotta go, Linda. Lovely to see you. Thanks for the flowers.'

Linda suddenly looked startled, 'Are you all right John?'

'Sorry, yes. Just remembered I'm expecting a call at the office. It's important. I must go,' he turned and began to walk out.

'Bye John. Take care. See you soon,' she called as his back disappeared through the door.

John scurried along the pavement, his heart pounding and his mind revolving in uncontrolled thoughts. His shoulders hunched and head down, he ploughed ahead, oblivious to people around him. He turned and stepped on the road to cross over to where his car was parked and a screech of brakes deafened him as a van halted so close to him that he was forced to lean over and hold his balance by resting his hand on the bonnet.

The young driver poked his head around the window and bellowed, 'Look where you're bloody going, idiot!'

John quickly put his hand up in submission and mouthed "sorry" and then stepped across the road. As the driver of the car moved off, he stuck his middle finger high in the air, but John didn't notice. He continued to his car and got in. Thank goodness, no parking ticket. Christ! That was close. He needed to calm down, pull himself together and think rationally.

He leaned back and closed his eyes, breathing deeply at the same time. He realised his first reaction to what Linda had told him was simply knee-jerk. He now had to look at things calmly without letting his imagination run away with him. Facts, that's what he had to look at, not too many of these silly assumptions which could lead one into a mine field. Okay, the caller's name was Bobby, that was fact, and her father was a magistrate which was also a fact. Now her best friend was Suzie and went to the same school, but it wasn't known what school that was, and it might not have been local. It was very possible but not certain. And there must be thousands of Suzies in the country; it didn't have to be his own daughter. The other important thing that he didn't know, and which was the crucial piece of evidence, was that he didn't know the name of Suzie's friend. Charlie had simply said she was a new friend, and that her father was a magistrate. That put a better slant on things. He'd probably jumped to conclusions too quickly, but in any case, he could easily settle things by finding out the name of Suzie's friend.

He took out his smartphone, connected to HOME and waited. It wasn't long before he got through and Charlotte answered.

'Hallo, John. Everything all right?'

'Yes, I'm fine. Just wanted to say I was sorry about this morning. You're right, as usual. I'll try and sort things out better in the future.'

'Oh, not to worry, darling. I know you do your best, and you've got a lot to contend with at the moment. But I worry about you too. You take on too much.'

'I'm fine. Suzie's going to her friend's after school, isn't she?'

'Yes, she'll be all right. I'll pick her up this evening.'

John inwardly sighed with relief that he could tell from the lightness in Charlotte's voice that she was no longer angry with him.

'I'm pleased. By the way, what's the name of Suzie's friend? I don't think she mentioned it.'

'Her name? Err, Roberta. Sorry, I thought I'd said.'

'Roberta.' John let out a deep breath and there was silence.

'John! John!' he heard Charlotte's voice down the phone.

'Yes, I'm here.'

'What's the matter?'

He quickly collected himself. 'Nothing. I'd better go.' He knew he had sounded odd.

'Are you all right, John?' Charlotte persisted, as if she had sensed something wrong.

'I'm fine. I'll see you later. Bye.' He switched off the phone and puffed out his lips as he blew out air. That settled it. No need to panic after all. He fired the ignition and set off back to work.

****

Simon lowered himself into the easy chair in the office behind the court room. He'd finished hearing all the cases for the day and his two colleagues who sat with him had gone home. He had not enjoyed listening to some of the scum – as he regarded them – he'd had to deal with as they trooped in one after the other. Some of them were scared because they'd not been before a court before, either because it was their first offence or because it was the first time they'd been caught. Some of their pathetic excuses and completely false expressions of contrition got up his nose, and he was going to have none of it. The bastards would have to pay. He had a responsibility to society, and that same society relied on him to do his bit to deal with trouble makers. People had a right to walk about in safety, without being mugged or robbed or have to stare at unlawfully dumped piles of shit. They shouldn't have to confront drunken thugs – male or female – as they walked through town on their way home from the cinema or theatre. They didn't want to have to live across the road from a house where they were pretty sure drugs were being used or sold by horrible-looking oiks who drove big cars.

Of course, there were exceptions and the accused could be innocent or there might have been extenuating circumstances, but they were rare. He thought his colleagues who sat with him on the bench were swayed too much in that direction. He knew that they thought he was often too hard, even prejudiced, but they had small lives and lacked the will to hand out punishment when it was obviously deserved.

He got up and went to a cabinet against the wall, took out a bottle of Macallan and poured some into a glass. It might just take him over the limit, but he wasn't going home just yet, so he could risk it. He stared out of the window and watched people walking by. Life was good at the moment. He had a nice home, a flourishing architectural practice, he was highly respected, his wife was devoted to him, and Bobby was the icing on the cake. There was a special sparkle in her eyes which made his heart beat faster, and when she smiled, which regrettably was never at him, her whole face lit up in sunshine. She was irresistible, and from the first moment he met her, it removed any doubts he might have had about marrying Pauline. Of course, he was fond of Pauline, even though her conversation never rose much above the level of talking about TV reality and quiz shows from which she seemed able to answer a surprising amount of the questions. She was kind and did her best to please him for which he was genuinely grateful. It suited him admirably that she didn't have a big sex drive and was thrilled to settle mostly for cuddling and hand-holding. If he had ever appeared ungiving in that direction, because he had secured satisfaction elsewhere in another way that met his particular needs, it had never been noticed. And Pauline had never felt she was being neglected. He was a lucky man.

Nothing in life was perfect, and it bothered him that Bobby could not show him more affection. In one way, it was still early days, and he thought she was more compliant now that they had shared their little intimacy on many occasions. But she still upset him with her coldness in front of Pauline. He had bought her presents, taken her out, tried to play with her and talk about her interests, but it was slow work. He would have to exercise dogged patience and, in the meantime, be thankful for the enjoyment he got with her.

There was another thing: Suzie, Bobby's friend. She was a lovely girl who gave his heart a flutter when he talked to her. It was on the cards that he would see more of her because of the growing friendship he and Pauline were building with Suzie's mother, Charlotte. Bobby and Suzie were definitely good friends, and if he put himself out to be especially nice to Suzie, she might see that Bobby's seeming lack of affection for him was not fair, and she could influence Bobby to be more considerate, even affectionate towards him. He would have to make plans to take them out together; perhaps to the theatre or cinema or maybe a daytrip to London or even a picnic. There was huge scope for developing friendship, affection and trust. There was also the possibility of one other big opportunity.

Once he had become properly friendly with Suzie – friendly in a way that she really liked him and thought of him as a person to whom she could talk to about anything – he would look for various opportunities where he could be with her on her own. Dropping her home after she had been over to play with Bobby might be a good time. He wouldn't try anything for the first few times, just to gain her confidence. It was simply a question of being alert to any opportunity that might arise and exploiting it to full advantage. If he ever did get Suzie on her own, there were various techniques he could try to get her to join him in that lovely world of the special union. If that ever happened, he felt sure she might persuade Bobby to be much more co-operative and that would mean there were possibilities which at the moment he could only dream about. Yes, there was much to play for. He would just have to be patient and proceed carefully. But then, that was half the fun.

He swallowed the remains in his glass and stared across the road at a group of young children who were standing around laughing and chatting. Two of the girls, probably about 11 or 12 years old, were wearing very short skirts, and he stared at them, imagining how the cheeks of their bottoms would be rubbing against each other as they jigged from one leg to the other. But enough of this. He was acting like a sex-starved teenager.

He went over to the wash basin in the corner and rinsed his glass and dried it before putting it back in the cabinet with the Macallan. He looked at his watch and realised he needed to call at St Catherine's Primary and speak to Richard Deakin before the men packed up for work for the day.

Richard Deakin was his foreman and handled all the on-site work for which Simon was responsible. He was a first-class man who knew his stuff and had worked with Simon for several years. Although their social backgrounds were very different, there was a strong element of friendship between them, which was born out of the fact that both Simon and Richard had the same sexual interest in children. Both he and Richard and one other – Jeremy Morris – had developed a tight group and met from time to time to exchange material which they guarded with paranoid endeavour. Loyalty and trust between them had created a tight bond which allowed them to enjoy their inner fantasies with a fair degree of confidence that their wrongdoings would never be discovered. *Long may it last*, thought Simon. It was too late to call at the school now. Richard would be coping with things all right. He gathered up his papers and went home.

****

John closed his laptop and stretched. He looked at his watch and saw that it was 8.45. He felt like a drink and moved over to the sideboard where there was a bottle of Glenmorangie. He poured some into a glass and took it over to an armchair and eased himself down into it. He decided not to turn on the TV. Too tired. He would just relax and enjoy his drink. No sooner had he closed his eyes than he heard a car pull into the driveway, and he knew that Charlotte had returned from collecting Suzie from her friend's. He waited before he heard a car door slam followed by a latch key in the door and then chattering between Charlotte and Suzie as they came into the room.

'Hi, John,' said Charlotte, as she came over and gave him a quick kiss. 'Have you been home long?'

'About an hour. You okay?'

'Fine. I stopped and gossiped for a bit. Are you hungry?'

'It's all ready. Remains of the ham.'

'Suits me. How are you, Suzie? Did you enjoy yourself?'

'She's filthy. Look at her jeans,' said Charlotte.

'I've had a brilliant time messing around Pansy's stable. I've had a ride on her around the paddock.'

'Good for you.'

Charlotte said, 'You'd better get straight into the shower and then off to bed. Half-term's not here yet.'

'This Roberta sounds a bit of a tomboy,' said John. 'Like you, is she?'

'Who?' replied Suzie with a frown.

'Haven't you been to your friend Roberta's today? That's what Mummy said.'

'Not Roberta, Daddy. Nobody calls her that. You mean Bobby,' Suzie snapped with a smile.

'Bobby!' John felt an electric current shoot through his body.

'Nobody calls her Roberta, it's such a mouthful. It's sort of Robby…and then Bobby. I think it's nice,' Suzie continued to explain, as if no explanation was really necessary.

'Pauline told me her name was Roberta, but it's true, they all call her Bobby,' added Charlotte.

'And she calls herself Bobby?' John persisted.

'Of course she does! What's wrong with that?' said Suzie.

'Err, nothing,' John said weakly, but his eyes were wide, and he seemed to be staring into space.

Charlotte peered at him questioningly, 'John?'

As if suddenly lost in a different world he didn't hear her.

Charlotte leant forward with a touch of concern, 'John, are you all right?'

Her voice pierced through and he came spinning back, 'Oh… Yes… I'm sorry. I just suddenly remembered. I left some important papers in the car. I've got to go and get them.' As if confused, he jerked himself up and strode from the room as Charlotte stared in bewilderment after him.

Almost in a daze, John went through the kitchen, out through the back door and quickly made his way into the garage. He needed to be alone to collect his thoughts and away from Charlie who would wonder what the hell was wrong with him if she saw him in such a terrible state. He leant over the car, resting his hands on the bonnet. For a moment, his mind went blank, and he was only aware of his pounding heart. He put his hand up to his face and felt the dampness across his forehead. His mind began spinning, and he felt a surge of panic he'd never experienced before. After what seemed like an age, he took a deep breath and leaned his back into the wall. He had to pull himself together and stop panicking. Hearing Bobby's name was a shock, but it didn't mean anything that should matter. Of course he was an idiot not to have realised that Bobby was the obvious alternative to Roberta. How dumb could he be? Not only that, there were too many coincidences. His name was Simon, he was a magistrate, her name was Bobby, and her best friend was called Suzie. It all fitted. It meant that there was absolutely no doubt now that Suzie's friend Bobby was the same Bobby that he had spoken to with her dreadful story of what that bastard Simon was doing to her. He knew the victim and he knew the perpetrator. What the hell was he going to do?

Chapter Three

John pulled into the Samaritan Branch Centre and parked in the small private car park. He was tense and was experiencing a kind of anxiety he had never felt before. He'd hardly slept all night and hadn't wanted any breakfast. He'd managed a cup of coffee which in itself was unusual because he normally drank tea for breakfast, and he could tell that it had sent alarm bells ringing for Charlotte. She hadn't pushed it, but she had told him to take care in that special way of hers when he set off for work.

He'd had to go into the work-shop first thing as there were some urgent matters needing attention, and he had to cancel a very important appointment with one of his best customers, but he decided he couldn't deal with them until he'd had a talk with Sarah, his branch director. He noticed that her car was already there and was glad that she had been free at such short notice to come in and see him. He had to put her in the picture and discuss what was going to happen over Bobby, although he knew he was kidding himself if he didn't, in his heart of hearts, know the answer to that already. Even so, he inwardly clung to the hope that she might come up with something that was a way out of the problem.

He got out of the car and released the lock on the volunteers' private entrance and went through into the Ops room. Tom and Pat, the two volunteers handling that shift, were occupied. Tom was on the phone with a caller and Pat was writing an e-mail – another means of communication that the Samaritans offered for those who didn't want to speak on the phone and preferred to unload their problems through e-mail. He didn't speak but gave a brief wave and a smile, and then made a face indicating that he was here to have a chat with Sarah. He went out and after briefly tapping on the director's office door, walked straight in. Sarah was sitting at the desk.

Sarah was in her mid-forties and had worked as a nurse for many years. She now did it part time. She was a handsome woman rather than pretty. Her dark hair was short and her brown eyes gave the impression of warmth and reassurance. John knew her well because they had joined the Samaritans at the same time and done their training together. She had been a good director and had one more year to go until her three-year term was up and somebody else would take on the role. She would then carry on being a "normal" volunteer. Although the Samaritans had branch directors and deputy directors it was essentially a non-hierarchical organisation.

Sarah smiled. 'Hi, John, take a pew. Do you want to get some coffee first?'

'No thanks,' said John, sitting down opposite her.

'You look as if you've got the world on your shoulders. Are things that bad?'

'Nearly,' said John with a frown. 'Can we keep this between you and me for the moment? I don't think anyone else in the branch needs to know unless you think it necessary, but then can we discuss it?'

'Fine,' said Sarah, but held back from saying any more.

John shifted in his seat. 'It's about Bobby.'

'You mean Bobby, the child that has rung us because she's being abused by her step-father?' Sarah nodded. She knew that another volunteer had taken a call from

Bobby, and there had been a very brief report made so that volunteers were aware of her situation when she came on the phone.

'Yeah. It was me who spoke to her first.'

'Yes, I know. Probably the worst kind of call we get. Has it been getting to you?' she offered kindly.

'Too bloody right it has, but not just for the reason you think.'

'What's happened?' There was a touch of alarm in her voice.

Tom stared straight at her. 'I know who she is, and who her abuser is.'

Sarah let out a long breath. For a moment there was a silence as she tried to take account of what he was telling her, 'Are you sure?'

'Oh, I know who she is all right. She's Suzie's best friend.'

'Your Suzie?' said Sarah slightly shocked. 'Fill me in.'

'I found out by chance. We know her name is Bobby; the abuser's a magistrate; his name is Simon, and he's Bobby's step-father, and Bobby has told us that she has a close friend called Suzie. They go to the same school. Suzie, well both Suzie and Charlie, have told me the same thing. It all came out in conversation.'

'You haven't said anything to Charlotte or Suzie, have you?' said Sarah with increased alarm.

'Of course not. Suzie hasn't a clue, and Charlie never asks me about anything to do with callers. She knows our absolute rule of confidentiality, and she has never questioned me. I wouldn't say anything anyway.'

'Does Bobby have any idea that you are a Samaritan?'

'No, I shouldn't think so. I've never met her myself, and Suzie is hardly likely to tell her. She only has some vague idea about a charity I belong to, and it's not something I discuss with her. I just don't know what the hell I'm going to do.'

'You're not going to do anything, John,' said Sarah, speaking quietly but authoritatively.

'For Christ's sake, Sarah. I can identify the bastard who's doing it.' He was showing his anger now and his frustration.

'We just have to be there for Bobby when she rings. You know what we do here,' she reminded him, but it was not a rebuke. 'She has come to us and talked to us in confidence. She trusts us; you know that yourself. And unless she gives us permission to break that confidentiality – no matter what we may think or want to do – we have to maintain it. Every volunteer knows that confidentiality is the rock on which the Samaritan organisation is built, and that holds true for children as well. Come on, John. You know that as well as any of us.'

John stood up and started to pace up and down. This wasn't real; it was the stuff of nightmares. 'I'm worried about Suzie, Sarah. She's my own daughter. There's no way I'm going to put her at risk.' He was glaring at Sarah now, and he couldn't conceal the element of hostility.

'Please sit down, John. We've got to talk about this calmly.'

John swallowed and took a deep breath. He knew that Sarah was not against him, and she was the only person that he could really talk to. He moved back to his chair and sat down with a look of despair.

'Of course I understand you're worried about Suzie, but let's not get ahead of ourselves. Is she ever likely to be alone with Simon, for instance?'

'Not yet as far as I know. I suppose it's unlikely, but it's possible that it could happen. Suzie hasn't a clue about these things. She'd be an ideal target.'

'This may sound a silly question, John, but if he did try anything, would Suzie come and tell you or Charlotte?'

'Christ, I never thought of that. I'm sure she would. Bloody hell, I hope she would,' said John, but he was looking confused again.

'Okay. You must carry on as normal. Don't go questioning Suzie or try dropping hints about suspicions of what you know is going on, and the same with Charlotte. She's your wife, and you can bet she'd soon pick it up if you were hiding something.'

John shook his head vehemently, 'No, there's no way I'd try anything like that. Don't worry on that score.'

'I also suggest that the easiest way to relieve your anxiety is to try and reduce, even stop, Suzie going over to Bobby's. Perhaps the friendship will fizzle out.'

'That's not going to be easy. I'm afraid Charlie is becoming quite friendly with Pauline – Bobby's mum – and she thinks that bastard Simon is charming.'

'I know it's going to be tough, but I can't see any other way at the moment. Do you want to go on sabbatical for a while?'

'Definitely no. I'm all right. I'm sorry I blew a fuse.'

'I don't blame you. It's a terrible situation. And I know you know all this, but I'm going to spell it out anyway. Agonising over the misery of all our callers goes with the job. But we can't interfere. The fact that we might know a caller makes absolutely no difference at all. Knowing the people involved doesn't allow us to do anything without the caller's express permission. As far as Bobby is concerned she has already told us that her mother has brushed aside her attempts to tell her what Simon is doing. Pauline's in love with Simon, and she can't believe he'd do such a dreadful thing to her daughter. She thinks he loves Bobby. That's what Bobby has told us. And suppose we did blow the whistle in some way, we don't know what Bobby would do. She might even deny everything and we don't know what kind of a hold her step-father has over her. Even her mother might continue to disbelieve her. In your report, you said that she told you she would kill herself if anyone found out what Simon was doing. There's all sorts of terrible things going on in the poor child's mind. I'm not saying she would, but she could take her life. We know it's happened before. We wouldn't want to be responsible for that.'

Sarah stared at him across the table. She had spoken firmly with the authority of director, but she had said it kindly and felt genuine concern for John.

There was a few minutes' silence as John mulled over Sarah's words. He nodded. 'I know,' he said quietly, 'I know.'

'I agree with you that maybe it is best if we keep the fact of you knowing who Bobby is between the two of us. There's no benefit in spreading it around all the other volunteers. If she calls again she'll be just like any other anonymous caller. Volunteers will know that she can also call Childline if she wants and give her the number but they mustn't press her. They are more experienced at dealing with children than us.'

'Would they take action?'

'It's unlikely but not impossible. When Clare took the call, she suggested to her that she could also call Childline but had to warn her that there was a possibility they may report what's going on. She was terrified at the thought.'

'They wouldn't know who she was anyway, would they, unless she told them and she's not going to do that. She thinks we don't know who she is or where she lives.'

'That's true. There's the issue of safeguarding as well. But I don't think we should go down that road at the moment. She's not knowingly revealed her identity and she's threatened to take her own life if we don't keep her secret. Even if she's approached sensitively, I think it's too risky.'

'God, what a choice. Carry on being abused or take your own life. She's done nothing wrong but terrified of anyone finding out.'

We'll keep in close contact over this, John. If you ever need to talk, call me. It doesn't matter if it's in the middle of the night. This is a heavy load for you, and I don't want you to feel it on your own.' She got up from her chair and came around to him. 'Will you be all right?'

He stood up. 'Sure. I hate to be in this position, but it's that poor child who is the one who's really suffering. I feel so helpless and guilty.'

'It's not your fault, John. Simon is the guilty one. At the moment our hands are tied.'

I should have joined a different organisation,' said John with a weak smile. 'Thanks,' he kissed her on both cheeks and went out the door.

****

It was lunch time, and Suzie had finished her last sandwich and eaten her fairy cake. They would have to go back to class soon, and she still didn't know where Bobby was. Bobby often slipped away on her own, and it always upset Suzie because they were friends and friends kept together. There was something about Bobby that worried Suzie. She had caught her crying a few times and often, when she had been speaking to her, she had seemed miles away and not listening to what she was saying. She had always dismissed the crying and said everything was fine except that it made her sad when she thought about her father. Suzie could understand that. It must be terrible to lose your dad when you're so young. Suzie had tried to comfort her, but she hadn't really known what to say or do. She dared not mention Simon because that always made Bobby angry. Suzie could understand that too. It was horrible to think another man could pretend to be your new father. She thought Simon was very nice. He was always smiling at her and being friendly, and he always seemed pleasant to Bobby, but even so, she could see that no one could replace one's own father.

Suzie suddenly thought she might know where she was. She had seen her furtively go under the arch at the foot of the clock tower and sit in a corner out of sight. That area was out of bounds to the children at the moment because of all the building works, but it was a place where you could be on your own as most of the workmen were working further along where the new classroom block was being built.

Suzie put her lunch box away in her bag and looked around to see if anyone was watching her. As it was lunch time, the workmen seemed to have congregated in their hut, and the other children were busy with each other. She sauntered across the playground, and then slipped under the barrier tape and skipped over to the clock tower. As soon as she had gone under the arch, she saw Bobby huddled in a corner. She had obviously been crying.

'I was looking for you, Bobby. I guessed you might be here.' She moved over to her and sat down next to her. Bobby didn't say anything. 'Are you okay?' said Suzie as gently as she could.

'Did anybody see you? We're not allowed here,' said Bobby.

'The workmen are having their lunch in the hut. Are you all right?' asked Suzie.

'Of course. I'm fine,' snapped Bobby, and Suzie knew that there had to be something wrong.

'I only want to help. We're friends, aren't we?'

'Of course. Sorry.' Bobby hesitated as she tried to think of a convincing answer. 'I just think about my dad sometimes. I'm all right.'

Suzie bunched her mouth in a weak smile.

There was a silence for a little while, and both of them seemed to think the silence was all right. Suzie suddenly noticed the photo poking out from behind Bobby's top blazer pocket.

'What's the photo?' she asked.

Bobby pulled it out and held it across for Suzie to look at, 'My dad. I've got my favourite one at home, but I always keep this one with me,' she said with a faint smile, but her face was sad.

'He looks nice,' said Suzie. 'I'm sorry for what happened. I think I'd die if I lost my mum or dad.' She pushed the photo back to Bobby. 'Have you eaten your lunch yet?'

Bobby shook her head. 'Didn't want it. I threw it in the bin.'

'Wasn't it very nice?'

'It was okay. Just not hungry.'

They were so engrossed with each other that they had not noticed the site foreman Richard Deakin standing against the wall of an adjacent building from which he was able to watch them without being seen. Just watching them chat quietly gave him a special thrill. They were so appealing in their school uniforms that he wished he'd got his smartphone with him, which he always kept on him but had left it on the desk in the site office today. The girls suddenly stood up and walked towards him but didn't notice him until they were nearly upon him.

'Hah! Caught you!' he said with mock severity. 'You're not supposed to be over here. It's out of bounds.'

They both looked guilty. 'Sorry,' said Suzie, 'we're just going. Don't say anything, please.'

Richard Deakin shook his head with a grin. It was so cute the way she said please. 'Trust me. It'll be our secret.'

The girls smiled at each other in relief, 'Thank you,' they called out as they ran off.

He watched them disappear round the corner and sighed with pleasure that he had such a lucky site to work on. He made his way back to the office and got the men back on the job.

****

Later that afternoon, Simon arrived at the school to assess the work in progress and discuss assorted queries that needed ironing out. The work was going well. The new classroom block was on schedule, and the work on the clock tower, which had been put temporarily on hold, would soon start again. Simon and Richard Deakin walked around the site discussing various issues and had a joke with the men on the job. Simon had timed his visit so that he would be on site when school finished for the day and he would be able to take Bobby home.

He walked with Richard Deakin across the playground and stood outside the site office.

'I thought you'd like to know, before you go, that I've got some new stuff. Usual source. Jeremy's coming around this evening to have a look at it. Will you be able to join us?' Richard Deakin said with a conspiratorial smile on his face.

'I'd like to. I'll have to let you know,' said Simon, and they both looked up as the school doors burst open and the children came pouring out. A group of girls came by giggling and chattering excitedly, and Richard Deakin watched them as they made their way across the playground to the main gates.

'Keep your mind on the job, Richard. Teachers are very alert these days. I don't want any of them getting any ideas,' said Simon with a hard edge to his voice.

Richard Deakin shook his head, 'It's all right. I'm not a fool. The children are not around most of the time, and I've got a good relationship with the staff. There's nothing to worry about.'

Simon nodded and spotted Bobby and Suzie come out of the door and begin crossing the playground.

'I'll try and get here tomorrow. Any problems, call me,' he nodded again and went to meet the girls.

'Hallo, you two. Out on time for a change,' said Simon, smiling at them.

'Hallo, Mr Hargreaves,' replied Suzie.

'Hallo, Suzie. Are you all right, Bobby?'

'Yes,' she didn't look at him and her voice was quiet.

'I'm collecting you both today. Suzie's coming home for tea with us if you'd like that, Suzie,' Simon kept his voice buoyant.

'Yes please,' said Suzie excitedly, grinning at Bobby.

'Right then, let's go,' said Simon, and led the way to the car.

The two girls got in the back, and Simon fired up the engine. As they travelled, Simon struck up a light-hearted and friendly conversation with Suzie; Bobby could see how much Suzie liked Simon and it made her angry deep down inside her. If only she knew what Simon was like. If only she knew what he did to her, and how he made her frightened and feel trapped. She didn't want Suzie to turn against her; to think she was not very nice; that she was bad. More and more she felt isolated, helpless and alone. Daddy was gone, and Mummy only cared about Simon.

'So do you enjoy school, Suzie?' said Simon with laughter in his voice.

'Yes, I do.'

'I bet you're one of the brightest students as well.'

'I don't think so. Bobby's much brighter than me,' giggled Suzie and gave Bobby a nudge, as if to get her to share in the joke.

'There's a good friend for you, Bobby. I can see you two bright sparks are a force to be reckoned with when you get together,' replied Simon, and he offered no more conversation for the rest of the journey. But inwardly, he thought that he was making a good impression with Suzie, and that here was a child with whom he could make a lot of progress. Yes, life could be so sweet.

****

It was after tea but still early when Simon had agreed to drop Suzie home. She thanked Pauline and said goodbye to her and waved at Bobby who looked down at her from her bedroom window which was at the front of the house. Suzie saw Bobby put up her hand and wished that she had seen her smile, but there was none and it made her sad.

The journey was short and would only take about ten minutes, but Simon began to chatter with Suzie in the front passenger seat.

'Sorry to have to take you home so early, Suzie, but I have to go on to a meeting,' he said, and slapped his hand gently down on to her knee.

'That's all right. Thank you for having me, Mr Hargreaves.'

'You mustn't keep calling me Mr Hargreaves. It's too formal. Simon is fine,'

'Oh all right,' smiled Suzie, ignoring his hand on her knee.

'We're friends, and you're welcome to come over to us whenever you want.'

'Thank you, Mr...sorry, Simon. Bobby is my best friend.'

'I'm pleased. You get on well together, and you're such a pretty girl,' he chuckled mischievously with a lean towards her, but he had to remove his hand from her knee to grab the wheel with both hands to avoid a car that had lurched in front of them.

For the remainder of the journey Simon concentrated on the road while Suzie looked out of the window. Simon was pleased with himself. He was making good friends with Suzie, and he was sure she liked him. Over time, their friendship would get better, and there was bound to be the possibility of opportunities for them to become very close. He would simply have to take things slowly, one step at a time. There was no rush, and he didn't want to blow a golden opportunity by becoming impatient and landing in a heap of trouble. He felt in very high spirits as he pulled up outside Suzie's house. Suzie jumped out and ran up the front path with Simon not far behind. She banged on the door and called out so excitedly that it was only a few moments before Charlotte came to open it.

'Hallo, Mummy. I'm home,' she beamed at her mother.

'My goodness, what a noise. Hallo, Simon. It was so good of you to bring her home. I would have happily come to collect her. Won't you come in?' said Charlotte, standing back.

'Just for a moment,' he said, and followed her into the house. 'It was no trouble because I'm on my way to a meeting, and it didn't take me out of my way.'

'Thank you for having her. I hope she was no trouble.'

'Absolutely the opposite. She's a delightful child, Charlotte. A credit to you.'

'You should try living with her,' laughed Charlotte and Simon laughed too.

'She and Bobby get on so well together. I'm glad they've become friends. We'll have to arrange for her to come and stay-over sometime.'

'Yes please, Mummy.'

'We'll see. Perhaps in the holidays. I shall never hear the end of that now. Bobby must come here.'

'That too, perhaps. You and your husband must visit one evening as well.'

'Thank you, we'd love to.'

I haven't got my diary with me at the moment, and I'm here, there and everywhere during the next few days. I'll get Pauline to fix up something in a couple of weeks or so. That'll give you plenty of time.'

'You certainly have a busy life,' said Charlotte barely concealing her admiration.

'Keeps me out of trouble,' Simon chuckled. 'Well, I must be off, Charlotte. Goodbye, young lady,' Simon looked down at Suzie who was smiling broadly.

'Goodbye, Simon. Thank you for having me.'

'It was a great pleasure,' he said, and, bending down and turning his head to one side and leaning towards her, he added, 'Are you going to give me a kiss?'

Suzie leant forward, and, although with a touch of embarrassment, pecked him on the cheek.

'My, you've certainly made a hit,' said Charlotte also with a slightly embarrassed laugh.

'Children are a great joy, Charlotte,' said Simon, with a small flurry of the arms. 'I'll say goodbye to you now.' He turned and walked to the front door, and Charlotte opened it.

'Goodbye, Simon. Thank you. And give my love to Pauline.'

'Will do,' he called back as he walked down the path to his car. Charlotte and Suzie watched him drive away, and then they went back into the house. *What a lovely man,* thought Charlotte.

****

Bobby stood looking out of her bedroom window. Now that Suzie had gone home, she felt alone. She wondered what Simon would have been saying to her as he drove her home. She reached across to the chest of drawers and picked up the photograph of her father. 'I wish you were here, Daddy,' she whispered, and her eyes filled with tears. She stood holding the picture for a little while and then put it back.

Across the road, a couple of children were playing in their front garden. They were sisters and went to the same school as Bobby, but she didn't know them much more than to say hallo. As she watched, their father came round the side of the house and called to them with a smile. They looked up and saw that he was holding out what looked like two small chocolate bars, which they ran up and grabbed excitedly. That's just what Daddy was like: always there and always bringing surprises. But all that was gone now. She was never going to look up and see him there; he would never be there so that she could take his hand. She watched the girls munch their chocolate with glee and then she turned away and opened the bottom drawer of her chest of drawers and pulled out her exercise pad which she kept hidden beneath her clothes. She knew it was safe there because those items of clothing she hardly wore, and her mother would never think to rummage in there.

She sat down on her bed and began writing in the book, but she hadn't been at it very long before she heard Pauline calling for her to go downstairs. She quickly put the book away and went down to her mother in the kitchen.

'What are you doing up there, darling?' asked Pauline.

'Nothing,' said Bobby with a shrug.

'Nothing. Oh dear.' She looked at Bobby with her motherly concern. 'I'm just making a sponge. Would you like to help me?'

'I'll watch.'

'All right. While it's in the oven, I'm going to make some icing, and you can have a taste,' she said, trying to elicit a smile from Bobby.

'Will Simon ever go away?'

'Good gracious, what a thing to ask!' said Pauline in utter shock.

'Lots of people get divorced, don't they?' Bobby persisted.

'Some people do, yes, but Simon and I are not going to get divorced, Bobby. We're always going to be together,' said Pauline, trying to keep her voice bright.

Bobby didn't say anything for a little while but then, 'Why did you marry Simon?' she asked as she fiddled with her fingers.

'Because he loves me. And I love him. He loves you too.'

'Daddy would hate him,' said Bobby in a flat voice.

Pauline stopped stirring the cake mix and came and sat down next to Bobby. She had to reach out to her daughter. 'Daddy wouldn't want us to be on our own. I know you miss him. I do too. But Simon is very kind and he looks after us.'

'I hope he gets killed in an accident,' said Bobby, but didn't look at her mother.

Pauline bit hard to suppress her anger and hurt, 'That's a dreadful thing to say, Bobby. And it's so unkind when Simon tries so hard to be nice to you.'

'I don't like him being nice to me,' said Bobby, but now there was a trace of pleading.

'That's so silly, dear. Of course he wants to be nice to you.'

'He kisses me and…' she stopped short, unable to say the words.

'That's because he loves you. That's why he kisses me. Daddy used to kiss you too.'

'Daddy didn't…' She broke off suddenly. There was a whole lot she wanted to blurt out, but she looked at her mother's face and knew that she couldn't understand and would accuse her of being bad and lying if she tried to tell her the real truth. She'd tried that once already. Then she would tell Simon who would become angry and want to punish her, and maybe he had the power to put her in prison for telling such awful lies. Mummy

60

wouldn't protect her because she loved Simon so much. Nobody would believe her and everybody would stare at her and then turn their backs on her, and even Suzie wouldn't like her anymore, and then there would never be any hope for her. She would have to kill herself because that's the only way she could be with Daddy.

She suddenly felt angry, 'You don't care!' she snarled at her mother as tears welled up. She jumped up and started to walk away.

'Bobby! Please come back at once!' snapped Pauline, but Bobby continued to walk out.

****

John sat down and was determined to try and stay calm. He was late home from work and was tired, so he was already on the edge of bad temper. But inside he was really fired up. The situation was going to get out of his control, and there was absolutely nothing he could do about it. And this was only just the beginning. Things were going to get worse; they had to because that was the nature of the problem. He would have to stand on the sideline and watch events being manipulated by others. The frustration and anger, even terror, would overcome him unless some quirk of fate took a hand and decided that good must overcome evil.

Charlotte stared at him in total bewilderment. Why he should make her feel guilty for having done nothing wrong was ridiculous. But for some reason, beyond her understanding, he was being completely unreasonable.

'I simply don't know why you didn't collect her yourself,' his voice was calm but unrelenting.

'I was going to. I didn't know he was going to turn up on the doorstep with her. It was very nice of him.'

Three times she had given the same answer, so why was he persisting in this pointless questioning?

'But it would have been better for you to collect her.'

'Why would it have been better? She was very happy to be brought back by him. She likes him.'

John started rolling back and forth in his chair, and he began to breathe loudly as he fought to control his emotion. Charlotte stared at him with a mystified frown.

'What on earth's the matter with you, John? Why are you being such a grizzly bear over something so trivial?'

'Trivial to you, maybe!' he snapped but realised, of course, that he must look like a complete idiot. He would have to get a grip and try harder, 'Look, I just think it was an imposition on them. Suzie has been over there, and it was our place to collect her.' It sounded weak, but it was a bit better.

'Well, all right. And I intended to. But once he'd turned up, I couldn't do anything about it.' *Surely he could see that*, she thought.

'Oh well, what's done is done. She's home safe.' His heart was slowing a bit.

'Of course, she's safe. Being over at Bobby's is one place I'm absolutely happy about. Simon and Pauline are a lovely couple and they want us to go over there one evening.'

'Oh, we can't do that,' Christ, what else was she going to tell him?

'Why ever not? Of course we'll go. You'll like Simon and Pauline is lovely.'

'No. It's absolutely out of the question,' his voice rasped, and again he knew immediately that if he didn't get a grip she would begin to suspect there was some hidden agenda.

'I don't know what kind of a day you've had, John, but you're behaving like a spoilt child. You're upsetting me, and I don't deserve it,' her voice trembled.

He'd blown it. All his good intentions had evaporated into thin air or rather hot air. Damn fool. He had to salvage the situation. 'I'm sorry, Charlie. Yeah, it's been a tough day. All I'm really trying to say is that I think we should slow things down a bit. I don't want Suzie outstaying her welcome there, and it might be better if Bobby came over here more often. And she should see Becky too. She used to be her friend.' That sounded a lot better and much more reasonable.

'That's fine with me. She's still friends with Becky, and I'm sure the three of them get on well together anyway.' Charlotte relaxed a bit. 'Suzie will want to go over to Bobby's sometimes, though. We can't stop her.'

'Okay. But I think you should collect her. Simon shouldn't have to do it, and I'm sure she'd rather travel with you,' he said, thinking that he had made a good concession.

'I'm not so sure about that,' laughed Charlotte. 'They seemed to hit it off just fine. She didn't even mind kissing him goodbye.'

'What?' John wrenched the words from his mouth, the muscles in his face twisting into an ugly contortion.

Charlotte jolted back at the blast from his attack but then spontaneously waved her arms at him dismissively, 'Oh, it was just a peck on the cheek. Kids have their funny ways sometimes. And it was him who initiated it.'

John was just about to cut loose with a tirade of outrage, but the phone in the hallway rang. Charlotte spun round and headed for the door. 'I'll get it,' and then she was gone. Immediately, he heard her mumbling, and guessing it was one of her friends, assumed she wouldn't be back for some time. He sank back in his chair, his mind reeling. He felt as if some dark and unstoppable force was closing in on him. He had been kidding himself if he had ever thought this nightmare would suddenly disappear. That evil bastard, Simon, had all the aces in his hand, and there was absolutely nothing he could do about it. Or was there?

In one way it looked so simple. All he had to do was go to the police and tell them that he knew that nine-year-old Bobby Hargreaves was being sexually abused by her step-father. It was his moral duty to do that, and the poor child would be put out of her misery. But deep down, he knew that things in life were not as black and white. He'd discovered that scores of times from speaking to callers on the telephone. Apart from breaking the rule of confidentiality he'd signed up to with the Samaritans, he would be betraying Bobby's trust that her secret was safe with them. Okay, she was a child but that made the situation worse. She was convinced that it was all her fault. She was convinced that nobody would believe her and think her a terrible person. She was convinced that she would end up with no friends. She was convinced that Simon would devise some terrible way to punish her and that her only way out would be to kill herself so that she could be with Daddy again. John had been over all this several times with Sarah. Suppose her mother continued to disbelieve her. That would certainly be possible in the early stages of any investigation and, during that time, Bobby would be devastated and would feel very vulnerable, even terrified. She might really take her own life. It was no good saying that she probably wouldn't do that. That would be a big mistake.

It was always dangerous to predict how any caller – child or adult – might think or behave. If it all went pear-shaped and was decided that she had made the whole thing up because she resented Simon taking the place of her father, she might really kill herself. It wouldn't be an easy thing to do, but it was possible. She'd certainly threatened it. Then where would they be? He and the Samaritans would be accused of being responsible for her death. But if he did nothing and it was discovered that the authorities had not been alerted, he could just imagine the howls of outrage from society for allowing Bobby to go on suffering from that monster, Simon. And what would Charlie think? Would she hate him? Christ, he couldn't bear that. He couldn't let this go on. He had to do something, but he hadn't the faintest idea what. As he sat there, with all the sensations of misery grinding away in the pit of his stomach, he suddenly felt the loneliest man in the world.

****

Simon retrieved the disc and shut down his computer. He'd seen enough for tonight. He put the disc in its sleeve and locked it away in his safe. It was just past midnight and the house was quiet. Pauline had gone to bed some time ago with a headache and would now be in a deep sleep. For a little while, he sat thinking about Bobby upstairs lying in her bed. The material he had been watching made him feel restless and frustrated. He sat thinking for a little longer, and then came to a decision. It was a bit risky, and he'd never tried it before, but Pauline was a heavy sleeper, so it would probably be safe if he was alert.

He left his study, went out into the hall and began to climb the stairs. Asleep in her bed, Bobby suddenly woke as she heard the creak of the fifth tread and knew that Simon was coming up the stairs. She waited for the creak of the ninth and fourteenth tread and knew he would now be stepping on to the landing. Her body went tense as she listened to hear whether any further sounds would be coming closer or away to his own bedroom at the other end of the landing. She heard nothing and began to relax. He had never come into her room at night while her mother was still in the house, but she dreaded that this might be a first time.

Simon eased open the door of his own bedroom and crept inside. He could hear the sound of Pauline's loud and even breathing and knew she was in a deep sleep. That settled it. She was unlikely to wake. He refrained from turning on any light and, in the darkness, slipped off his clothes and put on his pyjamas and dressing gown. He decided to leave off his slippers so that he could move more quietly. He crept back across the room and out again on to the landing.

Bobby was about to drop off to sleep again when she suddenly thought she heard a sound and immediately became alert. Was it her imagination or was it a sound? She must try and get back to sleep and not be silly. But there it was again, she was certain. She lifted her head off the pillow and strained to listen. Her heart began to pound as her sixth sense told her that he was out there, that he was moving along the landing. Then it was quiet. Was he going to go downstairs for something or would he continue on, in which case it could only possibly be towards her bedroom? She lifted her head higher and looked towards the door where she could see the strip of light from the landing shining along the bottom. The beat of her heart pounded in her ears as she watched to see if there would be a shadow. And suddenly there it was: a dark patch concealing the light immediately on the other side of the door. She dropped her head back on to the pillow but knew that the door was opening because a flood of light crept across the room and then disappeared as it was almost closed again. She kept her eyes shut as if asleep and waited for him to cross the room.

Back in his own bedroom, Pauline stirred and then woke. For a moment, she lay there blinking into the darkness. She turned and looked at the digital clock and saw that it was not long after midnight. She reached out to touch Simon and suddenly realised he wasn't there. She switched on the bedside lamp and immediately saw his clothes laid across the chair. That was odd. Why wouldn't he be in bed? Perhaps he had gone downstairs to get a drink or something had disturbed him. Perhaps the same thing that had woken her. She threw back the duvet and swung out of bed. She reached for her dressing gown and slipped out onto the landing. The house was quiet; perhaps she had better check on Bobby.

Inside Bobby's bedroom, Simon had moved over to her bed and was leaning over her. He could see she was asleep or was she feigning it? Her lids seemed to be trembling, and her breathing wasn't calm and regular.

'Bobby, Bobby,' he whispered, and moved his face closer to hers. 'I know you're awake. Be a good girl.'

She felt his breath on her face; it was warm and smelt of alcohol.

The landing light suddenly flooded into the room as Pauline opened the door and stood there staring at him.

'What's the matter, Simon?' she hissed, so as not to make too much noise.

Simon quickly stood up straight but avoided turning around so as to conceal his erection. 'It's all right, my dear. Bobby called out in her sleep as I was just coming to bed. Poor little thing had a nightmare, but she's gone back to sleep again.'

'Shall I look?' she asked gently.

'No, no. No need. Don't want to disturb her.' He held up his hand as if to suggest she retreat. 'I'm coming.' He pulled his dressing gown across him and turned as she moved out to the landing, and then he followed behind.

'Thank you, darling,' said Pauline and held his arm as he led the way back to their bedroom. 'If she called out, that's probably what woke me,' she continued as she slipped off her dressing gown and climbed back into bed.

'No harm done. You get back to sleep,' said Simon and climbed into bed next to her.

She gave him a kiss on the cheek and turned over, 'Goodnight, darling,' she whispered.

'Goodnight, my love,' he replied and turned out the bedside lamp.

In the bedroom at the other end of the landing, Bobby stared into the darkness. Her heartbeat had slowed, and she felt her muscles begin to relax. But frightened thoughts still swirled in her mind. Where could she go? What could she do? Who could help her? Why was this happening to her? Why, oh why, oh why? There was no answer so she lay there and cried herself to sleep.

Chapter Four

The nagging fears for Bobby and Suzie were never out of John's mind. He woke frequently in the night, and the first thoughts that came into his mind were always about how much Bobby was suffering and the increasing possibility of danger to Suzie. The thought that he knew she might be at risk and he was doing nothing about it to protect her consumed him with guilt. Wherever he was, whatever the time of the day, whether he was driving or at work, whether at home in the garden or watching television, his mind was always distracted.

In spite of his best efforts, all this had made him continuously bad tempered and both Charlotte and Suzie had been on the end of it. He had become an ogre in Suzie's eyes, and he had made her cry on a number of occasions. He had tried saying sorry several times, but now it was wearing a bit thin, and she seemed to be avoiding him. Charlotte had fared no better. He had snapped at her and been non-communicative when she had tried talking to him and her frustration and bewilderment was driving her to distraction. She knew that something was gnawing away at him, but when she had tried to ask him what was worrying him, he had clammed up and they always ended up rowing.

It wasn't just having the knowledge of what was going on but the secret and certain belief that things were almost bound to get worse. He didn't know what it would be, but some situation would arise that would put

Suzie in real danger, and he would be forced to turn a blind eye. He was becoming paranoid but felt helpless to fight it.

He had talked to Sarah when he'd felt at the end of his tether, and she had been sympathetic and encouraging, but he knew she was powerless to authorise a whistle blow, and as she had pointed out before, it could make a bad situation worse. Bobby had been on the phone a couple of times with two other volunteers recently, and each time she had expressed her fears that they might break their word and tell somebody. Each time, she had been assured that this would never happen unless she gave her permission. And in any case, without her permission none of them had identified her and wouldn't be able to take any action without her revealing who she was and where she lived. Such thoughts didn't help, though, and the same dreadful arguments kept going round and round in his mind. Was it just a question of high-flown Samaritan principles at one end of the pole and the suffering of a child at the other? He'd gone over the arguments time and time again and always ended up feeling totally helpless.

At the same time what weighed heavily on his mind was the thought that his own daughter, Suzie, could be at risk of becoming a victim of Simon's abuse. Vivid scenes of what she might suffer drifted in and out of his mind. The more he tried to blank them out, the more vivid they became. As he lay in bed each night, he was wracked with guilt at the thought of failing his daughter in such a terrible way.

As he drove home from work, his thoughts continued going around in circles. The weekend lay ahead, and he wondered about the possibility of taking Suzie and Charlotte out each day to give them a break, and that would ensure, at least, that Suzie was with him and not over at Bobby's home. The more he thought about the idea, the more he felt pleased. It would also be a good way of building bridges with Charlotte who was having a rough deal because of his behaviour. He knew that it was with good reason she had felt shut out each time he had closed down and been so obnoxious to her. She had only been concerned for him and wanted to help, but all he had done was hurt her. He didn't even dare to think it, but if things went on the way that they had been going, she might find him too unbearable and want to leave him. Even just the thought of it would send his mind reeling.

He wondered how much she might have said to her parents who were still alive and lived in Evesham, about 20 miles away. Charlotte was close to her parents and he got on with them reasonably well himself now, but initially there had been resistance to their beloved only daughter marrying him. He simply wasn't good enough for her. Her father was ex-military, whose approach to life was based on straight lines. He'd never said it to John himself, but John felt certain that her father had said to her mother that one day, he wouldn't stay the course and dump his daughter for another woman. John hadn't cared much. He understood that some parents, particularly fathers of only daughters, were often judgemental of prospective sons-in-law. Charlotte was totally loyal to him and would always stand up for him if her father ever made criticism of him, but it was not unreasonable to assume that she might talk to her parents if John continued to be so objectionable or bloody-minded. In any case, they would quickly spot that she was unhappy and start to ask questions. After that, it wouldn't take her father very long to make the huge leap of judgement that – just as he had always predicted – John was no good.

As he pulled into his drive and stopped in front of the garage, he saw Charlotte bending over a flower bed gently forking the soil and pulling out the occasional weed. How he wished he could tell her all about the dreadful situation they were in; he was in; Suzie was in; Bobby was in. She would be calm and thoughtful and come up with some brilliant solution. Yet, even as he wished it, he knew it was fanciful rubbish. She stood up and waved with a smile and John felt a warm glow at how lucky he was to have her. She was loyal and loving, and of late, incredibly long suffering of him. He knew too that she was such a good mother, prepared to scold only as the last option, always prepared to listen and give praise at every opportunity.

He waved back and got out of the car, feeling momentarily relaxed and contented. 'The garden looks lovely,' he smiled as he walked over to her and kissed her.

'All due to my hard work and green fingers.' She pushed back a few strands of hair that had fallen across her face. John leant down and picked a large daisy bloom and pushed it into her hair, 'Beautiful fairy queen of the garden, your slave stands before you.'

'Oh yes, and what special favour are you after?' she said with a twinkle in her eye.

'Any small crumb of your loving nature would be more than I deserve.'

'Hmmm, at last you're talking sense.' She poked his nose with a gloved finger and began to walk back to the house. 'Come on. Supper in ten minutes.'

'Coming, boss,' he said and followed her into the house.

They both washed and tidied up and came in together to sit down at the dining table which was already laid with ham, new potatoes and salad. A bottle of chilled white wine was also on the table.

'Looks good,' said John as he poured wine into her glass. 'Where on earth is Suzie?'

Charlotte took a sip of her wine and stared at him, 'Don't get all agitated, darling, but she's gone to Bobby's.'

'Bobby's?!' In an instant, his mood changed and the creases in his brow told exactly what it was.

'There was no reason for saying she couldn't stay when she had been invited. She enjoys it so much there.' Already she had gone on the defensive.

'Well, I don't want them bringing her back. You'll have to collect her.' He knew his voice sounded unreasonably hard.

'That won't be necessary. She's going to stay the night.'

Under the table, John squeezed his knuckles hard. His chest tightened and he could hear his breathing. The muscles in his face became so tight they hurt and, for a moment, he couldn't speak.

'You shouldn't have let her do that,' said John and couldn't stop his voice from quivering.

'Why ever not? They'll have a lovely time,' said Charlotte with a shrug.

'Because I want her here. I don't want her sleeping there.'

'It's been such a lovely day, and the forecast is good. Simon suggested the girls might like to sleep in a tent in the field he owns. They'll love it.'

Thoughts crashed around his mind so fast he could almost hear them. 'Simon suggested it, did he? Bloody Simon.' Now he was definitely snarling, and Charlotte shifted uneasily in her chair.

'Please, John. That's not very nice. Why are you so angry?'

'What's going to happen if they wake up terrified. It'll be very different in the night with a variety of weird sounds.' He glared at her as if she couldn't see that for herself, and it made a reasonable argument.

'There's no need to worry about that. Simon has agreed to sleep in a tent next to theirs and if they get frightened, he'll be there to sort it out.'

Before he knew it, he had slammed his fist down on the table and various items jumped. 'I want her home! Do you understand? She's got to come home,' he almost roared.

Charlotte jerked back in her seat in sudden fright.

'John, you're frightening me,' she started to plead.

'You should have asked me first. You'll have to go and get her!'

'I certainly won't do that. And since when did I have to ask your permission before letting her do anything?' Her voice trembled now in both anger and hurt.

'If you had bothered to ask me, I would have told you that I was hoping that we could all go out together this weekend. I thought it would be a treat. But that's impossible now because she spends more time over at that bloody family than she does at home.' His eyes glared and the veins in his neck stuck out.

'Then it's a pity you didn't tell us in advance. We're not mind readers. And the way you've been behaving lately, it's the last thing we would have expected of you.'

'Oh, so it's all my fault?' There was no let-up in his anger.

'Yes, it's all your fault. I can't take any more of this, John. I know there's been something gnawing away inside of you, and I've tried to ask you about it but you shut me out. You're continually in a bad mood and you've become impossible to live with. You're unwell, and I think you need to see the doctor.' She'd got it off her chest at last.

'Thank you, madam, that's all I need,' his words were laced with sarcasm. 'I'm off my head now.'

'I'm too upset to eat anything now. I'm going into the garden.' She turned and walked away as the tears began to flood her eyes.

'Charlie,' he shouted after her, but she kept on walking.

John sank back into his chair and dropped his head into his hands. He felt as if he had plummeted into a deep black hole. There was no way out, no escape. His whole being screamed in agony and yet he knew that it would only get worse. The more he had struggled to keep Suzie out of harm's way, the worse the situation had become. In spite of all his planning and resolve he had ended up as being the villain. And he couldn't expect otherwise. But what else could he do? To keep laying the law down like an uncaring bully would only drive Charlie and Suzie away for ever. The pain he was causing them broke his heart, but they'd never understand that from what they could see, from what they were having to put up with from him.

He desperately wanted to go out into the garden and take Charlie in his arms and tell her he loved her so much and needed her and had not wanted to hurt her, but he knew he couldn't do that without completely spilling the beans. And he knew, more than anything else, that if anything happened to Suzie because he hadn't protected her, Charlie would believe that he could have done something to stop it, and he would be blamed for that too. She'd never forgive him.

He stood up and went through to the kitchen door and looked out. He saw Charlotte sitting on a bench he had made for one of her birthdays. She was holding her head in her hands and sobbing. All he could do was stare and feel his heart breaking.

Chapter Five

John looked at his watch. His appointment was for ten o'clock but it was already quarter past. He looked at the dog-eared pile of magazines on the little table and decided that not much imagination had gone into their choice. On the wall across the room opposite hung the photographs of the staff: four doctors, two or three nurses and reception staff. He hadn't been to the surgery for many years, but he remembered Dr Henshaw who he had seen on that occasion. He couldn't remember why he had seen him, but he did recall him as being a fairly approachable, almost jovial kind of chap.

He shifted his view and gazed at the motley lot of sullen-faced individuals seated around the surgery waiting room. He wondered what their illnesses might be. With exception of one smart woman, they all seemed grossly overweight. A couple of women came in with babies, and he couldn't help noticing that one of them had what looked like dark nicotine stain on her fingers. He snorted to himself, but then realised that he had no right to sit in judgement of anyone else, and his conclusions would probably be wrong anyway. It occurred to him, as it had done frequently lately, that criticising everything and everyone he came into contact with had become a habit.

He couldn't kid himself any longer. His emotional state was almost in shreds, and because he felt so screwed up all the time, he was laying into everyone in sight. What the hell the doctor could do he had no idea, but at least he'd taken the bull by the horns and done what Charlotte had suggested. He knew he wouldn't be able to say what was worrying him, in spite of doctor-patient confidentiality, so there was a chance he would be recommended to a shrink. Jesus, what a state of affairs to get into.

'John Elliot to see Dr Henshaw,' came the voice from the internal PA system. John got up and went out to the corridor and along it until he found the door that said 'Dr Henshaw'. He tapped on it and went in. Dr Henshaw was sitting at his desk in front of his computer but looked up with a friendly smile, 'Good morning, Mr Elliot. Take a seat. How can I help you?'

John sat down and quickly took in Dr Henshaw. He was probably in his late fifties and a little overweight around the middle. His hair was thick and turning grey and his faced looked as if it had enjoyed some good living, most likely accompanied with alcohol.

John momentarily felt stumped for words, but Dr Henshaw didn't press him. 'The fact of the matter is that I'm completely stressed out.'

'Have you any idea why this is?' The doctor was calm and clinical.

'I know exactly why it is, but I'm afraid I can't tell you what it is,' and wondered if he was sounding rude. Probably. Dr Henshaw started tapping rapidly on his computer and watching the words come up on the screen.

'How are things at home?'

'Terrible, but it's all my fault. My wife and daughter are long-suffering, but they've had to bear the brunt.' John decided there was no point in holding back.

'How long have you felt like this?'

'Oh, I forgot. About three weeks, give or take. A certain problem has arisen that I've got to deal with. It's something I can't talk about, and it's not actually within my power to solve. I'm not saying it won't be solved; just that it can't be solved by me.'

Dr Henshaw kept busily tapping away. 'I can't help you solve it if you can't tell me what it is.'

'I know that, and I'm not expecting you to. I'm hardly sleeping, and I feel like shit. Sorry. I was just hoping you could give me something to help me sleep, and maybe give me a bit of a pick-up or, I dunno, a tranquiliser that does something?'

'I don't know that that would be the answer. I could give you something that might help you sleep and help you to calm down, but it won't solve the underlying problem.'

'I realise that, but if it can take the edge off things until the matter I'm having to cope with goes, I'll be thankful for that.'

'That's impossible. Losing any weight?'

'No.'

'Bowels all right?'

'Fine. Never had a problem there.'

'Do you ever cry?'

Christ, he hadn't expected that one although he should have done considering the amount of callers he's spoken to over the years who had cried because emotional stress they'd been under. 'Well, I've certainly felt like it. When the pressure's really on and I'm helpless to do anything. And I feel guilty too because I've put my wife through a lot.'

Dr Henshaw tapped in some more and then asked, 'And you are unable to talk about this problem with anyone else?'

'With one other, yes, which does help but it doesn't solve it.'

There was a long silence, and John could see that Dr Henshaw was not entirely happy about this situation. He obviously thought that he needed some counselling and probably a more in-depth discussion with a psychiatrist. John shifted in his chair and waited for the verdict.

'I'll give you something which should help, but the prescription is only for two weeks. If things don't improve, I want you to come and see me again.' Dr Henshaw wrote down his prescription on his prescription pad and handed it to John. 'I'm a bit concerned at not knowing more about what's giving you all this grief. I'm sure it would be beneficial to you if you could find a way of being able to talk about it. Would you consider talking to the Samaritans? They are an excellent organisation and completely confidential?'

John smiled inwardly. What an irony. 'Yes. I know of them. I'll think about it. I know it sounds crazy, but there's a good reason why I can't say what this is all about,' said John and stood up. 'Thanks a lot.'

He went out.

****

Sarah finished off the agenda for the next day's meeting and printed off some copies. Every few weeks, she held a meeting at the centre when volunteers were encouraged to attend and raise any problems or ideas they might want to air and discuss. It was something she had introduced to the branch during her first year of office as the branch director, and it had been useful.

Although there were 120 volunteers – unless their numbers were temporarily down as they had been for the last few months – they were all unified in their common purpose. They were all, never the less, of different ages and different backgrounds. They were all caring people with a sense of compassion for the less fortunate members of society, but they all had different personalities. The Samaritan organisation had started in 1953, consisting of a single branch with a handful of volunteers, but since that time it had spawned over 200 national branches and spread throughout the world. Several of the national branches, partly because of their location, could still only muster a small number of volunteers, and Sarah's branch was one of the best in the country. To keep the service that was offered open for business 24 hours a day, 7 days a week and 365 days a year was a big task, and it was an achievement for which the Samaritan organisation was proud.

The job of branch director was no little job. It demanded time, patience and a mountain of understanding.

Fortunately, Sarah had managed to pick a good team to back her up. She had a deputy director for Training, and others that were responsible for Selection, Caller Care, and Outreach which organised visits to schools among other events, and a deputy for the Prison Team. Even with all this support and a dedicated membership of volunteers, she was beginning to feel that by the time her third year in office came to an end, she would have had enough. On top of her work for the Samaritans, she still managed to do part-time nursing four days a week. She had a son who lived and worked in London, and although he got along to see her as much as he could, it was often difficult because of his own work commitments. Her husband had left her for another woman several years ago. Sarah was not the whingeing type and regarded her lot as a happy one.

The situation that had arisen over Bobby and John's involvement was constantly on her mind. She realised that John was in a very difficult position and was desperate to help him find a way out, but at the same time she knew that the Samaritan policy of confidentiality could never be compromised. The fact that John knew who Bobby was and that his daughter Suzie was Bobby's friend was something that she and John had continued to keep to themselves. She knew that she was the only one John could lean on and was conscious of how much he needed her support. She had decided, for better or worse, that there would be no benefit in advising other volunteers in the branch that Bobby was known to John. The two of them often talked and she was now waiting for his arrival to discuss the present state of play. She heard a car door slam and went to the door to let him in. As soon as she saw him, she noticed how tired and dark he looked around the eyes.

'Hi, John. Come on in,' she said, and he followed her in silence through to the living room. 'Coffee? I've just made it.'

'Thanks,' he nodded and sat down in one of her arm chairs. The smell of the percolated coffee in the corner drifted powerfully into the room as she poured him a cup and brought it over to him, 'Drop of milk and no sugar. Is that right?'

'Great. Thanks.' He said and forced a smile.

Sarah got her own coffee and sat on the sofa opposite him. 'You're looking tired. How are things?'

'Honestly? Shit!' he paused and took a sip of his coffee and put it down on the occasional table. 'Last weekend, Suzie and Bobby camped in Simon's field, and he slept in an adjoining tent. Charlie agreed to it and didn't tell me first – why the hell should she? – but I lost my rag and a mighty row ensued. I was scared. I mean,

Simon sleeping in a tent next to them! My imagination went into overdrive.'

'Was Suzie all right?'

'She came home full of it. Had a wonderful time.'

'So nothing happened during the night?'

'I don't think it did. I think he stayed in his tent all night. But I think he's a sly bastard. He's not going to go charging in. They've done it once and everything was okay. Next time he might briefly visit them so he gets Suzie's trust. Slowly, slowly, catchy-monkey. His brand of grooming.'

'Bobby has rung again. I think she relies on us now. From what she says, he's still abusing her. The fact that she still calls us must mean that we are giving her some comfort, though it can't help her situation. Simon may not be interested in Suzie,' Sarah offered encouragingly.

'Pigs might fly. The point is, I don't feel able to sit around and wait until something happens to her,' said John wearily. 'It's not just my fear for Suzie; my marriage is heading for the rocks. I'm so stressed out I've become unbearable to live with. A right bloody bully, to be honest. Charlie can't understand my nasty and totally unreasonable dislike of Simon and his wife. And who can blame her? Of course in her eyes I must look like a heartless bastard and frankly that's just how I'm behaving.'

'You're being too hard on yourself, John. Of course you want to protect Suzie. It must be difficult to stop Suzie being with her friend without coming up with a sensible reason.'

'To be honest, Sarah, the only way I can see for saving my marriage is to get Charlie on my side which means telling her about what's been going on. Telling Charlie isn't really breaking Bobby's confidentiality.'

Sarah suddenly felt alarmed, 'That's exactly what it would be.'

'Charlie's not going to say anything. Nobody else is going to know.' John was determined to put his case.

'You don't know that for sure, John. We volunteers make an absolute commitment to confidentiality. Partners might agree with it in principle but in an extreme case like this, they may waver. She could be so upset she might go and tell Simon's wife about what's been happening to Bobby. And don't forget Suzie. She'll want to put her before anything.'

'Of course I realise that. But I don't think she'd do anything if I told her not to,' replied John, but immediately felt his argument weakening.

'I'm sorry, John, but that's not good enough. It's too risky. She's a mother. She'd be under terrible pressure. She's not a Samaritan, and she would almost certainly believe that blowing the whistle was the right course of action. God knows, the plight of poor Bobby is taking its toll on us. If she tried spilling the beans, the outcome could be disaster. We've been over this before.' Sarah was harsh but not without feeling for him.

'What the hell am I going to do then, Sarah? Watch my marriage go down the pan? See my daughter begin to hate me? Stand by and do nothing when I think she might be at risk, never mind what's been happening to poor Bobby?' he replied with complete and utter despair.

'As long as Bobby's calling us and unloading her misery and asking us to keep it secret I'm afraid we can't do anything. I know it sounds brutal because of the situation you're in, but that's because it is brutal. I must have your word that you will keep Bobby's calls confidential.' She leaned towards him to emphasise her demand.

John began to breathe heavily, and Sarah could tell he was struggling with his answer.

'John…please.'

John took a final deep breath and then replied quietly, 'Very well.'

'I'm sorry. You know I didn't want to have to ask you,' she said as gently as possible. 'In the meantime, you'll just have to do your best with Charlotte and keep an eye on what's happening with Suzie. Bobby's never mentioned that Simon has tried anything with her, not that she would necessarily know, but it might be difficult for him to do anything involving Suzie without Bobby's knowledge. I know it's not a lot, but it's something positive to think about.'

John nodded but didn't speak, and Sarah realised he was as demoralised as some of their callers to the centre.

'Will you be all right, John?'

'Yeah,' he replied, without a shred of conviction.

'I'm truly worried about you. I think you should stop doing duties for a bit. I don't see how you can handle calls while you're in this state.'

'No, Sarah! Please don't ask me to stop doing duties. It's the one thing that's keeping me sane. I'm all right on the phone. I can remain focused, I promise.' He pleaded with a hard edge to his voice, expressing a defiance.

She thought for a few moments before replying, 'All right. Against my better judgement. But I've known you a long time, John, and I know you to be a super volunteer so I'll go with that.'

He nodded. 'I'll be all right. Don't worry. I went to see the doctor yesterday. I didn't tell him anything, of course, just that I was stressed out with a problem. I could tell he wanted more information, but he gave me some pills anyway. At least they'll help me sleep. He probably thought I was a nutter.'

'I'm sorry, John.'

'It's okay. It's not your fault. And I'm glad I've got you to talk to. In a way I'm glad you're not wishy-washy, otherwise I might weaken.'

'It breaks my heart to see you like this.'

He took a small medicine bottle from his pocket and stared down at it. 'This is the type of pill that many of our callers have been prescribed when they come on the phone screaming about their abdabs, the sort that many of them swallow all at once to end everything,' he said with a wistful smile.

'John?' said Sarah, quizzically tilting her head.

'Don't worry, I'm not going to try and top myself. That would only make matters worse. And I'd probably cock it up anyway.' He stood up. 'I'd better get off.'

Sarah stood up too. 'Keep coming and talking to me, John. I've told you, call me any time; even if it's in the middle of the night. I really mean that.'

'I know and thanks. If I ever do call you in the middle of the night, you'll know the bloody pills aren't working.' At last he managed a real smile.

They both walked out to the front door and gave each other a hug. 'Take care, John. Love to Charlotte.' She squeezed his arm.

She opened the door, watched him walk down the front path, get into his car and drive away. As she walked back into the house she was almost in tears.

Chapter Six

The atmosphere was icy and had been so throughout the whole meal. John and Charlotte had passed the occasional polite but completely inane comment to each other in the hope of concealing the frigid mood from Suzie, but it had not worked.

'I wish we could be happy again,' said Suzie.

'I'm sorry, darling. We are happy really, but Daddy's got a lot of things to deal with at work. Everything is going to be all right,' said Charlotte, and gave a knowing nod towards John who stretched his arm out towards Suzie.

'Mummy's right. It's my fault, really. I know I've been grumpy, but things are getting better now. We'll try and plan something for the weekend. Maybe we can take a trip to Bristol and visit the zoo. What do you think?'

'That would be brill, Daddy. Do you mean it?'

'Of course, if Mummy agrees.'

'Of course I do. That would be lovely.'

'It's settled then. If you've finished, you go and watch TV while I talk with Mummy,' said John.

'Thanks,' said Suzie, and sidled off to the living room with a bounce in her step.

'Thank you, John. She'll love that and it'll be nice to go out together. It's been ages.'

'I know. It's all been my fault.'

'I don't know what's been going on but you've definitely not been yourself. It's bad enough you being so unpleasant to me, but you've no right to be so unkind to Suzie.'

'I've not meant it. I've had to deal with…well, a number of difficulties at work, but I know that's no excuse.'

'Why won't you talk to me about them? In the past you've always shared problems, and I've always wanted to support you.'

John sighed, 'I know, but I've got to deal with what's going on, on my own. I don't mean to cut you out, but please let me deal with this.'

'It's all beyond me. I'm imagining all sorts of things. We're not going bankrupt, are we?'

'Good God, no. Things are not easy at the moment, but we'll pull through. You'll just have to trust me.'

'You may not mean to be, but I think you're being unfair and unreasonable.'

Charlotte stood up and began to clear the plates from the table. John knew she was right, but what else could he say? He stood up and gathered the remaining items on the table and followed Charlotte to the kitchen in a vague suggestion that things were normal between them. As he struggled to find something light-hearted to say, the telephone in the hallway rang. He began to move towards the door when Charlotte said, 'I'll take it,' and passed him as she went to the hallway. John opened the dishwasher door intending to load the machine when he heard Charlotte's voice. 'Hallo, Pauline. How are you? Good. Yes, I'm fine. Yes, I looked out for you but missed you. Oh really. Oh, well yes. That's really kind of you, Pauline. Yes, we'd love to come. Wednesday of next week sounds fine. I'll just check with John.' There was a pause and then, 'John, are we doing anything next Wednesday?'

John stood rigid and felt the blood rush to his cheeks. Pauline! Bobby's mum! Christ, what was she wanting? Love to come? What the hell was she arranging?

'Um...um,' he stammered as he searched for a stalling argument.

'John, we're free next Wednesday, aren't we? Hallo, Pauline. I'm sure we're free. Thank you so much. We'll look forward to it. See you about seven then. We will. Bye.'

John heard the receiver replaced and a moment later Charlotte returned to the kitchen. 'That was Pauline. They've invited us over for a meal next Wednesday. I'm certain we've nothing on. That's so nice of them.'

'A meal? What do you mean a meal?'

'A meal, John. They've invited us for the evening. That's so nice of them.'

'Well, we can't go.' The words were out even though he hadn't the faintest idea of what he could say for his objection.

'Of course we can go. Why ever not?'

'Well, we don't know them. What's the point of it?'

'Of course we know them. Well, I do. It'll give you a chance to get to know them as well. You'll really like them.'

He was well and truly on the spot this time, and he knew it. But how the hell could he wriggle out of it? Yet the thought of having to go and sit down with that man filled him with horror. He wouldn't be able to look him in the face without smashing his fist into it. He'd choke if he had to sit and eat with him and talk with him, to discuss their children and listen to him saying how much he loved Bobby, to laugh and joke with him as he tried to eat and drink without throwing up. The thoughts stampeded through his mind. He began to stammer. 'I'm not sure if I've got something on. I've got a feeling I have a meeting that night.'

Charlotte's eyes went into slits, and her voice was slow and cold. 'I've just about had enough of this, John. I don't know what's the matter with you, but if you don't come; if we don't go together, I won't forgive you. Your hostility towards Simon and Pauline is beyond me, and frankly, I'm ashamed of you. We're going and that's an end to it.'

John stood and stared in silence at her. There was nothing he could say. Nothing he could do. He'd have to go, and he'd have to get through it as if everything was normal. How the hell he was going to do that he hadn't the faintest idea.

****

John pulled into the Plough Pub car park. It was 11.45. It was a brilliant sunny day. He hadn't been to the Plough for a long time and it had always been with Charlotte. Their food was good and reasonably priced. He'd decided to come here now because it was well off the beaten track, and he wanted to sit in the garden with a pint and calmly think about his situation and what options were open to him to try and get himself out of the bloody mess he'd found himself in. He got out of the car, and made his way into the pub.

There were two men sitting at the bar and a young couple, holding hands, sitting by a window. He ordered a pint and went out into the garden and sat down at one of the tables. He took a long swallow of his beer and plonked the glass down on to the table wiping his mouth with the back of his hand at the same time. He should have been feeling good because he'd just come from a meeting with a new customer who had given him a healthy order which was going into a new design for a filtration and pumping system. He'd seen the "spec" a month ago and put in a quote which the company had accepted. The profit margin wasn't huge, but it would provide work and keep the firm jogging along. The order was a lucky break, but the pleasure he should have felt was blunted by the nagging strain of what was going on in his personal life.

He took another long swallow of his beer and let out a sigh. He really had to look at things calmly and sensibly and decide on a positive way forward. A crease appeared in his forehead as his thoughts began to filter through. Suppose he did blow the whistle on Simon. How would he actually go about it? Turn up at the police station and ask to speak to a senior officer? What would he say to him? There was a child ringing up the Samaritans who says her step-father is sexually abusing her.

'Who is this child?'

'Her name is Bobby Hargreaves. Her father is a local magistrate.'

'Ah yes, I know the man well. Has Bobby told her mother?'

'No. She's scared to. Well, I mean she has tried to tell her, but she doesn't believe her. She misses her father, you see.'

'Her father?'

'Yes, he was killed in a car crash and she doesn't like Simon because he's trying to replace her father. But that's not what this is about. I mean...' The policeman cut in. 'Has the child told anyone else about this, sir?'

'No, she doesn't want anybody else to know.'

'She doesn't want anybody to know?'

'No. She wants to keep it secret.'

'But you are telling us.'

'Yes, you see…look, I think you should question Mr Hargreaves.'

'I don't think we could do that without more evidence, sir. Will the Samaritans confirm your allegations?'

'Err, well, I'm not sure about that. We're supposed to be confidential you see and…'

Oh hell, blowing the whistle in that way was going to be useless. And in any case, Bobby would be too frightened to admit what Simon was doing. It sounded ludicrous in the cold light of day, but he had heard the dreadful anguish and fear in the child's voice when she had said that she was terrified if what Simon was doing ever came out. Whether her reasoning was right or wrong didn't matter. She obviously believed that he could do something terrible to her and her mother wouldn't believe her because she believed everything that Simon told her, and she would be branded by everyone for being a dreadful liar, and everyone would turn against her, including Suzie. Would she kill herself in those circumstances? Again, it seemed far-fetched, but it was not impossible, and such an outcome didn't bear thinking about. But he knew that it had happened before several years ago when a child had been calling his branch and had subsequently taken her own life.

There was, however, another important issue. The confidentiality policy in the Samaritans remained absolute with children as much as with adults, but the possibility of being criminally liable had recently gone into the melting pot. It wasn't impossible that the Samaritans or individual volunteers in the Samaritans could face a charge of aiding and abetting or some other similar criminal charge where a child was being sexually abused if it wasn't reported. Duty of care and safeguarding were phrases that kept swimming around in his mind. As for the fallout concerning the credibility of anything the Samaritans said, as well as their confidentiality in the future, would be seriously undermined. Some of the press would have a field day.

The only other option for him would be to continue doing nothing except trying to support Bobby on the phone when she rang. Perhaps, in the end, she would change her mind and tell them her name and address and ask for help in revealing what Simon had been doing to her. If they convinced her they cared for her and were on her side she might just go for it. He'd have to do his damnedest to keep Suzie from going over to her house which would mean more rowing with Charlie. The charade of his pathetic excuses had already blown up in his face. He'd have to think of some other reasons, a lot more convincing, if he was ever going to get Charlie to agree with him. Already his relationship with her was shot to pieces. If things carried on the same way, they could reach the point from which repairing the damage would be lost forever. He'd never get over that. Charlie and Suzie were the love of his life. To use the well-worn expression that he was between a rock and a hard place was pathetic. Whichever way any action was taken, people were going to get hurt. And it was all because of that monster Simon.

He drained his glass and stood up. He walked to his car and set off to his office, realising that he still had a business to run.

As soon as he arrived at the works car park, he made his way into the workshop to have a word with Eric, his chief supervisor. He was only a little way into his conversation when his secretary Jenny approached him.

'Sorry to barge in, but Mr Crawshaw's here. He insisted on waiting. I put him in your office. I didn't like to call you because I knew you were at a meeting with a customer.'

'Oh Christ', John mumbled under his breath. What the devil did his father-in-law want? 'Thanks, Jenny. That's all right. Tell him I'll be along in just a moment.'

Jenny turned and walked away. 'Have you got in-laws, Eric?' asked John with a wistful smile.

'Father's dead. Mother-in-law's not too bad in small doses.'

'Hmmm. Okay. Better put on my full metal jacket. Everything's all right here. We'll have to finish this later.'

'No problem,' said Eric and John walked off, making his way back to his office. As soon as he entered, he produced a bright smile. 'Henry. This is a surprise. How are you?' said John, and extended his hand which Henry took with a firm grip but accompanied it with a stony stare.

'I was in the area so I called in at the house.'

'Good. Charlie would have been pleased to see you,'

'What the hell's going on?' His voice was flat and hard.

'Sorry?' John tried to look surprised.

'You and Charlie. She was almost in tears. I've never seen her looking in such a mess.'

'What has she been saying?'

'It's what she's not been saying. Do you think I'm a bloody fool? I'm her father. What little she has told me I had to drag out of her.'

'I'd prefer it if you didn't interfere in my marriage.'

'Are you having an affair with another woman?'

'Don't be ridiculous.'

'Well something is going on. Don't try and pull the wool over my eyes.'

'I'm rather busy at the moment, Henry. And I'm not prepared to discuss my private life with you.'

'Don't think you can dismiss me as easily as that. This is my daughter I'm talking about. I'm not prepared to stand by and see her so miserable. What's going on between you two?'

John spread his hands as if to make a conciliatory gesture, but he kept his voice steady. 'The last thing I want is for Charlie to be upset or unhappy. We've just had a brief misunderstanding. Everything will be sorted.'

'And Suzie. It sounds as if you've put her through the ringer as well.'

'I'm not prepared to discuss Suzie with you. Charlie shouldn't have involved you in any of this.'

'Oh, you needn't question her loyalty. I've already told you I had to drag anything out of her. And that's why I know something's going on. She didn't dare tell me.'

'Nothing's going on.'

'If you're having an affair with another woman, I'll...'

'For Christ's sake, Henry. What do you think I am?'

'There's no smoke without fire. Get a grip, man. You have a wonderful wife. Prove that you deserve her.'

'I don't have to prove anything to you.'

'You'd better prove it to her or you're for the high jump.'

'I'd like you to leave, Henry. I'll tell you this. I love your daughter, and Suzie more than anything in the world. And I know they both love me. We've had a small upset, which happens from time to time in any marriage, but our marriage is solid. We'll soon sort it.'

'See that you do. I'll see myself out.'

****

John leant back in his seat and let out a long sigh. 'This is simply getting out of hand, and it looks to me as though it can only get worse,' he said and stared at Sarah across the desk. He had called in at the centre where he had arranged to meet her on his way back from work. He needed to bring her up to scratch with the developments, and he had just finished filling in about the visit he and Charlotte were making to Pauline and Simon's.

'You'll simply have to go, John, and carry on as if you know nothing about Bobby or Simon and what he's been doing to her.'

John rubbed his face and shook his head. 'I dunno, Sarah – sitting down with that bastard...'

'Do you know if Bobby will be there?'

'Very likely. It is her home, after all, and we won't be arriving there late so she won't have gone to bed or anything.'

'You're not taking Suzie, are you?'

'God no. Lady next door to us, Margery, usually baby-sits.'

'You've never actually met Bobby face to face, have you?

'No. Charlie's done the school runs over the last few weeks and on the odd occasions when Bobby has come over to us I've been at work or maybe down here doing a shift.'

'How many times have you spoken to Bobby on the phone?'

'Myself, oh, a couple of times. But of course I'm not the only one who has spoken to her.'

'The reason I'm asking is if you do meet her when you go to her house, do you think she might recognise your voice?'

'I've wondered about that myself. I don't know what that would mean or what she would do or think.

Probably assume my visit was for the purpose of spilling the beans to Simon.'

'That's a big assumption.'

'Well, she's so terrified that someone will blow the whistle and what she sees as exposing her, what else could she think if she recognised my voice and saw that I'd come to see Simon? She's not stupid.'

'It's a risk you'll have to take.'

There was a long silence as they both sat mulling over their thoughts and then John said, 'My biggest worry is knowing that I'm going to have to sit down with this swine and make polite conversation.'

'For God's sake, keep calm, John. Try and dismiss everything you know about what's been going on, and play the game as if he and his wife were a normal, decent couple.'

'I shall feel so guilty. Sitting down with a man and supposedly enjoying his company when I know of the dreadful thing he's doing, and yet I'm doing nothing to try and stop it. It's like collusion.'

'Look, John, you've got to stop thinking like this. It's the toughest part of this job. The one thing we would all like to do with all our callers whether we know them or not is wave a magic wand to remove the awful things that might be going on in their lives. We can't, and that's an end to it. All we can do is support her in the way we've been doing. Am I repeating myself? Yes, I am. I've got to because that's all we've got.'

John shook his head wearily. 'I'm sorry. I know. I'm just…sounding off, that's all.'

'Don't be sorry. I feel for you. It's a tough one. Let me know how things go and call me.'

John grunted with disdain. 'I shouldn't feel sorry for myself. Bobby's the one who's suffering. She's the only one who matters.'

'She sounds a gutsy little girl. She's calling us so we're obviously helping her. We just have to hope that things in some way might suddenly change for the best. That's all we've got.'

John nodded without speaking and stood up. It had been a useless meeting. He didn't mean that in a nasty way. It just meant that they had covered the same old ground again. Repeating the same old mantra about confidentiality, about acknowledging that they were helpless to intervene unless Bobby said they could. It could have almost been laughable if the stakes weren't so high. The arguments sounded so limp, even heartless. Yet he had to hang on to the thought that as long as they didn't betray Bobby, that was the right decision and that in some unfathomable way, everything would turn out fine for Bobby.

He kissed Sarah on the cheek. 'Thanks.' He turned and walked out.

****

It was 1.30 am when Jackie put the phone down after 45 minutes and came out of the booth in the Ops room. She'd come on duty at midnight to do a shift with Linda who looked up enquiringly.

'Eleanor,' said Jackie, and flopped into a chair.

'Bad?' asked Linda.

Jackie nodded with a grunt. 'I'll get coffee,' said Linda, and made her way to the kitchen where she quickly made a couple of mugs of instant coffee and came back with them to the ops room. They had both spoken to Eleanor who had called the branch on a number of occasions during the last two months. She had two children under the age of five and a partner who constantly beat her. She had put up with it for several years believing it was impossible to get away and too terrified to report him to the police. A few weeks ago, his assault had been so violent that he broke her nose and an arm, and she had ended up in a hospital. It had been too much, and the police had stepped in.

'The court case begins tomorrow, and she's terrified,' said Eleanor, and took a sip of her coffee.

'Poor girl. But he'll go down for it, won't he?'

'That's one of the things worrying her. Firstly, she's dreading having to appear in court, but more than that she's dreading the possibility of him getting off.'

'Surely not.'

Jackie shrugged, 'Don't ask me. Nothing surprises me today. Lawyers can pull all kinds of stunts, can't they? He may get away with a suspended sentence and a restriction order – is that what they call it – forbidding him to go anywhere near her.'

'Did you ask her if she wanted a follow up?'

'Yes. She jumped at it. I've said someone will ring between eight and nine tomorrow evening. She should have some idea of what's going on by then. Do you know who's on?'

'Pam, I think, so she'll handle it well.'

Jackie took a long gulp of her coffee and leant back into her chair. She worked in the office of a local builder's merchant and had been a volunteer for five years. She was an attractive girl in her late twenties and had moved in with George, another volunteer who had been with the branch for about ten years. They planned to get married the following year.

'I don't know why we do this, Linda. We must be crazy. The next call I get will probably be from some twit who wants to know if I'm wearing knickers.'

Linda grinned, 'All part of the service.'

'Like hell. How long have you been a volunteer?'

'About ten years.'

'I was told burnout usually happened after about three. Do you ever think of resigning?'

'No. Not yet. I know some calls are hard, but it makes it all worthwhile. I usually manage to dump it all before leaving the centre when I go off duty.'

The telephone rang.

'My turn,' said Linda and went into the other booth and picked up the receiver. 'Samaritans. May I help you?'

Silence. Linda didn't say anything. She decided to wait. She knew the person at the other end of the line was still there.

A minute went by but in the silence it seemed like an age.

'It's Bobby.'

Linda immediately leaned forward with the phone held tightly to her ear. 'Oh Bobby. We've been thinking about you. Are you all right?'

There was a long pause. 'They're in bed, asleep,' her voice was barely above a whisper.

'Is everything okay?'

'Mummy was out earlier. She went to her friends.'

'Who stayed with you?' the question was met with silence and Linda's experience guessed it was Simon. For a little while, Linda said nothing. Silence between the two of them was okay because Linda knew that Bobby found comfort in simply knowing that someone was there; that they knew what was going on and in part, was sharing her thoughts.

'Did anything happen?' Linda waited for an answer but nothing came. And instinctively, she knew that the silence, of course, meant that something had happened and that almost certainly Bobby would have suffered more abuse.

'It's all my fault.'

'It's not your fault, Bobby. You must never think that. What Simon does to you is bad, and he shouldn't do it.'

'No, it's my fault.'

'Why do you say that?'

'In the beginning, when I first met him, he was nice to me. He was kind and friendly, and I didn't mind holding his hand. He took me out, and he was funny and I was pleased. So you see, it showed that I wanted to be with him, and he understood that. He told me.'

Linda didn't reply immediately. The temptation to reply quickly and dismiss Bobby's thinking as completely misplaced would have been insensitive and useless because she realised that Bobby's understanding of the situation was too deeply embedded. Simon had obviously been able to terrify Bobby so that no one would believe her if she said anything, that she would be seen as a wicked liar, even by her mother, and would therefore be in serious trouble, with everyone turning against her, that it was she who was the one who enjoyed what he was doing and had led him on.

'Whatever Simon has said to you, Bobby, you are not to blame, and what he is doing is a very bad thing,' Linda said, with as much gentleness in her voice as she could.

'The only person who would believe me was Daddy.'

'We believe you, Bobby. We always will.' Again there was a long silence, which was the pattern of all the conversations that volunteers had shared with her.

'Just as a suggestion, Bobby, do you have a teacher at school who you like a lot and who you could talk to, as a first step towards stopping what Simon's doing to you? She would not be able to keep it secret, so I'm not telling you that you should do this, only if you want to. If you don't want to, that's all right. We'll still be here to support you and keep your secret as long as you say.'

Christ, Linda thought, *had she blown it and gone too far?* The last thing she and her colleagues wanted was to pressure Bobby into thinking that she ought to blow the whistle, and that they weren't really on her side.

'I can't tell anyone. I must never tell anyone. No one must know.'

'It's all right, Bobby. Your secret is safe with us. Call us whenever you like. We will always be here for you.'

There was a pause, and then Linda heard Bobby begin to cry. She could barely hold back her own tears. The thought of this child, lost and hurting, in fear and despair that no one – including her mother – would ever believe what was being done to her, was utterly heart-breaking. Bobby was talking to her and to other Samaritan colleagues from time to time, and it was good that she found some crumb of comfort in doing that, but they all shared an acute awareness that they were helpless to step in and stop this outrage as long as Bobby refused to agree. How long was her misery going to go on for? Would Simon ever make a slip-up and be exposed? Was there ever a chance that Bobby's mother, Pauline, would suddenly suspect that something was going on and eventually discover the kind of man she had married, and what he was doing to her daughter or would she always be so blinded by her love for him and dismiss even the slightest criticism of him?

Linda whispered into the mouthpiece, 'We care about you, Bobby. We think you're brave and know what Simon is doing to you is bad, and it's not your fault, whatever he tries to tell you.'

For a little while, there was the usual silence, and then Bobby said, almost inaudibly, 'I have to go. Thank you.' Linda didn't have time to reply before she heard the phone go dead. She slowly replaced the receiver and sank back into her chair. She'd done the job for a good number of years. But it never got any easier.

****

Charlotte pulled into the kerb outside number 12 Oakfield Terrace. She sighed and let her shoulders drop as she tried to relax. Was she over-reacting; being silly? What on earth would Linda think of her? Maybe she should drive away and forget it. She turned and looked at the house. Perhaps Linda wasn't at home. She should have rung first and told her that she was coming. No, it was better to take pot luck, and if she wasn't there, then she would take that as a sign to go away and forget the whole thing. If Linda was there, well, she was, after all, such a good friend of hers and John. She was sensitive and understanding and so easy to talk to. Damn it, what were friends for?

She got out of the car and walked up the front path, noting how nice the garden looked with a well-tended small patch of grass and a lovely display of flowers in the borders. She rung the door bell and a few moments later the door opened and Linda appeared.

'Charlie! How lovely to see you.'

'Hi, Linda. Hope you don't mind me dropping by unexpected.'

'Good gracious no. Come on in. Will you have some tea? I'll make a pot.' Linda led the way through to the kitchen and filled the kettle. 'Sit down. Will you have a biscuit? I've no cake.'

'Just tea would be lovely. I can't stop long.'

'So pleased to see you. Must be two or three weeks. Of course, I see John from time to time if we do an occasional shift together.'

'Yes, he often mentions that.'

'How have you been keeping, Charlie? Is Suzie all right?' said Linda as she busied herself getting cups and saucers off the dresser.

'Well I...' Charlotte hesitated.

'Is anything wrong, Charlie?' Linda suddenly stared hard at Charlotte. Charlotte looked down at her hands and fiddled with her fingers. There was a few moments silence. Charlotte mumbled, 'I um... I just wanted to ask you something. But I feel a bit of a fool now.'

'Don't feel that. Has something happened?' Immediately, Linda's voice was gentle. She moved over to the table where Charlotte was sitting and sat in a chair next to her.

'I'm probably being silly but I...' again she paused before gathering enough confidence to carry on. 'I wanted to ask you something about John.'

'John?'

'Well I was wondering if he has said anything to you about any problems he's got. I know this sounds ridiculous, but he's behaving in a way at home that is so unlike him. To be honest, he's become unbearable. And I know it's not the real John. It has to be something that's upsetting him. Maybe at work. Maybe we're in trouble, although he assures me everything is okay.'

'I am surprised, Charlie. He certainly hasn't talked to me about anything, and I haven't noticed that he's different. What do you think it can be?'

'I just don't know. I've asked him to tell me, but he says everything is fine.'

'He's not just being a grouchy old man, and it is just a phase that will fizzle out, is it?'

'No. I don't know. I feel guilty talking to you about him like this, but I don't know what to do.'

'I'm glad you have. You and John are two of my dearest friends. Do you want me to speak to him?'

'I'm not sure that would be wise.'

The kettle began to hiss. Linda stood up. 'Hang on. Let me make the tea.' She moved over to the work surface and poured the hot water into a tea pot. 'How do you want it?'

'Oh, milk. No sugar, thanks.'

Linda poured out the tea and came back to the table with the two cups.

'We seem to row about things on which we would normally be pleased about. Together.'

Linda bunched her mouth and looked at Charlotte questioningly.

'Well, for instance we've been invited out to a meal with a couple we know. Well, I know. Through the school. I met the mother, Pauline, on the school run. Pauline's daughter and Suzie have become good friends. I've also met Pauline's husband – well, her second husband. Her first husband died. The point is that they are a lovely couple. Her husband is charming. Anyway, I thought that John would be thrilled to meet them and go over to their house for a meal, but he went mad and said it was out of the question.'

'That sounds unlike John. Did he give a reason?'

'Not a proper one. He simply went on about us not pushing things too quickly; that they were new friends, and we should slow things up. Absolutely ridiculous.'

'I don't know what to say. If there is something wrong, he hasn't confided in me, and I haven't noticed anything. Are you sure you don't want me to have a word with him?'

'I'm not sure that would be a good idea.'

'I'd only do it if the moment was right. I won't go charging in with heavy boots on.'

'I know that, Linda. I'm sorry to burden you with this.'

'Rubbish. We're close enough to be able to talk about something like this, aren't we? Look how I've unloaded to you and John about me and Clive. That's hardly a happy story.'

'I know. I'm sorry. How are things?'

Oh, well, we're jogging along. A kind of truce at the moment.'

'God, I admire you, Linda. You're so down to earth and...well...' Charlotte shrugged her shoulders, 'forgiving and kind.'

'Don't you believe it! You want to see me when I'm riled up. Especially with Clive.' She smiled, and Charlotte gave a little chuckle which suddenly relaxed the atmosphere. For a few moments, there was silence as they hung on to their thoughts.

'What makes it worse', said Charlotte, 'is that he's being so unkind to Suzie,' she shook her head in dismay.

'Good gracious. That's not like John.'

'None of it is like John. It's one thing to be unkind to me, but it's so upsetting to see him be nasty to Suzie. It's totally uncalled for.'

'Well, I must say you surprise me, Charlie. I thought he doted on Suzie.'

'He does but... oh I dunno. Suzie loves to go over to her friend's house. They get on so well together. But John's always objecting without giving a sensible reason. Bobby's a lovely child, but John always gets riled up and says she can't go. There's always a row.'

Linda's brow suddenly creased, but she spoke as calmly as she could. 'Who's her friend?'

'Bobby. Pauline and Simon's daughter. She's a lovely child.'

Linda suddenly jerked her elbow and slopped her tea from her cup over the table. 'Drat it.' She quickly turned away to hide her expression and moved over to the sink. 'I must get a cloth.' She bent over the sink to pause as the implication of what Charlotte had said slammed into her. A surge of thoughts rushed around her head. God, it was suddenly all so clear. John had identified Bobby. She'd have to explain the situation to Charlie. Charlie had to know. Christ, she couldn't do that. What the hell was she thinking? She moved back to the table and began to wipe up the spilt tea.

'And John has given no real reason why he doesn't want Suzie to go over to Bobby's?'

'No. He just loses his temper and makes Suzie cry.'

'Perhaps he's just being over-protective if Bobby is a new friend. Fathers tend to be a bit silly about their little daughters.' Linda knew it sounded weak. No wonder John was having a problem in coming up with something sensible.

'I thought that as well at first, but I've told him that Bobby is a super child, and her parents are really nice. Simon is a magistrate. He's charming.'

Linda let out a big sigh. 'I don't know what to say. I'm not being much use to you.'

'Just talking has helped. I'd better be on my way, Linda. Sorry to unload on you like this.'

'It's lovely to see you, Charlie. Do try not to worry. If I get the chance, I'll have a friendly chat with John.' She tried to remain calm and hope the quivering in her voice was not too obvious.

'Be careful. He might be very touchy if you mention too much detail about what I've told you.'

'I'll tread carefully. It's probably strain of work.'

'He says not but we'll see.'

'I'm sure things will settle down soon, but call again if you need to talk.'

Charlotte stood up and kissed Linda, and then made her way to the front door. 'You've got enough on your own plate with Clive without having to listen to my worries.'

'I'm fine, Charlie. It's just bloody men.' Linda smiled and opened the front door. 'Take care and try not to worry.'

'You too, Linda. Thanks. Bye.'

Linda waved as Charlotte drove away, and then made her way back into the kitchen. She flopped down on to a chair and rested her hands down on the table. She needed time to take in what Charlie had told her. Bobby was Suzie's best friend. John couldn't fail to realise the implication. Of course, he'd kept it to himself. What else could he do? He obviously wouldn't have said anything to Charlie. He'd have to have kept it confidential from her. No wonder he was in such a state. He was probably the only one who knew, unless he'd confided in Sarah. That would have been the best move and knowing John, he would have done that. At least, he would have had her to share the load.

But how long could he go on like this? If he was behaving as badly as Charlie had said, he might crack and tell her everything. What would Charlie do? He'd tell her to say nothing of course, and she might agree, but there was no guarantee. She might believe in what the Samaritans did, but in a case like this, she might easily think an exception had to be made. A lot of people would. But then she wouldn't have thought through the implications of what it meant if the confidentiality was broken. John would have to try and hang on. Maybe she should try and talk to him as Charlie wanted. Maybe she'd tell him she knew that he knew who Bobby was. She was doing a shift with him in a few days. It might provide an opportunity. She'd tread carefully. Maybe he'd tell her himself. Maybe he wouldn't. Christ, what a mess.

Chapter Seven

Charlotte slammed the front door shut and followed John down the garden path to the car parked in the road. She had feelings of both pleasure and anxiety. Pleasure because she was going to have dinner with Pauline and Simon and anxiety because she knew that John – for some reason unknown to her – still didn't want to go and she was nervous about what he might say.

They were odd feelings which she hadn't experienced before because whenever they had gone out to socialise they had always been on the same page. In equal measure, they both liked their friends, and their tastes in enjoyment were pretty much the same. John, particularly, was normally fairly laid-back about going along with Charlotte on something he didn't much care about but which she enjoyed. It wasn't the fact that he had not moaned or complained about going as they had got ready, it was because he had said nothing but moved about with a tight-lipped and sullen expression. A ridiculous tension had arisen between them, and she had a slight sense of guilt that she was dragging him along somewhere he didn't want to go. That was putting it mildly. He definitely didn't want to go. It didn't make sense. Simon and Pauline were a lovely couple. They were friendly and liked Suzie. Why John should have been so hostile about them was a mystery to her. And it was infuriating because it was so unnecessary. In reality, she thought he was behaving like a spoilt child, and he would just have to pull himself together.

'You've been to the house before, haven't you? You'll have to show me the way when we get nearer,' said John in a toneless voice that she interpreted as saying "let's get this misery over as soon as possible".

'Of course, John. It's not very far.' Charlotte kept her voice upbeat.

'I don't want to be late tonight. I have to make an early start tomorrow. You know I'm off to the conference.'

'Let's not talk about coming home before we've even got there.'

'I'm just saying, that's all. You know I find the conferences quite stressful. I could well have done without this.'

'You've made it quite clear all day, all week, since we had the invitation that you don't want to go. And you've always said you've enjoyed the conferences otherwise you wouldn't go.'

'I don't like visiting people I don't even know.'

'Well, now's your chance to get to know them.'

'We have our friends. I'm glad you're pally with Pauline, but Simon's not my sort.'

'That's ridiculous. How can you say that about someone you haven't met?'

'I don't have to know him. We're perfectly happy as we are.' Each time he opened his mouth he realised how pathetic and utterly stupid he must have sounded. But he couldn't stop himself.

With every passing moment he was drawing closer to when he would be confronted by a man for whom he only felt disgust and terrible anger. He was going to have to smile and shake his hand and smile and say stupid, platitudinous rubbish. He couldn't do it. He couldn't trust himself. He knew he had to. But he couldn't.

He was almost certain to blow it. He'd lose his cool and come out with some totally out of line comment which would be too near the mark for Simon to not realise that he was – in some inexplicable way – on to him. The balloon would go up. There would be a terrible scene with accusations, and then tears from Charlie so that they would have to leave. Charlie would never forgive him.

As soon as they would get back in the car, she would scream at him in rage and total disbelief that he could have behaved in such a dreadful way. Then she would cry and not even want to look at him. It would take weeks, months before she would even consider forgiving him, if she ever did. It could end their marriage. She'd tell Suzie what had happened, and she would also be devastated because it would mean that she wouldn't be able to see her friend again. They'd probably hate him, and he would have to leave. And on top of all this, he would know that he was to blame.

He would be filled with shame because he would realise that he had let Charlie and Suzie down, and he would have let himself down. And all because he couldn't control himself when it was vital that he did so, no matter how difficult or how he felt.

He would have also let Bobby down. God knows what the repercussions would be in her household. Pauline would presumably be outraged at his odd but unfriendly remarks but not fully understanding of what the hell he had been implying by his remarks, whatever they had happened to have been. Simon would act as if he hadn't a clue and dismiss his remarks as pure rudeness because he'd had a drink – even though he intended to hardly drink anything.

With a bit of luck, it would all fizzle out as far as they were concerned, and there would be no reason for Bobby to experience any kind of backlash. Of course, Simon and Pauline would regard him as a boor, and feel sorry for Charlie. They would wonder how she could have married such an oaf, and Pauline would probably eventually ring up Charlie to see if she was all right. Charlie would be so embarrassed and try to explain things away, not for his sake, but to cover her own humiliation.

'There's a turning to the left about a hundred yards further on. Take that and then second on the right,' said Charlotte and John nodded silently.

No, he wouldn't do it. He couldn't. It was a step too far. Okay, he accepted the rule of confidentiality and absolutely believed in it. And that meant he couldn't by some circuitous route or by some vague comment to someone somewhere that could in some equally vague way compromise that confidentiality. If the trust of the caller – in this case Bobby's – was exposed in any way it would be nothing short of betrayal. Never mind about any personal considerations that might cause him discomfort. Tough. He'd have to put up with it in a way that was professional and which was expected of him.

'There it is. Number 24. The one with the Audi in the drive.'

John slowed and eased the car into the kerbside and switched off the engine. For a moment, they both sat in silence. Charlotte held a bunch of flowers and a bottle of wine on her lap. She reached across to John and handed him the bottle of wine. John stared at her for a moment and forced a weak smile. 'Come on, then,' he said, and got out of the car.

No sooner had they reached the front door when it sprung open, and Pauline stood there with a beaming smile on her face. Simon stood behind her. A moment later, she was excited and laughing as greetings were exchanged amongst three of them. Charlotte and Pauline hugged, and Simon leant forward and kissed Charlotte on both cheeks. John forced a smile and extended his hand to Pauline who gave a giggle, 'Oh so formal, John. How are you?'

'I'm well, thank you.' He held his smile.

'Good to meet you, John,' said Simon, and extended his hand. John mechanically took it, and he pushed the bottle of wine towards him. 'A small contribution.'

'Ah, thank you, John. That's great. Come on through to the living room.' Simon led the way down the hall to the living room and waved his arm expansively. 'Take a seat. Wherever you like. There's plenty of room.'

The room was large and expensively furnished. John inwardly snarled in recognition that Simon was probably loaded. Just one of those things: male competition.

As John and Charlotte each took a comfortable arm chair Charlotte said, 'I do love this room. It's lovely, isn't it, John?'

John replied with a quiet grunt and a nod.

'The fireplace is new. It cost an arm and a leg but what doesn't today,' said Pauline.

'What would you like to drink, Charlotte? We'll have wine with our meal, of course?'

'I'd love a fruit juice, Simon. Do you have apple?

'No problem. How about you, John?'

'Nothing, thanks.' John shook his head.

'Would you like me to drive, John, so you could have a drink?

'No thanks.' He held up his hand in an odd way to indicate that that was the end of the matter. Charlotte did not miss the quick glance that Simon made in the direction of Pauline, obviously indicating that he was thinking that John was some kind of oddball.

'I'll get the drinks. How about you, darling?' said Simon.

'I'll have some of the wine we're having with our meal please, Si,' said Pauline. Simon left the room.

While he was away, Pauline and Charlotte chatted about their children's schooling, and John sat in sullen silence. He snatched a cursory look at the clock on the mantelpiece, and inwardly groaned when he saw it said 7.30. They hadn't even started the meal yet, for which he had absolutely no appetite, and which was going to be a nightmare anyway. If they managed to get away by 10 o'clock, at the earliest, that still meant another two and a half hours. He'd never last that long being able to sit down with this man who he knew was abusing Bobby.

'Is Bobby coming to see us?' said Charlotte, trying to keep the mood up-beat.

'She's not very well this evening so she's gone off to bed early,' said Pauline.

'That's a shame. Is she sickening for something?'

'Just a bad cold, I think. Simon's been fussing over her as usual.'

'I'll go up and see her shortly,' said Simon. Immediately, John clenched his jaw and rubbed the back of his hand as his only means of controlling his discomfort.

'Simon has been absolutely wonderful with her. It's been hard for her since Roger died. He's so patient with her and spoils her rotten.'

'We think she's a lovely child, don't we, John? We're so glad she's friends with Suzie.'

'Yes. We think she should spend more time over at our place instead of always coming here.' Damn, had he said that too quickly and aggressively?

'Whatever they want, John,' said Simon, 'But we're very happy for Suzie to come over as much as she likes. She's a delightful child.'

You keep your filthy hands off her. John felt his cheeks burning, and he clamped his jaw tight as he struggled to conceal his thoughts.

'Absolutely,' chipped in Pauline, 'they get on so well together, and she's no trouble.'

'Even so...'

'Oh, it doesn't matter, John; whatever the children want,' said Charlotte.

'No! I think Bobby should spend more time with us!' Shit, he had definitely spoken with what looked like a ridiculous outburst of hostility. He quickly added, 'I just think it is only fair.' *You're not going to get your own way so easily, you bastard.*

There was an embarrassing pause and the others searched frantically for something g to say.

'Whatever. These things work themselves out okay in the end,' offered Simon.

'Simon's so easy-going about these things. He loves children.'

I bet he does. John diverted his eyes towards the carpet so as not to look at the man in front of him.

'So, you're in engineering I understand, John,' said Simon.

'Yes.'

Simon stared at John, expecting him to elaborate but nothing was forthcoming.

'Is business good?'

'Yes.' There was an awkward silence in the room, and Charlotte realised that Simon and Pauline were trying to fathom out what made John tick.

'You must find it very interesting being a magistrate,' said Charlotte brightly.

116

'Yes indeed,' said Simon.

John licked his lips which had gone dry. How do you deal with paedophiles, you bastard; congratulate them?

'I suppose you get all sorts?'

'Certainly do. A lot of young people too.'

How wonderful for you. What a thrill – especially if you get young girls; little children you can ogle at. John nodded grimly and squeezed the knuckles of one hand with the other.

'It must be difficult for young people today. So many come from broken homes, it's not surprising they turn to crime,' said Charlotte.

'That's an excuse that's often used. Of course, one has to weigh up all the facts, but I think we get it right most of the time.'

'I'm sure you do. I'm sure you do a wonderful job, Simon,' said Charlotte, smiling in admiration.

John breathed out noisily. God, how long was he going to have to suffer this drivel? The thoughts swam around in his head. He didn't want to listen to it. He didn't want to be there. He shouldn't be there. He should be doing everything he could to nail this bastard. Oh shit! What was the matter with him? He knew the score so why torture himself about what should happen; what ought to be done? The die was cast, and he had to accept it in the hope that something out of the blue would burst on the scene and put everything right. Yes, pigs might fly. And until he looked in the sky and saw that happening, he'd have to accept things as they were and be certain he didn't blow it. Whatever happened he mustn't make some stupid remark that would alert Simon that he was on to him.

Pauline returned to the room having visited the kitchen 'I think everything is ready so shall we all go in to eat.'

The others rose from their seats and followed Pauline to the dining room. As they moved through the doorway Charlotte shot a glare at John which clearly told him she was unhappy with his unfriendly manner. What the hell was the matter with him? He responded with a shrug which implied he couldn't care less. She turned away and quickly felt her appetite draining away. Why was he doing this? This was something she'd never experienced before. They'd been welcomed by a warm and friendly couple, but already he had turned the mood into an atmosphere where everyone was feeling awkward. Her stomach muscles were becoming knotted and the muscles in her face were so tight she was finding it difficult to smile. This was so unlike John. Everyone liked him because of his friendly and easy-going nature. She didn't know what was wrong with him, but if he didn't show a little more courtesy and friendliness towards their hosts, her embarrassment would be unbearable.

'If you would sit by the window, John, and I'll sit next to Charlotte,' said Simon as he lifted a bottle of wine from an antique dresser. They all sat down, and a moment later, Pauline came in with a steak and kidney pie.

'My! That looks beautiful,' said Charlotte, 'Isn't that beautiful, John?'

'Yes,' said John and endeavoured a weak smile at Pauline.

'I didn't bother with a starter, I hope you don't mind.'

'Good gracious, no. I'm sure this pie will be more than enough. It's so kind of you to ask us.' Charlotte smiled and swallowed hard.

'Nonsense. It's time we got together. The girls get on so well. I'm sure they'll stay friends for a long time.

We're going on holiday in France in July. We'd be very happy to take Suzie along with us if she'd like to come.'

John felt his stomach grabbed by an icy hand. The bastard was determined to have her; to get her on holiday with them where he would have a massive opportunity to get his dirty hands on her. No way. Over his dead body.

'We couldn't let you do that, Simon. She'd be a burden. It's really too kind of you,' said Charlotte.

Well done Charlie. 'I think Charlie's right. You will have had enough of Suzie by then.'

Pauline jumped in. 'Of course not. She's no trouble, and it would be such good company for Bobby. They'll love being together.'

'Well, it would be wonderful for Suzie if you really didn't mind. I'm sure she'd love to go,' said Charlotte, beginning to be persuaded.

'It's settled then. The girls will be thrilled, and Pauline and I will enjoy having them together.'

John clamped his jaw in silence for a few moments as his thoughts raced. The bastard was going to pull a fast one.

'When are you actually going?' he asked as calmly as he could manage.

'Last week of July.'

'Ah, then it won't be possible. We're going on holiday ourselves that week.'

'Are we?' Charlotte looked totally surprised, 'I didn't know that.'

'It was going to be a surprise.'

I thought we weren't going to manage a holiday this year, things being so tight. Where are we going?'

John hesitated. Shit. It would have to be somewhere good to compete with a visit to France. Where? Where? Where? He hadn't got the bloody money anyway.

Charlie was right. They had planned to not go on holiday. 'Um, I thought we... might try the Canary Islands.' Jesus, that was going to cost a packet.

'The Canary Islands. Well, well, well. I had no idea. Does it actually have to be the same dates? Have you booked it?'

'Well, yes I have.'

'Sounds wonderful, John. Even so, I think Suzie would have a much better time with Bobby than us. It would be good for us to have the time together. You've been under a lot of stress lately. It'll be good for both of us,' said Charlotte with enthusiasm.

'Absolutely. Much better for both the children if they're together,' said Simon with renewed confidence.

'Simon's right, John. Let's let Suzie go.'

'Well, I was thinking that perhaps Bobby would like to come with us. The girls will be together then.'

Charlotte stared at John in amazement. What on earth was going on inside his head? It was becoming impossible to keep abreast of what he was thinking. There was a silence all around as each of them thought of what they might say next.

Charlotte said, 'I think that Suzie would much prefer to go on holiday to France with Bobby, John.'

'Excellent,' said Simon with a beaming smile. 'You have a lovely time with Charlotte, John. We'll take the children. You can be sure we'll look after Suzie and see that she has a great time.'

'It's some way off yet. We'll see,' said John curtly, whilst thinking that he was not going to let this monster get the better of him. He picked up a piece of meat and began to chew on it in silence. The atmosphere around the table suddenly took a dive, and the two women gave weak chuckles in an attempt to conceal their embarrassment.

A few moments passed, and they turned the conversation on to television programmes that they watched. John sat in silence without comment as the meal progressed but pretending to listen to what they were saying. He managed an occasional nod and a suggestion of a smile to indicate that he was also participating, but it wasn't lost on Pauline and Simon that he was some kind of a misfit and on Charlotte that his behaviour was the worst she'd ever experienced.

John knew what the others must be thinking about him. He'd behaved in a way foreign to himself, but he had no regrets. They could think what the hell they wanted. It was hard on Charlie, and he bitterly regretted that, but at least he had managed to stop himself from saying anything that might alert Simon that he was on to him in which event all hell would let loose. His apparent controlling attitude towards Suzie could well have been the response of any protective or overbearing parent. But he couldn't kid himself that he hadn't let himself down. And worse, he had let Charlie down. Regardless of what he knew and felt about Simon, he should have put that to one side and behaved with courtesy and polite conversation. Underneath it all, he couldn't help feeling like a snivelling little rat. All he'd done was think about his own feelings of revulsion and contempt for his host which would do nothing to help his suffering relationship with Charlie and Suzie and not benefit Bobby in any way.

The trouble was, well, the actual root of the problem was that he felt so guilty about being there as a supposed friend of Simon's. He couldn't state the true reason why he detested the man, but he needed to demonstrate in a way – if only to ease his conscience – that he wasn't his friend, and that he was against him and would like to string him up if he had the chance. The thought that on

121

one day he would talk to Bobby as her friend and listen to her unload all the misery that Simon was inflicting on her and now, on another day, sitting down with Simon as a buddy and enjoying his company was tearing him apart. He knew he couldn't do anything about it, but it made him recoil at his sense of betrayal and hypocrisy.

'Would you like some pudding, John?' said Pauline, and John quickly dragged his attention to what was going on around him.

'John, it's something you haven't had for years. Pauline's actually made a steamed, suet spotted dog. It looks wonderful,' said Charlotte with genuine enthusiasm and hoping that this would at least brighten him up.

He didn't want her wretched pudding. He just wanted to bloody well get home. 'Oh yes, thank you Pauline. Just a little please. The first course rather filled me.' He surprised himself that his response actually sounded friendly and that his smile had warmth. Good. And why not? The meal would soon be over and time was getting on. In any case, it wasn't her fault that her scumbag of a husband was abusing her daughter. She didn't know anything about it so there was no reason to be unfriendly towards her.

'It looks such a beautiful pudding. I wish I hadn't eaten so much of the first course.'

Pauline smiled back, 'It's a treat for us too. I don't make it very often.'

'The whole meal was wonderful. You've gone to so much trouble. You ought to go on Master Chef,' he smiled.

Everybody laughed. Good, that was a bull's eye. Maybe he'd escape Charlie's wrath once they got out of there. Dream on. His behaviour had been obnoxious all evening, and he'd definitely get the sharp sting of her tongue once they were alone. Well, if that were the case, he'd just have to take it. She'd calm down in the end.

As soon as everyone had been served their pudding, there was a slight injection of merriment with the odd joke and banter, and although John hardly participated, he didn't dampen the mood. But he did himself no favours when he announced, after they had finished eating, that they would rather not stop for coffee as he needed to get off for an early start in the morning. He resisted glares of disappointment from Charlotte and pleas from Simon and Pauline for them to stay a little longer, and still insisted that it was time for them to go. The well-worn script of thank yous – how enjoyable it had been, getting together must take place soon, the kissing and handshakes from those who wanted them – were quickly rolled out on the doorstep, but then the door closed and John and Charlotte were on their own. The atmosphere was cool as they walked down the garden path but solid ice as soon as they got into the car. John turned on the ignition and pulled away, but neither of them spoke the whole journey home. He pulled into the drive and turned off the engine. For a long time, the silence was maintained, but both of them knew it spoke volumes. There was nothing for it, he would have to face it head-on.

'All right, say it, and let's get it over with.'

She didn't look up and although she spoke quietly, she couldn't disguise the quivering in her voice.

'Why? Why would you want to behave like an ill-mannered oaf? If it's because you wanted to humiliate me, hurt me, and at the same time show yourself up to be someone who had been dragged up in some god-forsaken shit-hole and deprived of any teaching of basic manners, then you succeeded with flying colours.'

Increasingly, as she spoke it took all her strength to restrain herself from screaming at him.

'I'm sorry, Charlie.'

'Sorry! Sorry! Is that all you can say and expect that to be the end of it?' He knew she must have been terribly hurt, and if it had not been dark he would have seen her face burning red with rage. Everything she said was true. He'd been a bloody stupid, indulgent fool who could have blown the whole thing wide open. As it was, he'd achieved nothing good and everything bad – especially for himself.

'I'll make it up to you,' he reached out his hand to take hers.

'It's too late. The damage is done. I shall have to ring up and apologise to Pauline and Simon and make up some pathetic excuse. God knows what they must think. They probably pity me for marrying such a ghastly moron.'

'I'll speak to Pauline.'

'No! I can't trust you. Don't you dare go anywhere near them.'

'How can I make things right?'

'You can't. This is one step too far. I'm going to stay with Mum and Dad.'

'What?' Her words triggered alarm bells.

'This has gone on for too long, John. I've had enough. The last few weeks you've been aggressive and uncommunicative. I've tried to help, but you've shut me out. And you've been horrible to Suzie. I can't take it anymore and neither can she.'

'Don't do that, Charlie. I can't manage without you.'

'You should have thought of that before.'

'When will you go?'

'Tomorrow. After you've set off for your conference.'

'What about Suzie and her schooling?'

'It's only 20 miles. I can still bring her in and collect her.'

'But that'll be so difficult for you.'

'Don't try and tell me you care.'

'Of course I care.'

'Too late. Whatever the problems, I'm going.'

'How long will you stay there?'

'As long as it takes. The way I feel at the moment, for good.'

John sunk back into his seat, utterly deflated. A feeling swept over him that he'd never sensed before. He mustn't lose her. He'd never cope without her. She was his life, his everything. They did everything together. And Suzie? Was he going to lose her as well? He'd go to pieces. Surely Charlie understood that.

'Charlie, please…'

'I've nothing more to say. I'm going in and going to bed. And I'd prefer you to sleep down on the couch tonight.' She stepped out of the car and went on up to the house without waiting for him.

Chapter Eight

He hadn't slept. It was impossible. His world had come apart, and he was in a hole he'd never get out of. It was almost six o'clock and he moved around the kitchen like a zombie, trying to fix some breakfast. He had to leave home in about ten minutes to drive to Birmingham. Once there, he would pick up a train to take him to Manchester, where he was going to attend his engineering conference. It was an annual affair, and he always tried to attend. It was a good place to find out everything new coming along and get a general overview of many aspects associated with his profession and business.

He had agonised over whether or not he should attend this year, but he felt that Charlie would welcome having him away for at least 36 hours. It always meant that he stayed away the one night, and because of the cold atmosphere that had developed between them, he had decided that attending again was a good idea. But now things were much worse, and it was tearing him apart, and the fact that Charlie was still asleep, or pretending to be asleep, and had not come down to say goodbye and wish him well as she had always done in the past was breaking his heart. He dreaded spending the night in a hotel which he would feel as the loneliest place in the world because Charlie wouldn't be with him. Last night had been bad enough, but at least he had been in the same house. And would she be there when he came home again or would she really carry out her threat and stay with her parents?

Maybe he should cancel his reservation and stay to try and put things right. No. Everything was too raw. It was best if he went and was out of the way for 36 hours. A change of scene might help him see a way through the misery he was in. He might recognise a few faces, but he wouldn't want to be sociable like some of the delegates who tended to drink well into the night.

He swallowed his mug of tea and got his things together to leave. He made his way out to the front door and paused to listen. Could he hear Charlie getting out of bed to come down after all? It seemed not. She really had dug her heels in. He quietly opened the door and went out to the car and drove off.

The traffic on the road at that time of day was not too bad so his journey to Birmingham took under the hour, and he was in good time to catch his train. He found a seat and tried to settle himself. He had hoped that the drive to Birmingham and general business of finding and boarding the right train would have distracted him from his problems at home, but it was a forlorn hope. He picked up his newspaper and read the headlines, but a minute later, he couldn't remember what they had said for he was taking nothing in. It was only after the train had set off and was well on its way that – thankfully – the rhythm of the carriage allowed him to doze until he arrived at his destination.

When the train came to a stop, he became more alert and realised that he must now pull himself together and focus on the reasons why he had come there. He took a taxi to the hotel and went to check in. He was signing in the register when someone touched his arm. 'John, hallo,' said the light-hearted voice, and he turned to see Carole Cooper.

'My God, hallo Carole,' said John in pleasant surprise and instinctively had a wide smile on his face. 'Great to see you.'

'You too. How are you?' Her face was beaming.

'Fine. You're looking well.' It would have been pathetic to say he felt like shit, but he really meant it when he said she looked great.

'Older,' she said, and continued to smile.

John had known Carole from his university days. They had been on the same course, she being one of the few female students. She was a very attractive girl then and had lost none of her looks now that she was in her very early forties. Her hair was still long and dark and her brown eyes wide apart and always shining. Her flashing smile came easily to her and held one's attention. Her figure was still good, and John thought she probably attended a gym. Carole had a warm and outgoing personality and was very popular at university. Against much competition, he had had a bit of a fling with her. It had been nothing heavy: a few lunches together, some clubbing and some brief petting, but it all came to an end when she fell in love with Derek Cooper, another student on the course. Derek was brilliant and John had liked him even though he had swept Carole off her feet. In the event, after university, Derek and Carole got married. John had gone to their wedding. After that, they set up their own small engineering business. Tragically, Derek had a heart attack two years ago, and Carole had not attended last year's conference. John had more or less lost touch with her since Derek's funeral, principally because she lived at a different end of the country from him. Prior to that, he had only ever met up with Derek and Carole once a year when they had all attended the annual conference.

As he stared at her, John found himself wondering what Carole's situation would be since she had become a widow and without Derek to help oversee their business. Regardless of the business, she would have been utterly heart-broken by his death. He must have been only about 40 when he died and had always seemed in good health and was very athletic. Poor Carole, she had obviously soldiered on.

'We'd better find our rooms, John or we're going to be late for the kick off. I'll catch you later,' she said and scurried away with a jocular wave of her arm.

'Fine,' said John but wondered if she had heard him as she disappeared into the lift. It was really good to see her again, and she was obviously back in the saddle, work-wise. He looked forward to finding her later and catching up with all her news, and it would probably be a distraction from his own problems. He signed the register, took his key and headed for the lift which was already being loaded with guests going up. He exited on the third floor and found his room. It was reasonably sized but was just like most hotel rooms which he always considered had no souls.

He dropped his overnight bag on the floor and opened his brief case where he found the day's programme. When he had scanned it at home a few days before, he had felt enthusiastic, but as he ran his eyes over it now, he struggled to feel interest. Still, he had booked his place and arrived so he knew he had to make the effort and give it his best shot. He picked up his brief case and went out.

The whole day became something of a trial for him. As he listened to conference speakers on subjects which should have held his attention, he found his mind constantly wandering. Of course, there was a variety of subjects: design and new design patent, links with industry, new tools and techniques, government input and future needs, rising costs, apprenticeships and problems with surviving the recession. And Brexit was prominent in everyone's mind. As the day wore on, he found the whole thing a struggle, and a couple of times, he felt his eyes closing and had to make an effort not to drift away.

During the coffee, lunch and tea breaks he had kept much to himself, dreading the need to make either polite conversation or in-depth discussion about his work. He spotted Carole a couple of times during the breaks, but she had been kidnapped by various groups of men who gabbled away at her with intermittent bursts of laughter. At the end of the final session, after which he had listened to a constant drone of words and looked at a stream of material on a huge screen, he was thankful that he could creep back to his room and grab some shut-eye before going down to dinner.

He opened his door, dropped his brief case on the floor and collapsed on to his bed. He closed his eyes and breathed deeply in an effort to completely relax, but in spite of feeling wiped out, sleep evaded him. He laid there occasionally opening his eyes and staring at the ceiling. There were no windows in the room and no pictures on the walls. He felt he was in some kind of a cell, albeit a luxury one compared to the real thing. He began thinking about what Charlie would be doing at that moment, and whether Suzie would be with her or whether she would be over at Bobby's. Would they already be at her parents', Henry and Martha's, home? They would have been shocked at what was going on, and he wondered how serious a picture Charlie would have painted. No doubt, Suzie would chip in which would confirm that she had not exaggerated. He quite liked her parents, but was a bit wary of Henry when his background in the military came to the fore. They could be in the kitchen at that moment, chatting about him and wondering what was going to happen. More likely, they would be glad that he was away so they could be happy together without him being a bully and laying down the law and stopping them from doing things and making them unhappy.

His spirit was so low, and he felt so alone that he felt he would cry, but even that seemed too difficult, and he felt the muscles in his face begin to hurt. He wanted to be home, to be happy with his wife and daughter; he wanted Suzie to be safe and Simon to move away, even though he knew that wouldn't help Bobby. He wondered if it would all end in tragic disaster or would something unexpected and miraculous suddenly burst on the scene and bring everything to a happy conclusion.

Even though he knew that such an idea was never going to happen, it gave him a little pleasure to imagine it. He picked up his mobile phone and turned it over and over in his hand trying to make up his mind if he should ring Charlotte or if it would be better to leave things be. Finally, he sat up and punched out the number, but then almost immediately after, cancelled it. *Christ*, he thought, *what a state to be in*. To think that things could have got so bad that he was unable to call her on the phone. Well, she hadn't rung him either when she could have done, so maybe it was for the best to leave it. After all, if he did ring, he didn't know what he would say. Tell her he loved her, of course, and that he was sorry, but she would want to witness him being more reasonable over Suzie as well as Bobby's parents, but he couldn't see that would happen. No, he'd leave it and try and steer an easier course when he got home. He swung off the bed, washed his face and hands and decided to go down to the dining room and have his dinner. After that he'd have an early night and get off first thing in the morning.

****

The dining room was fairly busy, and most of the diners seemed in an upbeat mood. Nearly all of them were delegates from the conference and were in animated discussion punctuated with laughter, and the staff were busy visiting tables with bottles of wine as well as food. He spotted Carole sitting with another woman and two men at the far end of the room, and when she looked up and saw him, she waved at him. He waved back, and then – much to his relief – found a table tucked away in a corner, with two places only. He took one of the seats and thought it unlikely that anyone else would take the vacant chair. The waiter arrived, and he ordered a glass of wine and a main course of poached salmon plus the trimmings. The wine arrived quickly, and he waited for about 15 minutes for the salmon, but the way it was presented made him think it was worth waiting for.

He drank some of the wine and concentrated on eating, gradually becoming detached from the general hubbub surrounding him.

He had not felt hungry and was surprised that when he put his knife and fork down, there was nothing left on the plate. Even so, he would dispense with a sweet and ordered coffee which he said he would take in the lounge. He finished his glass of wine and stood to go when he felt a hand slap him on the back. 'Hi there, John; thought it was you,' said a voice behind him. John turned to acknowledge Douglas Horner who was a heavy-weight in his line of engineering and who John knew from previous attendances at the conferences.

Although John liked him, he was the kind of gregarious character that John was desperate to avoid.

'Hallo, Douglas. It's good to see you. How are you?' John put on his best front.

'Great, lad. Everything's great. Worried about bloody Brexit. Don't sit here alone, lad. Come and join us. I'm on a big table over there,' he pointed with a beaming smile.

'Well I've just ordered my coffee in the lounge, Douglas. Perhaps I could join you later.' John thought that sounded good.

'Stuff that, John. Tell the waiter to bring it over to my table. We'll squeeze you in all right. I want to hear how you're getting on and get your thoughts about Brexit. I take it you're still afloat?' Douglas maintained his beaming smile.

'So far so good, but who knows?'

'Too right. We're all going to be in the bloody shit if this government doesn't get its finger out.'

'You go ahead, Douglas. I'll catch up,' said John and tried to sound convincing.

'Okay, lad. See that you do. May as well make a night of it, eh?' said Douglas, and slapped John on the shoulder.

'See you in a minute,' he added and was already walking away back to his table. John watched with relief as he went away and quickly made his way through to the lounge. He found a comfortable chair, and the waiter soon arrived with his coffee.

There weren't many people in the lounge, and he knew none of them personally, though he recognised a couple from previous conferences. He sipped his coffee and hoped that he'd be able to leave the hotel in the morning without getting caught up with any of the other delegates. There were one or two he had seen during the day whom he had come to know as colleagues rather than friends who would have expected him to join them for at least a chat, but he simply couldn't face even that prospect in his present mood.

It was only just gone nine o'clock when he finished his coffee. He thought that if he went up to his room then and went to bed it would be too early for him to be able to get to sleep. Perhaps, if he found one of the quiet bars and had a couple of drinks over the next hour, he could then go to bed and probably fall asleep more easily.

He left the lounge and was directed by a member of staff to the quietest bar in the hotel. There were a few people in there, but he was thankful that he recognised none of them. He sat on a stool at the bar and ordered a Jack Daniels, a double, which he sipped and felt the warmth of it roll down into his stomach. He hadn't bothered with his medication, which he considered had either been of no benefit or even made him feel worse, so he wasn't worried about drinking alcohol. As he continued to sip his drink, he idly stared at the array of bottles against the mirrored wall on the other side of the bar. Occasionally, the pleasant barmaid would pass a friendly comment to him about the weather, and as to whether he had enjoyed his stay, and if he had far to travel. He hadn't found her obtrusive and felt that it helped pass the time.

After 15 minutes, he had finished his drink so he ordered another double, and then idly watched the barmaid moving up and down the bar, serving drinks and smiling pleasantly at the customers. She certainly knew her job and he thought the hotel was lucky to have her. Staff in that line of work could make or break a business. He suddenly took out his phone and wondered again whether or not to ring Charlie. He desperately wanted to hear her voice but was terrified she might give him a cold response and would make him feel even worse. *When in doubt, don't,* he thought and put the phone back in his pocket.

'Hallo, stranger. Why are you hiding away in here?' said the voice next to him, and he immediately saw it was Carole.

'Hallo, Carole,' he smiled but in relief, 'I just... um... just didn't fancy the high jinks tonight,' he fumbled his words.

'I know what you mean. I had a job to escape, myself.'

'Can I buy you a drink?' he said, glad she had found him.

'Thank you. What are you drinking?'

'Jack Daniels,' he grinned sheepishly.

'Hmmm, hard stuff. Then I'll have a gin and tonic. Gordons,' she smiled mischievously.

John nodded and ordered her drink and another Jack Daniels for himself. For a few moments, they watched the barmaid in silence. She gave them their order and put the bill on John's tab.

'Happy days,' Carole laughed and raised her glass to him. But in an unguarded moment, he responded with only a nod, and a wistful smile reinforced with a quiet grunt.

She immediately noticed his mood but pretended not to.

'Had to give the conference a miss last year,' she said conversationally.

'I'm not surprised. How have you been... I mean since Derek died? Christ knows how you have managed,' he said, feeling genuine concern for her.

'It was a terrible shock when he died and initially I went to pieces. I simply couldn't believe what had happened. My parents were wonderful and tried their

135

best to help me, but it wasn't easy for them to see their daughter so distraught, and they themselves had been terribly fond of Derek.'

'I'm sorry, Carole. I can't even imagine what it must have been like for you.' He reached across to put his hand on hers in affection.

She managed a weak smile. 'Well, life goes on, John, and slowly I picked myself up. Of course, I still miss him dreadfully, but I'm still here and have to get on with things. I was amazed that, unbeknown to me, he had taken out a very valuable life policy from which I benefited quite a large sum of money. I invested nearly all of it in our business; took on a manager who has been brilliant and got stuck into the work. At the moment, we are doing reasonably well, but like everyone else we're wondering about the future.'

'You're amazing, Carole. I always thought that about you anyway, and you're looking fantastic. No wonder you've had all those lecherous engineers hanging round you like a swarm of bees round honey, all day.'

She quietly scoffed with a wave of her hand, 'Agh! Imagination, John. They just wanted to pick my brains.'

They both chuckled and stared at their glasses with silent thoughts. He noticed her glass was empty. 'Have another?' he said.

'My shout. I insist. Same?'

'Bloody hell, I'm no drinker, Carole, but what's the harm?' He was feeling a lot more relaxed than he had done half an hour ago.

'Good. You look as if you need it anyway,' she said, not unkindly.

'Does it show that much?'

'I've never forgotten you, John. We were very close at one time, unless you've forgotten, you cad, and I know a little bit about what makes you tick.'

'It's complicated. You don't want to know.'

The barmaid handed them their drinks and after holding them up to each other with a smile they both took a sip. For a little while, there was another silence, and they knew that in their silence their thoughts were beginning to mingle together.

This time she reached across and laid her hand on his.

'Can I help?' Her voice was so gentle.

John looked into her eyes and felt such a tenderness. The huge battle he'd waged to protect the secret that was causing him so much pain suddenly seemed so futile. His sense of despair and isolation flooded over him in such an overwhelming surge that he thought he would simply crumple up and disappear. 'No one can help, I'm afraid,' he said quietly. 'I'm in a hole that was not of my doing and nobody else's fault either. I'm unable to talk about what it is because it involves another person and by not talking about it to Charlie, because I can't do that either, my marriage is heading for the rocks. I've had to play the role of the bad guy and without any means to fight back. I'm on my own, Carole, and I can only make things worse.' He sounded like a broken man. For a few moments there was a silence. He fiddled with his glass and looked down into it. Was it possible that he was suddenly with someone with whom he could unload all the awful stress he'd been under for what seemed like an eternity? Was Carole just about the only person in the world who was not a Samaritan with whom he could feel safe in revealing the terrible dilemma he faced? He knew that she was the one person who would not break any confidentiality and that she was so far removed from the situation it really made no difference. He gave a sigh and sunk his drink and then banged his glass decisively down on the counter. He couldn't do it. It didn't matter the circumstances. It didn't matter that Carole would not breathe a word of what he might tell her. Like all Samaritans he'd given his word to abide by confidentiality and that didn't change just because the screws were on.

She squeezed his hand, 'I remember you too well to know you're not a bad guy, John. I'm not asking you to tell me what's been going on, but I can see you are desperately unhappy, and I feel for you.'

'You haven't lost that lovely, caring touch I remember from our uni days, Carole.'

She smiled at him. 'Only for the people I had affection for.'

'We had some good times together, you and I, before that handsome hunk Derek shoved his oar in.'

'I know, but I still remember the good times.'

'Do you still remember the night I came to your room? It was snowing, and we'd been to a party. I think it had been at that private house.'

'Colin Harris. His parents were very wealthy and lived close by.'

'Yeah, that's him. Your memory is better than mine. It was damn late, and when we got to your room we...' his voice petered out and he looked down at his hands.

'We nearly made love but...' she offered and then paused.

'Yeah, but I chickened out. Christ, I was so scared, and I felt like the biggest bloody fool under the sun.'

Carole smiled at him encouragingly. 'At first, I thought it was because of me.'

'I know and I hated myself for causing you that. It was my first time, you see or would have been, and I was so embarrassed.'

'It was all right. It was my first time too. Later on, your not being gung-ho in the bedroom and a well-practised sexual athlete I found endearing.'

'I lost my chance, after that,' he said with a wistful smile.

'If I remember rightly, you went down with the flu, and nobody saw you for a couple of weeks.'

'That's right. Yeah, I remember being on my own all that time feeling sorry for myself and thinking of nothing but you. Let me see, I must have been about 19. God, I remember feeling so lonely,' he said as if the memory had suddenly become very close.

'I know about loneliness, John. It's crept up on me a few times during the last two years,' and he felt the sadness in her voice.

'I guess you have,' he nodded and then after a few moments as if he were in deep thought added, 'I've had a bit of that myself recently.' Then there was a silence.

They stared at each other, and both of them felt as if something had moved each of them into a single space. It was a space that was quiet and warm and away from the world; it was distant and was pulling them together. They were suddenly two people who felt a bond, perhaps because they recognised the nature of each other's loneliness; perhaps because it was the bond that had laid dormant from the past.

'I don't want to be here. Shall we say goodnight in my room?' She asked it as a simple question without any sign of a hidden message.

'I would like that very much,' said John and with a touch of unsteadiness and taking her by the arm he led her out of the bar. No one looked at them; no one stared. They were simply two friends moving on to somewhere else.

Neither spoke as they travelled up in the lift, then along the corridor until they reached her room. She opened the door, and they went in. In the darkness, she moved across the room and switched on the bedside lamp, and then turned and faced him. John was now shaking, though she wouldn't have known, and he slowly moved over to her and stood in front of her. She put her arms round him and pulled him in close. 'Goodnight, John,' she said in a whisper, and her lips brushed his.

'Good night, Carole,' he replied, and eased her down on to the bed.

****

It was eight thirty when John entered the dining room and ordered poached eggs and a pot of tea. He had planned to be up and away much earlier but, unusually, he had overslept. *So what?* he thought. It wouldn't matter if he got a later train.

He'd got back to his own room at about three am, and he now wondered if Carole was up and about or if she was still in bed. The answer to his question came as he finished his eggs, and the waiter took away the plate. Carole was suddenly standing there.

'Hi,' he said and stood up. 'Have you had breakfast?'

'Ages ago,' she said with a smile and sat down opposite him beckoning him to sit down too. 'I've only come to say goodbye. My taxi is due in five minutes.'

'Right,' he replied, and wondered at the directness of her words.

'It was lovely last night, John. But it didn't happen. It'll just be another memory.'

'Well...' he started, but she cut him short. 'Better that way.' She stared at him and smiled. He only nodded, but it was enough. Words would have got in the way.

'I suppose I won't see you again until next year's conference.'

'I won't be here next year,' she said.

'But surely –' he started. She held up her hand to cut him short again, but not unkindly.

'I've sold my business. The deal will be completed next month. I put the agreement in motion a couple of months ago. My life is changing. I'm moving down to Cornwall and buying a house near my sister.'

'But why?' he said, completely taken by surprise.

'It's what I want. My sister and her husband have a small-holding, a horse livery really, and they have a lot of other animals, mostly rescued: donkeys, goats, sheep, some chickens and ducks, that kind of thing. It's the sort of thing that Derek and I had planned on doing one day. I have money, and I'm putting it in with them. It'll be the best thing for me.'

John didn't speak for a few moments but then smiled at her with enthusiasm. 'Sounds wonderful. It'll be very different for you.'

'I'm sure it will. But I won't miss the business. I'm a country girl at heart.'

He laughed. 'I'm sure you'll look just as wonderful in muddy wellies and straw in your hair.' She smiled back at him and for a little while, neither of them spoke.

'This'll be goodbye, John,' she said quietly.

He nodded. 'I know.'

'You're a good man, John. Don't beat yourself up over last night. It didn't mean anything. Loneliness has a will of its own.' Her voice was gentle and full of understanding. She knew that only he would understand.

Again he nodded but remained silent.

'Whatever mess you're in, you'll find a way out in the end. Goodbye, John.' They stood up, and she leaned forward and kissed him on the cheek, and then turned and walked away.

He stared after her as she moved across the dining room. 'Goodbye, Carole,' he whispered and watched her disappear.

Chapter Nine

Richard Deakin sat in the site works office at St Catherine's Primary school. It was ten thirty, and the rest of the men had gone back to work after their short morning break. Richard was content with his life. At 45, his health was good although he had recently started to put on too much weight, but he'd succeeded in pretty well managing his life the way he wanted it.

He had a good responsible job by his association with Simon, and the money he made was adequate for his needs. He'd got married in his late teens, but it had only lasted two years, undeniably as a result of his obsession with children. Over the years, he had managed to satisfy his cravings, at least to some extent, and had still managed to keep free of the law except for two cases some years ago, but there had been insufficient evidence, and he never went to court.

He was able to present himself as a decent, hard-working chap, which in fact he was, at least as far as work was concerned. He had a nice little house in an out of the way cul-de-sac where he stored a huge collection of child pornography DVDs and child photographs. They were his pride and joy which he had built up over many years.

He looked at his watch and thought it was time to try his luck. Since he'd been working at the school, he had endeavoured to make a note of the times when classes changed; the morning breaks when the children would stream out into the playground, and especially, the times of the classes when the PE took place. He knew exactly where he could take up a position on the other side of the buildings where he could observe the children in secrecy. There were a few bushes around there, and in any case if anyone saw him he would simply say it was necessary for him to keep an overall eye on the whole site.

He checked and made sure that he had his smartphone with him and went out of the office. There was nobody about except the workmen who didn't take any notice of him. He sauntered over to the main school block and walked along the side of the building and turned left at the corner.

Further along, there were bushes growing close to the wall, and they were immediately outside the windows that looked into the large gym where PE took place. He moved along the wall slowly and could already hear the teacher's voice shouting out what he guessed were exercises for the children to follow. He reached the windows, the sills of which were about four feet from the ground. It meant that he had to keep well crouched, but he decided to position himself behind a bush which would keep him well concealed whilst at the same time allow him to have a clear view of what the children were doing.

His heart began to quicken as he surveyed a class of about 30 who were in three lines of ten. The exercises in which they were engaged consisted mainly of stretching and bending, and he smiled with pleasure as he watched the girls in their tiny gym shorts touching their toes and displaying their backsides in his direction. Then they began stretching from left to right and touching their toes in rhythmic swinging movements. Richard Deakin thanked his lucky stars he had picked the right time. He poked his smartphone through the foliage and began to take photos, but there were too many leaves interfering. He decided to move away from behind the bush and get close to the window where he would have unrestricted view. From that position he was able to take several pictures which he hoped were of such good quality that he would be able to add them to his huge collection at home.

Miss Prentice was resting in the teachers' common room situated at another part of the building. She had a free lesson and was resting because she had a bad headache and had not been feeling too well. After a little while, she decided that what she needed was some fresh air. She stood up and made her way to the playground. For a few moments, she watched the builders at work, and then decided to wander round the building. She made her way towards the clock tower, and when she got to the end of the building, she turned around the corner to investigate an area she had not seen for a long time. Straight away she saw the site foreman Richard Deakin. What on earth was he doing? She looked around to see if there were any other workmen close by but couldn't see any. She pushed her glasses up her nose and peered more intently to see what he was seemingly trying to investigate. She suddenly realised he was holding a camera up to the window of the room in which she knew children were having a PE lesson. She froze in horror, not knowing what to do. She felt scared and vulnerable. If he saw her, would he become aggressive and attack her, or would he try to run away? She knew instinctively that something was terribly wrong, and she must tell somebody. She hesitated for a moment, and then very slowly, she moved backwards and retraced her steps around the corner and out of sight. He, in any case, was so absorbed with what he was doing that he did not notice her.

Again she paused, feeling flustered and shocked, but then with a determined step, she set off to the headmistress' office. She would know what to do.

It was about 20 minutes later when a police car pulled up outside the school at the same time as Richard Deakin walked back to his site office. PC Ann Jenkins and PC Brown got out of the car and walked up to the main entrance to the school where they were met by the headmistress, who, after a brief conversation pointed towards the site office. The two constables nodded and made their way over to the office and went inside. Richard Deakin was sitting at his desk, and his smartphone was on the desk in front of him. When the police entered, he looked very surprised and with a knee-jerk response, stood up. 'Is something wrong?' he asked, trying to conceal the alarm in his voice. An unexpected visit from the police couldn't possibly be good news.

'We've had a call from one of the teachers complaining that a workman here has been taking pictures of children during their PE class and that workman has been identified as you,' said PC Jenkins.

'What member of staff? I don't know what you mean,' he said and felt his mouth go dry.

'The member of staff is not important, sir. You were seen taking photographs through the window at the back of the building.'

'I often take photographs when I'm on site as the building works progress. There's nothing unusual about that,' replied Richard Deakin with a touch more confidence.

'Our witness says she definitely saw you taking photos through the window where the class of children

146

doing PE was taking place,' PC Jenkins persisted calmly.

'A simple mistake, I can assure you,' said Richard Deakin with a shrug.

The constable reached down and picked up Richard Deakin's smartphone. 'Is this your phone, sir?'

'Hey, that's mine,' snapped Richard Deakin and reached out to grab it back.

'It's all right, sir. We're not going to keep it.'

'Damn right you're not. That's my property. You've no right to take that!' said Richard Deakin, suddenly alarmed.

PC Jenkins ignored his protests and said, 'Is this what you took your photographs with, sir?'

Richard Deakin suddenly changed his tone, 'Look, what's on there is nothing. It's just harmless stuff. I'm just interested in children, that's all. There's no crime in that, is there?'

PC Jenkins was already running through the photographs that Richard Deakin had taken of the children. 'These are hardly the sort of innocent photographs of children that one would expect to be taken by a complete stranger without the permission of the school staff or parents,' said the PC severely.

Richard Deakin began to bluster with hand gestures and wide grins, 'Well yeah, I guess not. I can see it was silly now. I'll get rid of them. No harm done, eh?' he said, and reached out as if expecting to be offered back his mobile phone.

'I think we'll need to hold on to this for a little while, sir,' PC Jenkins said without a smile.

'What do you mean? I have to have that phone. I can't manage without that. I need it for my work and everything,' Richard Deakin began to demand.

'I understand, sir,' persisted the PC, and then turning away, she nodded to her colleague who nodded back and stepped outside the office and spoke into his phone.

Richard Deakin peered around the side of PC Jenkins with a strained expression on his face. 'What the hell's going on? What's he doing?' he said with alarm.

'No problem, sir. Won't keep you a minute.'

'That's all very well, but I've got things to do. Are you done, and when can I have my phone back? I've explained everything.'

'All in good time, sir. Just keep calm.'

'I won't keep calm. This is bloody harassment by police. I shall make a complaint,' said Richard Deakin and he began to shout. PC Brown came back into the office and nodded at his colleague who immediately turned back to Richard Deakin. 'Richard Deakin, I'm arresting you on suspicion of collecting indecent photographs of children. You do not have to say anything, but it may harm your defence if you do not mention something when questioned which you may later rely on in court. Anything you do say may be given in evidence. Do you understand?'

'What?' Richard Deakin's eyes bulged, 'This is an outrage! Taking a few photographs like this is not a crime!'

'You've not been charged with anything, sir. We just need to ask you some questions down at the station. Please come with us,' said PC Jenkins more firmly but still remaining calm.

'I've not done anything wrong!' shouted Richard Deakin becoming very agitated.

PC Brown took Richard Deakin's arm, 'Shall we go, sir?' he said and began to lead him out of the office.

Richard Deakin said, 'Look, is this really necessary? It's all a mistake.' He now looked pale but did not resist as the PC led him to the police car. PC Brown got into the back with Richard Deakin, and PC Jenkins got into the driver's seat.

As they drove away, the headmistress and Miss Prentice watched them disappear.

****

DS Harris leaned back in his chair and sighed. He had been questioning Richard Deakin with DC Jones for 25 minutes but had got very little out of him. Deakin was being stubborn. DS Harris could see that he was nervous, but he was still not cracking. He should be nervous because he was in deep trouble.

Henry Phillips, a solicitor who had been dragged in to represent Richard Deakin, sat stony-faced, next to his client. If expressions revealed anything, it looked as if Henry Phillips would have rather been at home or on the golf course.

'You're not doing yourself any favours, Richard. You need to think about what it will be like in prison. Not a very nice place for people like you.'

'I didn't know I'd been found guilty of anything.'

'You will be. The material we discovered in your house and on your hard drive is more than enough to get you a prison sentence.'

'They're pictures, that's all.'

'Yeah, pictures of children being horribly abused.'

'Okay, they're bad pictures, but I'm not in them. I've never done things like that. They're just pictures.'

'You were arrested five years ago for exposing yourself in front of a couple of kids.'

'I was never charged. I never went to court. Those kids just made it up.'

149

'Are you part of a ring, Richard? Are you in a network that shares this stuff?'

'No, I'm not.'

'If you gave us some names, things might go better for you. You help us, and we will do what we can for you.'

'There are no names. I know nobody.'

'Just give us one name. You need to start thinking about what's going to be best for you.'

'I've told you. I don't know what you're talking about.'

'One name, that's all.'

'My client has already answered your question,' interrupted Henry Phillips.

DS Harris let out a long sigh. This was going to take a lot longer than he thought.

****

Lucy Carter was sitting at her desk when DS Harris and DC Jones arrived at the Architectural Offices of Simon Hargreaves. Lucy had worked as secretary and personal assistant for Simon since he'd arrived in town just over a year ago. Lucy was 22, and liked her job. She also liked Simon and always tried to be as efficient as she could for him. Lucy was pretty and had a pleasant manner with anyone who called at the offices.

As soon as the two male police officers entered, she stood up and smiled pleasantly. 'Good morning, can I help you?' she asked.

DS Harris and DC Jones took out their ID cards, introduced themselves and said they would like to speak to Mr Hargreaves if he was there. Lucy was flustered for just a moment, and then asked them to wait a moment while she went through to Simon's office. She knocked on his door and as soon as she went in, she whispered conspiratorially that two detective policemen were outside who wanted to see him. Simon immediately reassured Lucy that there was no problem, and asked her to show them in.

When DS Harris and DC Jones entered Simon's office, he stood up and smiled broadly at DS Harris. 'Good morning, Sergeant. This is an unusual visit; I usually see you in court.'

'Good morning, sir. Sorry to trouble you. We're here to make some enquiries about a Richard Deakin who I understand is your foreman at St Catherine's Primary school,' said DS Harris with a slight touch of deference.

'That's right. My goodness, is there a problem with the work? I haven't been to the site since yesterday, I'm afraid. But I'm sure he would have let me know if anything was amiss,' offered Simon, keeping his voice upbeat.

'Nothing to do with your work, sir. Could you tell us how long you have known Mr Deakin?'

'Quite a long time. Several years. He's first class at handling things on site, and he's very reliable. I've never had cause for complaint,' replied Simon in a matter-of-fact voice.

'Do you know anything about his personal life?' asked DS Harris, keeping his voice friendly but formal.

'Personal life? Well, I can't say that I do,' said Simon and immediately felt a sense of uneasiness.

Christ! What was he asking that for? Had Richard been a bloody fool and let something slip? Why would they want to know about his personal life? He'd have to be on his guard. He smiled and stroked his skin in thought. 'I've always thought I knew him well, but of course that's only been on a work level. I believe he was divorced many years ago, but as far as I know, he lives alone.'

'And you've no idea about his social life, hobbies or clubs that he might belong to?'

Simon put on his most innocent expression, 'Absolutely none. Is that important? Would you mind telling me what this is all about, Sergeant?'

DS Harris cleared his throat. 'Well sir, it seems that a member of staff at the school spotted him taking photographs of the children doing their PE lesson this morning. Many of the pictures were of the children in slightly revealing positions.'

'Good God. Richard? Are you sure there's no mistake?'

'Absolutely not, sir. We have the photos, and he admitted it, saying it was a harmless thing to do, and he meant nothing by it,' continued DS Harris.

Simon's heart began to quicken. Shit! What the hell did Richard think he was doing? What else had they found out? Would Richard keep his mouth shut? As long as he didn't panic and start blabbing, there was no way he could be connected. They had never exchanged incriminating e-mails, and they had never written anything down or kept records so there was no way of linking them except on work matters.

'So is he in custody, Sergeant?'

'We are just holding him for questioning at the moment, sir. He hasn't been formally charged,' said DS Harris.

'Well, how long are you going to keep him, do you think?' Simon's voice was steady, as if it was a reasonable thing for him to know.

'We ran his name through the system and it has shown up a couple of previous arrests. Some time ago now. One was for apparently interfering with a child, but the witness dropped out, and it never went to court. We have obtained a search warrant of his house and removed his computer and a large quantity of DVDs.'

'Well, what's on them?'

'I can't tell you that at the moment, sir, except to say they are undesirable.'

'Well, Sergeant, I can tell you that this has come as an enormous shock.'

'Yes, sir. It shows that when we sometimes think we know someone we find we know very little at all.'

'Indeed. I wish I could be more helpful.'

'That's fine, sir. We're sorry to have bothered you.'

'Absolutely no bother at all.'

'Thank you. We'll get off then,' said DS Harris and turned with his colleague and went out.

Simon sank down into his chair. Shit! His mind was racing. What the hell had happened? All Richard's DVDs? They'll have a field day and find enough evidence to put him away for some time. At all costs, he must distance himself from him. He must maintain his sense of shock and disbelief and there would be no point in saying anything to Pauline about it. Sometimes he would talk to her about how the work was going at the school, but there was no need for her to know that one of his workmen, his foreman in fact, had been arrested. Even though, of course, she would know that his association with Richard was purely to do with work, the fact that he knew him well and had done so for years would naturally mean an unfortunate connection between the two of them. That was only one thing he had to consider. Now that Richard would be out of the way he would be left without a foreman and Richard would be difficult to replace. He remembered then that he had to go to Belfast on Saturday for a week to assist on a project that he had negotiated some time ago. Still, that may be a blessing in disguise. Better to be out of the way while all this was going on.

He decided that he had had enough for today. He put his things away in the desk drawers and went home.

Chapter Ten

John pulled into his drive and switched off the engine. He stared at the house through the windscreen, and although he wouldn't have been able to see Charlie if she was inside, he knew she wasn't there. On the journey home from Manchester, he had tried telling himself that after all she wouldn't have gone to her parents and that she would be waiting for him to kiss him and welcome him back. He got out of the car and went into the house. It was still and quiet and empty, and he felt an awful sinking feeling in his stomach. He walked into the kitchen and then the living room to see if she had left a note, but there was none. Well, it was no more than he deserved or expected.

For the past few weeks he'd become a monster and behaved in a way to those he loved and would condemn if he'd witnessed it in anyone else. Apart from anything else, he'd gone off for the night and slept with another woman. There was no other word for it but betrayal. It was no good saying that all this had come about because a monster by the name of Simon had penetrated his psyche and was squeezing the life out of him. Everything in his life at the moment seemed unreal. Standing alone in his empty house wasn't real. It couldn't be. This sort of thing only happened in other people's lives, not his. Was it a fate he deserved? He tried to tell himself that it was all because he'd had to deal with the misery of standing aside while poor Bobby was being sexually abused by that bastard Simon; that the strain of it and the crushing loneliness he felt had led him to behave completely out of character. It didn't work. Whichever way it was sliced it up, he'd slept with another woman, and that was betrayal. He felt a sudden urge of hate for Simon. 'You cruel, bastard, this is all because of you,' he spoke the words out loud.

He took off his coat and opened the drinks cabinet. He took out a bottle of whisky and a glass but immediately decided to put them back again. He took out his phone and rang his office and spoke to Jenny, his secretary, to tell her that he was back and ask if there was anything he needed to know that had happened since he'd been away. She told him everything was fine, and he replied that he would not be coming in for the rest of the day. He hung up and went into the kitchen.

He stood still for a few moments, feeling the emptiness surrounding him. He needed to talk, to hear a human voice. He bunched up his mouth wondering whom to call. Sarah, he could talk to her. He took out his phone and brought up her name. As soon as he heard the ringing sound, he cancelled the call. No, he couldn't speak to her. He didn't know why, but he couldn't, that's all there was to it. He'd ring Linda instead; he could talk to her about anything. He brought up her name and listened to the ringing sound. Suddenly he cancelled it. He shouldn't ring her. Not now. She'd be in the shop and dealing with customers. It wouldn't be convenient for her to talk. It wouldn't be fair. Damn and blast it. What was the matter with him? He sighed and looked round the room again. Christ, he simply had to pull himself together.

He opened the fridge and peered inside. Ah, that was better. There were a couple of lamb chops and half an apple pie in there. She hadn't completely left him high and dry. It suddenly made him feel closer to her. 'Thanks, Charlie. I love you.' He smiled and began preparing a meal. He put the chops under the grill and the apple pie in the oven. He quickly put some new potatoes in a saucepan to boil and some broccoli in another. Everything was done mechanically, and he tried to believe that what he was doing was perfectly normal and he should relax and enjoy the meal. It didn't work. He felt lousy and knew bloody well that what he was doing was not normal. It would have been normal if he had been a young bachelor living on his own but he wasn't. He was a married man with a lovely wife and a wonderful daughter, and he loved them both dearly.

He went back into the living room and got the whisky out again and poured a double into a glass. He returned to the kitchen, took some ice out of the fridge and put it in the glass. He drank some and wondered if he should ring Charlie. He desperately wanted to but strangely felt nervous in a way he'd never felt before. It reminded him of how he felt as a young man ringing her up for a first date. That was natural. But now he'd been married to her for years, for God's sake. He shouldn't be feeling like this. Maybe it wasn't a good idea. Maybe he should just sit tight and take his punishment until she returned. Maybe, she would be back later that evening and had only stayed away when she knew he would be returning to an empty house, in order to give him a real scare. If that was the case, it had certainly worked.

He took his chops out from under the grill and served them with the vegetables. He sat down and stared at the meal in front of him. Charlie, where are you? Come home, honey. I can't handle this. He picked at the meal, moving the meat and veg round the plate. Twenty minutes later, most of it was still on the plate but was looking a mess. He pushed the plate away and leant back into his chair. A moment later, his mobile rang. He looked at the name. *Jesus, it was Charlie.*

'Charlie! Hallo!'

'You got home safely then.'

'Yeah. I've been back about half an hour. Are you okay?'

'I'm fine.'

'Are you… are you coming home?'

'No.'

'No? I mean… well, what's happening?'

'Nothing's happening.' Her voice was flat and calm.

'Aren't you ever coming back?'

'I haven't decided what to do.'

'Charlie, I can't live without you. Come home and we'll talk.'

'I've got to go.'

'Charlie, Charlie… is Suzie all right?'

'She's fine.'

'Give her my love.' The phone went dead. 'Charlie!' Shit! No, better not call her back, it would only make her angry. He sat for a little while trying to work out how he was going to manage without her and wondering how long it would be before she came home – if she ever intended to. Surely, she'd do that some time. Things hadn't gotten that bad between them. Not so that they were going to separate. Had they?

He got up from the table and cleaned his plate into the bin. The land line telephone rang in the hallway. He went out and lifted the receiver.

'Hallo.'

'Hi John, it's Sarah.'

'Oh, hi. How are things?'

'Any chance of you coming around to see me? There's been a development with you know who, but I'd rather not discuss it on the telephone?'

'Um, well I s'pose I could, yes.' She detected the sombre note in his voice.

'Is everything all right, John?'

'Not exactly. I'll talk to you when I see you. I'll be there in about 20 minutes.' He put the phone down without waiting to hear her say anything else or goodbye. What did she mean by "development"? He suddenly felt completely drained. It seemed as if he'd been hacking his way through an insolvable problem since he couldn't remember when. He felt as if he'd changed from being a reasonable kind of human being into an objectionable tyrant and loathed himself for it. His marriage was on the rocks, and he was involved in a horrible situation which he was unable to change. There was no good end in sight.

It only took John a few minutes to drive to Sarah's and he wondered what could have happened. As soon as he arrived, she led him into the living room, and they both sat down.

'Oh dear, John, you look terrible. Is everything all right?'

John made no reply but looked down at the floor.

'John?'

'You may as well know. Charlie's left. At least, she's gone to stay with her parents. I don't know when she's coming back.'

'What's happened?'

'It's complicated. A mess. It's all my fault, and I was a bloody fool.'

'Come on, John, I don't believe that.'

'It was the dinner. The meal. I told you about it. I had to go, and the whole thing was a bloody disaster.'

'What happened?'

'I behaved badly and completely humiliated Charlie. I should have had more control, but my good intentions went out of the window.'

'You didn't row, did you?'

'No, that came later.'

'I'm so sorry, John. It put you in a terrible position.'

'Just sitting down with that bastard, shaking his hand, eating his food and having to laugh at his fucking jokes...sorry.'

'It's okay. You didn't say anything that might... well, you know?'

'If you mean did I say anything about Bobby, of course I didn't. I kept right off the subject of children. The only time they were mentioned was when the others said how well they got on together. Oh yes, and they want to take Suzie with them on holiday to France. I can't let that happen.'

'Is that going to be easy?'

'No. I asked what date they were going, and then made up a story that we were going to the Canary Islands and would want to take Suzie with us. Of course, dear Charlie knew nothing about this. Of course not, it was pure fiction. In any case she said Suzie would have a better time with Bobby so she'll want her to go with them. I'm digging a bigger hole for myself every day.'

'Will you go to the Canaries?'

'I may have to now. But Christ, things are very tight at the moment. We haven't really got the money.'

'I don't know what to say, John. Anything else?'

'No, not really. Most of the evening I hardly said anything. It was quite obvious they thought I was a real weirdo, and poor Charlie suffered all night with the embarrassment of it. The evening was the last straw for her. I'm hoping she just wants a break and will come home in a day or two. I just don't know. I could never have imagined this in my worst nightmares.'

There was a long silence as they sat mulling over John's situation. Sarah wanted to try and give him some comfort, but there was little she could say. Yes, he was in a hole, all right.

John looked up and said, 'Anyway, what's your news? Has something happened?'

'I was on duty earlier, and Bobby came on the line. She was speaking very secretively, and I think she was ringing on her mobile from her bedroom and didn't want to alert Simon or her mother,' said Sarah.

'How was she?'

'Much the same. She went on a lot about missing her father, and she cried a lot. Simon's been at it again, and I think his abuse is becoming more frequent.'

'Bastard,' said John, almost choking on the word.

'But this is the good part: she says he's having to go away to Ireland for a few days. Something to do with his work, she says.'

'When's he going?'

'In a day or two, I think. I'm not sure.'

'Thank God for that. That'll give her a few days' relief.'

'Yes, but that's not all. Apparently, she has been asked by one of our volunteers during a call whether she would want to talk to anyone else: perhaps to a teacher at school who she liked; or if she ever felt she wanted to escape Simon, did she know she could talk to her doctor or someone from Social Services? She was never told that that's what she should do or that it would be best for her or that it would be a good idea even. It was just discussing options though it was impressed on her that if she told any of these people, then they would have to report it to the police.

'How did she react?'

'She's always said she couldn't or didn't want to do that. She's always been desperate to keep it secret. But when I was on the phone today she brought up the subject herself and said she would like to think about talking to someone else. She knew that what had been happening would no longer be kept secret, but if we could promise that she could be protected and that people wouldn't disbelieve or blame her she would think about it.'

'Good for her. She's a gutsy little girl,' said John with a sudden excitement.

'Hold on, John. Of course we want this terrible thing that's happening to Bobby to stop. But we have to be very careful not to push her into a course of action which suits us. We simply can't predict the outcome of any of this. We both know how slippery paedophiles can be. This Simon has huge standing in the community, and his wife, from what we can gather from everything Bobby tells us, is besotted with him. You will have probably gained some idea about this yourself now that you've been to their house and seen them together. Of course she loves her daughter, but we can't guarantee that she will believe Bobby's word against Simon's. He's put the fear of God into her in some way, and it could all get messy and become too much for Bobby, and then she might suddenly change her mind and pretend she had made it all up. Then she'd be back to square one, totally at his mercy. I know it sounds far-fetched, but her emotional state is in shreds.'

John gave a long slow sigh, blowing out his cheeks as he considered all the different ways in which Bobby's dilemma might pan out. 'There's not going to be a happy ending to this, no matter what happens, Sarah. She's going to be scarred for life, that's for sure. And even if the whistle is blown and her secret is revealed, resulting in Simon's arrest and her abuse comes to an end, it's still going to be a traumatic time for her. And it will be terrible for her mother too,' he said, shaking his head despairingly.

'We'll just have to try and be there for them, John, if that's what they want. It's all we can do.'

'So how did the call finish?'

'In the end she actually said she wanted to go ahead and tell someone else but she didn't want to do it alone.'

'What can we do about that?'

'She wants one of us from the centre to go with her. I've asked Linda and Mary if they will do it, and they've readily agreed. I think it would be better if there were two of them, and they would be the ideal pair,' said Sarah.

'I agree. They're brilliant, and Bobby will soon feel at ease with them. So what's going to happen?'

'I'm not exactly sure, John. It worries me, I can tell you. We've never done anything like this before. She said that after she's had her tea when she gets home from school tomorrow she's going to say she wants to go down to a corner shop in Wilmot Street near where she lives, to buy some sweets. She said it also has a post office counter in there, and I said I knew it. I have a friend who lives not far from there, and when I've visited her, I've called in there myself. She said she'll try and get there around five o'clock. Linda and Mary will be there to meet her.'

'And then what?' asked John, looking a bit doubtful.

'This is the bit I'm anxious about. There's too many unknowns. She wants us to take her to the house of one of her teachers. She's been there for tea with a group of other children from her class, and she says she likes her. From there on I'm not quite sure what will happen. If she tells the teacher what she's told us, I imagine the teacher will call the police and Social Services. At the moment, her teacher knows nothing. Bobby may want her to call her mother as well. I don't know the answer to that,' Sarah explained, and John could see that she was worried about the whole plan.

'Do you not want to go through with it?' asked John, sharing her own misgivings.

'We've no choice now, and if it's what Bobby wants, we must support her.'

John pondered for a little while, trying to imagine what could go wrong. 'Are we free to tell Social Services or the police or even her mother, after this, about what Bobby has told us?'

'We'd have to check with Bobby. At this stage, she may still want us to keep it secret, but if she wants us to help her through this, she's going to need our back-up evidence. We'll play it by ear. Linda and Mary know the score; they'll know what to do.'

'How will they recognise each other? Bobby doesn't know any of us, and we haven't seen her. As you know, even I have never met her,' asked John.

'Linda's got a summer, orange jacket. She's going to wear that. I've seen it; it's very distinctive. I don't think they will have difficulty recognising her. The shop is unlikely to be crawling with small children,' said Sarah.

'Okay then. We can't do anything now except wait and see,' said John and stood up to go. 'Thanks for letting me know.'

'The least I could do. I'm sorry about the strain it's putting on your marriage, John. It's an impossible situation but our hands are tied.'

'I'll get through it somehow. It's good to be able to talk about it.' He smiled, but she could tell his pain.

'If this mess with poor Bobby is resolved, you'll be able to explain everything to Charlotte, and she'd understand, I'm sure,' said Sarah, trying to offer a crumb of encouragement.

'I think that's a long way off. We'll see. Anyway, I'd better get off.' He kissed her and made for the door.

'It's good to see you, John. Let's hope for the best tomorrow,' she said and opened the door.

He smiled with a wistful smile and a nod but didn't speak. She watched him get into his car and drive away.

Chapter Eleven

Bobby sat at her desk and briefly looked out of the window and watched the clouds drift by. She'd spent all morning thinking about what was going to happen after school and her teachers had had to call out to her to pay attention more than once to what was going on in class. She'd tried to look at her books, at the blackboard and listen to the teacher, but she was so tense about what she had planned that her mind remained anywhere except in the classroom. She began to imagine what would happen if she wasn't allowed to go to the corner shop and meet the ladies that were going to look after her when she went to see Miss Prentice. And supposing the ladies weren't really going to protect her but take her straight back to Simon so that she would be punished for being a wicked girl? And what would Mummy say? She would be so angry and punish her in some way.

'Bobby, will you please stop looking out of the window and pay attention. Are you unwell?' said Miss Hobbs, the teacher who was taking this class.

'No, Miss Hobbs,' said Bobby

'I think you've hardly heard anything I've said,' persisted Miss Hobbs, but then decided to leave it at that and turned back to writing on the blackboard.

By making a big effort, Bobby managed to keep facing the front of the class until the bell went for lunch break.

As they poured out of the classroom, Suzie caught up and tugged at her sleeve and giggled with a kind of moral support because her friend had been told off. Bobby smiled back, and the two of them went and sat in their favourite place to eat their sandwiches. For a little while, neither of them spoke, and then Bobby said, 'Will you always be my friend?'

Suzie looked at her with a frown, 'Of course I will. Why are you asking me that?'

'Nothing. Even if you found out something bad about me? Would you still want to be my friend?'

'What do you mean, bad? You haven't done anything bad,' Suzie stated quite firmly.

Bobby didn't reply but munched her sandwich, and Suzie began to feel that something was wrong.

'Are you okay, Bobby?' she asked.

'Yes,' she said, and there was another silence. Then Bobby said, 'Do they ever send children to prison?'

'I don't know. They might do if they did something really bad,' replied Suzie seriously.

'How bad would it have to be?'

'If they stole lots of money or if they killed somebody. That would be bad.'

'What about if they were accused of lies. I mean really big lies?'

'They might do. I don't know. Why do you want to know?' said Suzie and looked at her friend with a mystified frown.

'Just wondered, that's all,' said Bobby, and then wrapped up the rest of her lunch because she wasn't hungry. After that, they just sat and chatted about nothing in particular until it was time to go back into class, but all the while Suzie thought something was wrong with her friend.

During the afternoon, Bobby paid even less attention to her lessons than she had in the morning. She simply couldn't get out of her mind what she was going to do later. It began to cross her mind that if the ladies tried to take her back home she could make a run for it. She was a good runner, and they wouldn't be able to catch her and she could hide somewhere until they gave up. She wouldn't know where to go, but she would think of something. But even as the idea came into her mind, she knew it was impossible, and she would be much too frightened to even try. *Why, oh why did Daddy have to die?* The bell suddenly went and jolted her out of her dreaming.

'Off you go, children. See you tomorrow,' said the teacher.

Bobby gathered up her books and followed the rest of the children out of the classroom. On their way across the playground to meet their mothers, Suzie said to Bobby, 'See you tomorrow, Bobby.'

Bobby replied, 'Maybe,' and Suzie couldn't understand why there was so much uncertainty in her voice.

****

Linda managed to leave the florist shop by four o'clock and got home shortly after to get ready for her meeting with Bobby at five. Mary turned up at four fifteen, and the two of them sat down with a cup of tea to discuss the plan. Mary was in her late twenties and had been a volunteer for only three years but had a quiet and comforting presence which drew people to her. Linda had been her mentor when she joined, and the two had become good friends and often did shifts together. They had both spoken to Bobby on the telephone over the last couple of weeks and were glad to be part of the plan to help Bobby.

Mary took a sip of tea and stared at Linda, 'I don't mind admitting, Linda, but I'm a bit nervous about all of this. I've never done anything like this before.'

'Nor have I. I don't think it's ever happened before,' Linda agreed. 'I don't think we had any choice, though, when Bobby asked if we could be with her if she told somebody what's been happening to her.'

'No, of course not. But she must have got herself into such a terrible state to want to do it. She's always been so adamant that her abuse should remain secret. She's terrified no one is going to believe her, and that she'll be blamed.'

'That's down to Simon. He's put all that stuff in her mind and has frightened the life out of her. Can you think of anything more wicked?' sighed Linda. 'I'd like to cut his balls off.' They both smiled, but they weren't happy smiles.

'I'm mostly concerned with how Bobby's mother will react. She'll want to believe her daughter, but it will be difficult for her to accept that her husband is such a monster. I can't imagine a worse situation,' said Mary.

'I suppose there will need to be evidence. Is there any of that?' put in Linda.

'I don't think so. In the end, it will probably be her word against his.'

'That means that with his intimidation, which I'm sure he can apply very cunningly, and his innocent protestations, Bobby is simply likely to fall to pieces, and they might think the whole thing is a fantasy. That sort of thing has happened before. Or maybe they'll put it down to a slur she's dreamt up against Simon because she resents him trying to be her real father. They'd think it a very likely possibility.'

'Please, Linda, you're beginning to really depress me,' said Mary.

'Sorry. That hasn't happened yet. And anyway, Social Services and the police are much more on the ball these days. They may want to dig deeper.'

'Let's hope you're right.'

'We'd better get going. I think we should get there at least 15 minutes early. She could get there early herself. We can park across the way and watch for her. If we see her coming, we can go over to the shop and meet her then,' said Linda.

'I'm ready,' said Mary and stood up.

Linda grabbed her orange coat. 'Right. Let's go,' Linda nodded, and they both went out.

****

Bobby sat on her bed, writing in her exercise book. It was four o'clock and she was feeling anxious. When she had got home from school, her mother had looked at her with that penetrating look she sometimes produced and asked if anything was the matter. Bobby had been huffy and dismissed her question almost too emphatically so that Pauline looked at her questioningly. But she'd managed to escape to her bedroom where she could be alone for as long as possible before she was going to set off to the shop.

She finished what she was writing and returned her book to underneath her clothes in the bottom drawer. She looked around her room which was in a state of chaos, with an assortment of clothes strewn about the floor, and wondered if she would be sleeping there tonight. She didn't really know what would happen to her once she was at Miss Prentice's house.

The lady on the phone had told her that the police or Social Services would have to be contacted. She wasn't sure what the Social Services did, but she had a vague idea that they were supposed to help people. The thought of the police coming really scared her because she knew that Simon knew so many of them because he was a judge or something like that. She imagined the police turning up outside Miss Prentice's house in a police car with the siren blaring. She saw people running out of their houses to watch the police leap out of their car and race up the front path and hammer on Miss Prentice's front door. They would come in and surround her and demand to know what she was accusing Simon of. They would tower above her and look from one to another and then whisper to each other with nods and shakes of the head, and she would stand there not knowing what they were thinking or what they were going to do to her, whether they would smile down at her and say that now she would be safe or whether they would put handcuffs on her and march her away.

'Bobby, will you come down for your tea please,' called Pauline from downstairs. Bobby looked at her watch and saw it was half past four. If she took ten minutes or so eating her tea, she would then have just enough time to get to the corner shop by 5 o'clock. She looked at herself in the mirror and tried to calm herself as she felt her heart begin to beat with excitement, and then went down stairs.

'I've done you a boiled egg. You usually have that on a Thursday. Is that all right?' said Pauline as she fussed around at the sink.

'Yes, thank you,' said Bobby, but really she had completely lost her appetite. She gritted her teeth and stuck the spoon into the egg and shoved it in her mouth with a piece of bread and butter, but she had to push it

171

around her mouth several times before she could swallow it.

'Did you have a good day at school today?' asked Pauline.

'All right,' said Bobby as she struggled to eat some more egg and bread and butter.

'Can I go down to the corner shop after tea and get a magazine and some sweets?' asked Bobby, desperately hoping there wouldn't be a problem.

'You're not going anywhere until you've tidied up your room, young lady. It's a shambles. Simon popped his head around the door this morning and was appalled at what he saw. You know he likes things to be tidy,' said Pauline, and Bobby could tell that the hard edge to her mother's voice meant that there would be no point in arguing. She looked at her watch and saw that it was a quarter to five.

'I'm not very hungry. Can I leave the rest?' asked Bobby and held her breath.

'Of course you'll finish it. You love your egg. And if you're hungry enough to eat sweets then you can eat your tea,' said Pauline and continued fiddling at the sink. 'Simon's going away for a few days the day after tomorrow. He has to go to Belfast, so we'll be on our own,' said Pauline across her shoulder.

'Good,' said Bobby, thinking that it would have been better if he had never been with them in the first place.

Suddenly, before she could help herself, Bobby asked, 'What do Social Services do?'

'That's a funny question. Why do you want to know that?'

'Just heard a girl talking about it at school that's all,' said Bobby, trying to act as if it was of no particular interest.

'They deal with all sorts of things, mostly to do with people who are poor or in some kind of family trouble. It's a very big organisation run by the government and local council. You'll learn about them as you get older.'

'I've finished.'

'Don't you want a piece of cake? It's your favourite?'

'No, thank you. Had enough,' said Bobby and stood up.

'You go and tidy up your room now; and I don't mean just stuffing things into drawers. Fold everything and put them away properly,' said Pauline as she saw her daughter skip out the door and heard her run upstairs.

As soon as Bobby reached her bedroom, she frantically began gathering up her clothes and putting them away in drawers, but she wasn't too fussy about folding them neatly. Even so, it took her longer than she wanted because different clothes went into different drawers, and all the while, the clock was ticking. If she didn't get to the shop by 5 o'clock, would the ladies wait? As she stuffed the last article of clothing away she looked at her watch and saw the hand was on five. She rushed downstairs and ran into the kitchen.

'All done. Can I go to the shop now?' she panted at her mother.

'Goodness gracious, what's all the rush?' said Pauline.

Bobby inwardly scolded herself for being so stupid. If she didn't calm down, she would blow it. 'Sorry. No reason. I just don't want them to sell out of my magazine.'

'Oh. I'm sure they won't do that. Let me give you some money,' said Pauline as she went for her purse and took out some coins. 'I hope you've done your room properly,' she said as she handed Bobby the money.

'I have. Thank you,' said Bobby and was out of the door in a flash.

'Don't be long,' shouted her mother and then went back to the sink.

****

Simon gathered up the last of his papers and put them in his brief case. As he was going off to Belfast on Saturday and had planned not to come back into the office before going, he wanted to make sure he left everything shipshape. Lucy had been given all her instructions, and although Richard Deakin was no longer on site at St Catherine's Primary school, he had spoken to the men and knew them to be a reliable lot. He had arranged a schedule of work and expected them to stick to it until his return.

He suddenly thought about his absence from home and how much he would miss Bobby. She was such a darling girl who melted his heart when he was with her. He did so wish she showed a little more enjoyment when she was with him. Perhaps he would take her for a little drive this evening and say a special goodbye to her as he wouldn't be seeing anything of her for a few days. He looked at his watch and saw that it was ten to five. He decided that he would have time to call at the corner shop on his way home and buy some stamps before the post office shut and get a box of chocolates for Pauline and Bobby. He went to the outer office, said goodbye to Lucy and then walked to the car park to get his car. He put his bag on the passenger seat and drove away.

****

Linda and Mary sat in their car about 20 yards down the road from the corner shop. It was five minutes to five, and they had arrived there 15 minutes ago. Fortunately, being parked where they were was not a hazard and did not necessarily look out of place so that it didn't draw attention to themselves. They sat quietly, chatting and watching the road ahead of them feeling more anxious with every passing minute.

'I've got a feeling she won't turn up,' said Mary.

'It's early yet,' responded Linda.

'It's a huge decision for her. Poor little girl must be in a dreadful state. I know how nervous I feel, and I haven't got anything to worry about.'

'I feel the same, Mary, but I still think she will come. I don't mind waiting until half past even if necessary. We did tell her we would wait,' said Linda.

Mary nodded, and as the clock on the dashboard showed 5 o'clock, they both idly saw a big BMW pull up outside the corner shop and watched a tall, white-haired and distinguished looking man get out and go into the shop. A minute or two later, they spotted who they both instinctively thought must be Bobby running down the road towards them. Linda nudged Mary. 'That's got to be her,' she said. 'Wait in the car, Mary. I'm going over,' she continued, as she got out of the car and walked across the road and followed the little girl into the shop. As soon as she got inside, she saw the little girl standing by the magazine rack looking bewildered around her. She suddenly spotted Linda in her orange jacket and when Linda smiled at her, she smiled back and started to walk towards her.

'Bobby,' called out a voice, and they both looked up to see the tall distinguished man walking towards them. In a split-second Linda took a step to the side and walked past the little girl without looking at her and

175

carried on up to the post office counter which was just closing. Immediately, she opened her bag and began to fiddle in it.

It wasn't rocket science to realise that the man was Simon and the little girl was Bobby. Linda's heart was pounding, but she got a grip and walked back to the magazine rack and stood next to Bobby and her step-father so that she could hear what was being said.

'I'm just on my way home, Bobby. I was getting you and Mummy some chocolates. What are you after?' asked Simon.

'I was just getting my magazine,' said Bobby, and Linda could see out of the corner of her eye that Bobby was struggling to keep her composure.

'Ah, which one is it? I can't remember,' said her step-father

'This one,' replied Bobby and pointed to the magazine that she wanted, and as Simon reached down for it, she quickly turned her head and catching Linda's enquiring expression, quickly shook her head. The message was unmistakable, and Linda, after managing the quickest of smiles, turned away and began to look at the magazines herself.

'There you are,' said Simon, handing Bobby her magazine.

Bobby said, 'Thank you,' and took the magazine.

'There's no rush for us to get home, Bobby. We can go for a little drive if you like, as I'm going away for a few days on Saturday. We can park somewhere quiet and enjoy the scenery. You keep your money. I'll pay for the magazine and chocolates,' he said and walked to the counter to pay.

Bobby turned and stared at Linda, and Linda could see the frightened and sad look in her eyes. She gave an understanding nod and a smile and walked out of the shop and back to her car.

'It's her step-father, Mary,' snarled Linda.

'What?' replied Mary in alarm.

'Pure chance. He's on his way home and called in at the shop. Christ, he would have to choose that one time.'

'My God, I can't believe it. What happened?'

'I nearly blew it. It's all right; he didn't suspect anything. He saw her before Bobby, and I had a chance to speak. She signalled for me to do nothing,' said Linda, feeling devastated.

They suddenly looked up, and saw Bobby and her step-father come out of the shop and get into his car. He leant across to her in the passenger seat and gave her a brief kiss on the cheek and then drove off.

'Did you see that?' said Mary.

'I saw,' said Linda scowling, 'and the bastard's just taking her off for a quiet *tête-à-tête* in the woods.' Her face was tight and grim as she watched Simon's car disappear in the distance.

Chapter Twelve

It was a quarter to ten in the evening when John swung off the road and pulled up in his drive. He'd had a long day at work and was glad to get home. He was just about to get out of his car when his mobile phone rang. He saw the number and lifted it to his ear, 'Hallo Sarah,' he said.

'Hi, John. Is it okay to talk?' replied Sarah.

'Sure. I'm alone in the car.'

'Just to let you know it all went pear-shaped.'

'What! How!?' said John, completely stunned.

'Bobby turned up at the shop all right, but by pure chance, her step-father turned up as well, apparently on his way home from work.'

'Bloody hell! What happened?'

'Linda says that she and Bobby were able to make eye contact to acknowledge recognition, but then they had to ignore each other.'

'So he didn't suspect anything?' asked John anxiously.

'No. But unfortunately she had to go off with him and Linda heard him say he was going to take her for a drive into the countryside before going home. I dare not think what that meant,' continued Sarah.

'Jesus, Sarah, when's it all going to end for the poor little thing?'

'I wish I knew the answer to that, John. All we can do is be there for her if she needs us,' said Sarah, with a tone of resignation.

'Christ, is it enough? Is it enough? 'Do you think she'll want to try again?'

'I don't know. We won't know anything unless she decides to contact us again,' said Sarah, wearily. 'I know she's a child, John, and so it is particularly terrible, but she is just the same as any of our other callers. All we can do is listen to them, believe them and tell them that we care,' said Sarah, knowing that he had already lived with that situation for years as a volunteer. She heard him sigh and for a few moments.

'I know, but the way things are it just looks as if we don't care.'

'We both know that's not true. But we just have to do what Bobby wants. To do otherwise is too risky.'

'Okay. We'll have to wait until she contacts us. We won't know anything until then,' said John.

'At least we know he's going to be away for a few days from the day after tomorrow; she's told us that. Hopefully, that will give her a few days when she can relax. I know it's not much but it's something.'

'Yes. He's going to Belfast. Pity it wasn't Syria; he might get shot,' said John grimly.

'Yes, and I know what area of the body I'd aim for,' said Sarah.

'As far as that guy's concerned, even that's not enough.'

'Pointless thoughts, John. Any word from Charlotte?'

'No. Afraid not.'

'We'll keep in touch,' said Sarah, bringing the call to an end.

'Okay. Thanks for letting me know. Goodbye, Sarah.' He sat for a few minutes thinking about what had happened. What unbelievably bad luck that Simon should have turned up at the critical moment. Thank

God, he didn't twig anything. That was something, at least. It must have been a tough call for Linda.

He looked through the windscreen at the house in semi-darkness. It looked bleak and uninviting. Obviously, Charlie hadn't returned. He hadn't eaten since lunch time, but the thought of rustling up a meal at this time filled him with despair. Maybe Charlie would return at the weekend. He'd have to try and talk to her. It was frustrating that she wouldn't even answer her phone. That was really putting the boot in. Maybe he should drive over to her parents on Saturday if she hadn't returned by then, and try and reason with her. Of course he'd have to face her parents if he visited. He wondered what Charlie would have told them. They'd obviously want to know what the hell was going on. No doubt, Suzie would have plenty to say. He couldn't blame her. She was only a child and would have been only too happy to confide in her grandfather, who was very fond of her. One way or another, the whole miserable saga would come out, and there would be nothing he could say to excuse it.

He sighed and got out of the car and slowly walked up to the house. He went to put the key in the front door when he suddenly noticed that it wasn't quite closed. Damn, he thought, he really was going to pieces. Going off in the morning without shutting up the house. What would he be doing next? Going to bed and leaving the cooker on? He'd burn the bloody house down while he was asleep. He pushed the door open and stepped into the hall. And then he heard a sound and suddenly froze. Christ, somebody was in the house.

He remained absolutely still and felt his heart begin to race as he listened for more sounds and to detect where they were coming from. It was definitely the living room and it sounded as if stuff was being moved around. Burglars? It had to be, there was no other explanation. What the hell was he going to do? Quietly call the cops? Investigate and tackle him or them? Probably get stabbed. Cut to pieces and left to die in a pool of blood. Should he be scared? By Christ, he was scared. But this was his house. His property. Who the hell did these bastards think they were that they could just barge in and help themselves?

He was no wimp; he'd been good at rugby; he didn't mind a few knocks and could hand out a hefty punch or two if push came to shove. Still, there could be two of them. He slipped his mobile phone out of his pocket and punched out the 999 number. He got through quickly and whispered that he wanted the police. Another transfer and he told them his address and that he was being burgled and asked if they could come ASAP. He was told not to confront the thieves. He put the phone back in his pocket and crept forward to the living room door which was ajar. He couldn't just stand there and wait for the police. Whoever it was wouldn't want to hang around. He'd grab whatever he could and want to get away. He'd probably come flying into the hallway and run smack into him. So if he came out before the police arrived, he'd see him and have the shock of his life. The thief would probably have his laptop. If he imagined that to be a rugby ball and if this was a game of rugby, he should go for his legs and bring him down.

The idea suddenly calmed his nerves. Before he had a chance to think about it further, the thief came out and sure enough, carrying the laptop. He immediately saw John who was already charging forward. John thumped into him using his shoulder just above the knees. The thief dropped the laptop and crashed to the floor with John sprawling alongside him. Instinctively, John thought he would have the better of the man he'd brought down, but before he could push himself up from the floor, he felt a hefty thump in the side of his rib cage and an explosion in his head, and he collapsed back on to the floor. He vaguely heard a voice shout something, but he couldn't make out what it was. As if in a reflex action, he went to push himself up but couldn't feel his arms working, and he dropped down again with everything going blank.

****

John sat up in bed and fidgeted. He'd been awake for ages and wanted to go home. He thought he should never have been in hospital in the first place. It was fortunate that he had called the police when he did before tackling the burglars, and although he'd been told that nobody had been picked up yet as suspects, they got to the scene in good time to call an ambulance and get him to the hospital. Because he had had such a crack on the head which had sent him unconscious, the hospital had kept him in overnight as a precaution.

His rib cage hurt like hell if he moved in certain positions and he had a lousy headache but otherwise he felt fine. He had already been to the toilet and looked in the mirror allowing him to see the state of his face which was swollen on one side, causing his eye to partly close up. The massive bruising was beginning to spread in a dark shade of purple and was the result of the boot that had slammed into his head from the second burglar who must have been hiding in the kitchen. The doctor and nursing staff who had looked after him had been wonderful and had told him they had kept him in for his own good. But as they had told him, he was in the clear now, so he wanted to get off home as soon as possible.

He had work to do, and his staff would want to know what had happened.

One of the curtains round his bed space was suddenly pulled back and a nurse came in with his neighbour, Margery. 'Okay for you to go home now, Mr Elliot. Your neighbour has kindly come to take you.' The nurse immediately disappeared.

'Hallo Margery. Christ, it's good to see you,' said John and began pulling on his clothes.

'And you. You look as if you've been in the wars.'

'I'll live. It's really kind of you to come.'

'What are neighbours for? I've telephoned Charlie and told her what happened.'

'Oh thanks. What did she say?'

'Shocked of course. But I didn't alarm her. I told her you were all right except your looks had improved a bit.'

'Anything else?'

'No.'

John wasn't sure how much Margery knew about the problems he and Charlie were having in their marriage. They were good friends and would no doubt unload problems on each other. On the other hand, it would not have been completely out of the ordinary for Charlie to go and stay with her parents for a day or two – if that's all it was. But as yet, he didn't know when she was coming back.

'The police have been around and have asked me a load of questions, but I couldn't really tell them much. I didn't even see their faces or what they were wearing. I got the impression that one of them was young, but that was all. I don't suppose they'll catch 'em.'

'They could do. They've probably got a list of well-known villains in the area that have the hallmarks of this kind of break-in,' encouraged Margery.

'I don't know if they managed to get away with much stuff. I imagine they left in a hurry. I'm relieved it didn't happen while Charlie or Suzie were in the house. It would have terrified them.' He suddenly wobbled and had to steady himself by putting his hand on the bed.

'Are you all right?' Margery looked at him with concern.

He waved his hand dismissively. 'I'm good. Don't worry.'

The nurse popped her head between the curtains again. 'No going to work today, Mr Elliot. You have an easy day at home. Any concerns, you call us.' She smiled.

'Trust me. And thank you for everything.'

'You're welcome,' replied the nurse and disappeared.

'They're lovely, but talk to you like children. I'm ready.'

Margery walked close to his side as they went out. The hospital had said he was okay, but she didn't want to take any chances of him falling down. They reached her car in the car park and got in.

'Would you like to stay at our place for the day, John? I don't like to think of you being on your own.'

'I shall be fine. As far as I know, they didn't have time to pick up my laptop. I know he dropped it when I hit him, so if it's not been taken or damaged, I can contact the office and then get on with some work at home.'

'You shouldn't have tried to tackle them, John. What they did is bad enough, but it might have been worse.'

'I didn't realise there were two of them. Anyway, I've survived.'

Margery switched on the engine and began to drive out of the hospital car park. 'You must come in and have

184

lunch anyway. You need to keep your strength up,' she laughed.

It only took them five minutes to get home and even though Margery lived next door she pulled up outside John's house. He immediately spotted Charlie's car in the drive, and a moment later, the front door of the house opened and she rushed out. As soon as he got out of the car, she ran up to him and threw her arms round him.

'Are you all right? Oh my God, you look terrible,' there was a tremor in her voice. John gave a wince.

'I'm sorry, darling. Are you in pain?' she said in fright.

'My ribs. It's okay. Just a bit tender.'

'It's terrible what's happened. You could have been killed. I should have been here. Margery rang me first thing this morning. I've just arrived. I was about to come to the hospital. Thank you so much, Margery.' Her words were pouring out uncontrollably.

John held her gently but firmly. 'I'm fine. I'm fine. I'm so glad you're here. I didn't know if you'd come.'

'Of course I'd come. I'm your wife. I love you.'

'Yes but I…' he was suddenly lost for words.

Margery said, 'I'll leave you two. Glad you're all right, John. Call me if I can do anything.' She pulled forward the short distance and swung into her own driveway.

John called across the front garden as she got out of the car. 'Thanks for everything, Marge. You're a gem.' Margery waved and disappeared into her house.

'Come on, let's get inside,' said Charlotte as she held John's arm. 'I can't believe we've had a break-in. The place is a bit of a mess.'

Suzie had been watching from the front door step slightly bewildered and frightened at the sight of John's face.

'Hallo, Daddy. Are you all right?'

'Hallo, Suzie. Don't worry, luv. It looks far worse than it is.'

'The three of them walked on into the house.

'I'm so glad you're back. This place has been like a morgue.'

'I wish I'd never gone now.'

'Oh, it's all right. You did the right thing. I'm sorry I pushed you to it. It was all my fault.'

'Never mind about that now. You need looking after. Shall I make tea?'

'Just what I need. The cuppa that makes everything okay. But don't fuss, Charlie. I'm not ill. Look at this place. You're right: they made a hell of a mess.'

'I'll soon clear it up. It must have been a terrible shock. It has been for me and I wasn't even here. And you had a nasty crack on the head.'

'Oh well, it's knocked some sense into me.'

'Something I've been trying to do for ages.' She said it with good humour.

It had crossed John's mind while he was in hospital that if Simon was going to be away for a few days, he wouldn't be around to abuse Bobby which meant that Suzie would be safe too if she went to play with her. He had thought it rotten luck that as Charlie was away at her parents he couldn't take advantage and be easy-going about Suzie visiting Bobby. But now, since she was home, the opportunity was there and he could be much more reasonable. He'd be able to repair some of the damage to his relationship with Charlie and Suzie at the same time. Okay, it would only be temporary, and he would probably be faced with the same problems again in a few days, but what the hell, he should do his best on a day to day basis. He'd have to deal with the issue as and when it changed.

'I realise I've been a... well a bit of pig about Simon and Pauline and really unkind in making such a fuss about Suzie going over there. If she wants to go, that's fine. I'll even take her myself or collect her if it will help.'

'Oh thank you, Daddy. We don't do anything wrong anyway.'

'I know. I'm sorry, luv. I've been a bit grumpy. I didn't mean it.'

'Well, this is a turnaround. That kick on the head must have done something to you. Sorry, that was unkind.'

'I wouldn't have lasted long without you, Charlie.'

'I didn't want to go, John. But I was at my wit's end.'

'I know, I've given you a hard time lately. I'm not going to try and make excuses. I haven't any. I'm just sorry. I'll make it up to you.'

'Well, there's been a lot I haven't understood. And yes, you have been a pig.' She stared down at him with a look of disdain, but then, with a twinkle in her eye she said, 'Fortunately I'm of such a forgiving nature and will therefore let you off this time.' She bent over him and kissed him. 'I'm going to have to get Suzie to school now. She'll only be a little bit late, and I'm sure they'll understand. Will you be all right?' He was about to respond when they both heard the letter box rattle.

'That'll be the post,' said Charlotte.

'I'll get it,' said Suzie and ran out. A moment later, she returned holding a letter.

'Addressed to both of you,' said Suzie as Charlotte took the letter off her and peered at it. She slipped her thumb into the opening in the corner and tore it open.

'It's from the school. The headmistress. Good gracious, one of the builders, it says the foreman here,

187

was arrested by police for apparently taking photographs of the children during PE class. Rumours and panic have been flying around the school, but she assures all parents that there is no need for alarm. The man is no longer working there, and the police are confident it was an isolated incident from that one man. My God, John, you've got to be on your guard all the time.'

'He must be one of Simon's men,' said John as steadily as he could manage.

'Oh dear. Poor Simon. He'll be shocked.'

'I suppose he will. But he must know something about the men who work for him – especially the foreman.'

'He won't know anything about their personal lives, I shouldn't think. These sorts of people can be very clever.'

'The letter doesn't say he's in custody, does it?'

'No. Do you think he should be?'

'Not if they've no other evidence. They'll probably search his home and look at his computer and any other stuff to see if he's a really bad lot. He may be in league with others, too. So they'll obviously search for names and addresses. If there are any others, they'll want to question them as well.'

'Oh dear. You're making this sound really serious.'

John didn't say anything for a moment. His mind was racing. It had to be too much of a coincidence for Simon's foreman to have such an interest in children without him knowing it. The most likely scenario was that they were in collusion together, part of a paedophile ring. Is that how they operated? In secret groups passing material to each other and supporting each other in their nasty games? It was a dark and secret world. Still, this could be the break he had been waiting for. If the police found any kind of evidence that began to point the finger at Simon, or even if his foreman ratted on him as a means of currying some favour if he got sentenced, then it could be the beginning of the end for Simon and the start of a new life for Bobby. That would be poetic justice: for Simon to be brought down by one of his own nasty cronies.

'I'm sure the police know what they're doing and will suss out any other wrong-doers,' he suggested.

'All I can say is thank goodness they caught this foreman chap before he did any harm.'

'Yeah. Brilliant,' said John, but she didn't detect the irony in his voice.

****

Bobby put her exercise book away in the bottom drawer and quietly went downstairs. She could hear her mother and Simon talking in the living room as she slipped out through the kitchen door and made her way down the garden. She opened the garden gate and went into the paddock where Pansy was grazing. She walked over to her and stroked the top of her neck under the mane which she knew the pony loved. When Bobby felt miserable she often came to talk to Pansy. Pansy was her friend and understood how unhappy she was.

'Simon's going away tomorrow for a whole week. Good riddance, eh Pansy?' she confided. 'The plan I told you about all went wrong. I knew it would. Everything goes wrong for me. The lady was there, the one I told you was going to meet me, but then Simon turned up. I was terrified at first. I thought he must have known about it, and it was a trap, but the lady pretended that she didn't know me, and I knew it was just by chance he turned up at the same time. I had to go with him then. I wanted to go back home but he took me for a drive into the country where nobody else was and he made me... well you know what he made me do; what he always makes me do. He said he wanted me to be happy but I cried afterwards. He said that what we did, what he always calls our lovely secret, was a wonderful thing between us, and because of that, he would always look after me.' She broke off and put her arms round Pansy's neck and gave her a cuddle. 'I wish Daddy were here, Pansy. I miss him so much. He loved me, and he loved Mummy, but now Mummy loves Simon. How can she do that, Pansy? I don't understand. I shall never be happy until I'm with Daddy again.' She put her arms round Pansy tightly and pushed her face into her mane and cried.

****

Miss Charles, the headmistress of St Catherine's Primary school, smiled across her desk at Simon and Pauline. Pauline returned her smile but shifted uneasily in her seat.

'Thank you for coming. I'm so glad both of you were able to come. So often only one parent can make it,' said Miss Charles.

'You did suggest in your letter that it would be better if both of us came,' replied Pauline. 'You've got me quite alarmed.'

'That wasn't my intention. I just wanted to have a chat with you about Bobby.'

'She's not done anything wrong, has she?' said Pauline, a touch of panic in her voice.

'No, no. She's a lovely girl. Both her teachers say she makes no trouble in class, but she seems unable to concentrate.'

Pauline turned with a confused expression and looked at Simon. He shrugged and said, 'Could you be more specific, Miss Charles?'

'She spends a lot of her time as if day dreaming; looking out of the window. Often she hasn't heard a word the teacher has said.'

'Has she been asked about this?' asked Pauline.

'On several occasions. It's as if she's in another world. I understand she's not been crying but she...' Miss Charles hesitated, 'Well, she seems unhappy.'

'Oh dear. I don't know what to say. We haven't noticed anything at home, and she's not told us she's unhappy,' said Pauline. 'She's moody at home sometimes, but that's not unusual, is it?'

'Children vary so much. I don't think you should worry too much, but I hope you don't mind me mentioning this to you.'

'Of course not,' said Pauline. 'We're only too grateful you've told us.'

'It's my fault,' said Simon. 'I'm to blame.'

Pauline turned sharply and looked at Simon again. 'Darling?'

Simon spread his hands disarmingly. 'Look. She's only nine, and she's lost her real father. She misses him. I'm no substitute. I'd be surprised if she didn't sometimes appear to be thinking of her father. It's barely two years since Roger died, isn't it Pauline?'

'Oh, Simon darling, it's not your fault. Of course, she misses Roger, but you've been wonderful to her. You're patient and kind with her and you're always making a fuss over her.'

'Well, I love her as my own daughter and she's a loveable child, but I can't help feeling a bit guilty that she must see me as a poor replacement of her father.'

'She's so lucky to have you, Simon. Please don't blame yourself.'

'Your wife is probably right, Mr Hargreaves. I'm sure you do your best in a difficult situation.'

'Forgive me for saying this, Miss Charles, but is there any chance that she's being bullied?'

'I think it unlikely. We keep a very strict eye on anything like that. We've only ever had one case of bullying, and that was several years ago. She has a very good friend, I believe. Suzie Elliot.'

'Yes. They're great friends. And we're pleased. She often comes around to us. They get on so well. Bobby seems perfectly happy at home, except as I say, for the occasional bad mood. But that's her age, surely.'

'Well, as I say, I thought it worth having a quick word with you. She is a lovely child and we'll just be watchful. If we think there is cause for concern, I'll call you again.'

'Please do, Miss Charles. In the meantime, I'll talk to her.'

Miss Charles stood up. 'Thank you for coming in. The new classroom block is making great progress, Mr Hargreaves.'

'It is, yes. A few more weeks and we'll be done.'

'Excellent,' Miss Charles put out her hand and firstly shook Simon's and then Pauline's. 'Goodbye.'

Chapter Thirteen

John came into the Ops room carrying two mugs of coffee as Linda put down the phone in the booth. 'Just what I need,' she said and sat down in the chair opposite him.

'Long call,' said John

'It was a quarter to ten when I started. Just over an hour then,' said Linda and took a sip of her coffee. 'She's in her fifties, married for 25 years, and her husband has been having it off with a younger version from his work place. He's admitted it and said he's sorry and is going to end it, but she knows he's still at it. She says she should leave him but she can't. She still loves him and hopes one day it will just fizzle out.'

'Must be awful for her,' said John, and then the two of them remained quiet for a little while.

John liked doing a duty with Linda. She was brilliant on the phone and really cared about her callers. Although she was one of his closest friends, he had not told her that he knew who Bobby was and that she was his daughter Suzie's best friend. Normally, he would have done that, but as he and Sarah had agreed to keep it between the two of them, he had stuck to the arrangement. In a funny way, he felt a kind of protectiveness towards her. He knew she and her husband were having real problems and that her husband resented her being on the Prison Team. A few years ago, she had become pregnant, and she had told him and he was mad as hell. In the event, she had a miscarriage and went into a long bout of depression. Linda had told John that her husband Clive had no patience and no understanding. As far as he was concerned, it was about time she got a grip and pulled herself together. It had been a hard time for, her but she had stuck at it and tried to make the marriage work. They jogged along, but there wasn't much in it for her.

Linda suddenly said in a voice that couldn't hide its urgency. 'John, I want to talk to you.'

'What?' He immediately detected the change in her mood.

'It's difficult.'

'Difficult? I don't understand.'

'Charlie came to see me.'

'Charlie? She came to see you?'

'Yes. She's worried about you.'

'Me? I'm all right.'

'She thinks you've got trouble at work, and you're not telling her. You're grumpy. No, what she means is you've been behaving like shit. Sorry. She really is worried.'

'Oh Christ.'

'She's not going behind your back to talk to me. You know that.'

'Of course not.' He didn't say any more, and she waited in silence expecting him to be forthcoming about what had been going on. But he said nothing, and she assumed that he was going to keep it secret. She could understand that. The less people that knew, the better. There was nothing to gain by her or anybody else in the centre knowing Bobby's identity. And she now thought it better not to reveal that she had accidentally found out from Charlotte that he knew of Bobby's identity.

He suddenly looked up. 'It's complicated.'

'I don't want to pry, but she is worried, John.'

'Oh shit! I know. It's true. I've been a bit of a sod. It's all my fault. She deserves better, and Suzie too.'

'It's unlike you, John. And you two have been so close.'

'I've hated myself for what I've said and, Christ, for what I've done.'

'I'm sure you're being hard on yourself.'

'No way. I've been a bully, and I don't deserve her.'

'You're beginning to worry me now, John. What's happened?'

John began to breathe heavily and rock his head from side to side in frustration.

'Do you want to talk about it or do you want me to shut up? I had to bring it up because Charlie wanted me to.'

'Oh, it's all right. I'm glad she talked to you.'

'Can I do anything?'

'I'm afraid not. That's the trouble, nobody can.' He dropped his head in despair as if he were contemplating a big decision. Linda didn't press him and waited in silence.

He suddenly looked up. 'All right. I trust you above all others, Linda, you know that. I'll tell you. And it's because you're a Sam, it's okay.' He paused again as he struggled to think how to start. 'The thing is, I know who Bobby is.'

Linda sagged into a chair and spread her hands across the table. 'I know. Or I was sure I knew.'

'What! How?'

'It's only recent and by accident. When Charlie came to see me, she mentioned that Bobby was Suzie's best friend. When she told me more about her parents it became pretty clear. It was obvious you would have sussed it out.'

'My God. You didn't say anything, did you?'

'Of course not. I quickly put two and two together and could see the position you're in.'

'Have you told any other volunteer?'

'No. I wouldn't do that. There would be no point. Does Sarah know?'

'Yes. I had to tell her. She's the only one. We both thought it best to keep it to the two of us – at least for now.'

'I agree. I'm sorry, John. I can see how difficult it's been for you.'

'You don't know the half of it.'

For a few moments, neither of them spoke. Linda said, 'What are you going to do?'

'I don't know. I can't do anything.'

'Does this Simon know that you're a Samaritan and that Bobby has been talking to us?'

'No, of course not. They don't know anything. I've never actually met Bobby. Charlie's made good friends with Bobby's mother Pauline and she thinks the sun shines out of Simon's backside. That's how we got an invitation to spend an evening with them. Of course, I didn't want to go. It was terrible. I had to sit next to that bastard and act as if I was Charlie's lovely husband. It was a disaster. I behaved like a demented pig. Charlie was devastated, and I can't blame her.'

Again Linda tried to grasp what John was saying. 'Did he suspect anything?'

'No, thank goodness. I've had to keep my mouth shut because of Bobby. She's begged us not to tell her secret. You know the score.'

'You know we talk about this scenario in training, but nobody really thinks it will happen in reality. Now here we are. What a dreadful situation. No wonder you've been under such a terrible stress.'

'You can't imagine, Linda. Suzie's always around at their house. She's invited there all the time, and she loves going there. But don't you see, I'm terrified for her safety. That bastard may want to get his hands on her.'

'Oh John, that's terrible.'

'So far it's been all right. At least, I think Suzie would come to me or Charlie if he'd tried anything. But that doesn't mean he won't. The trouble is that Charlie's encouraging Suzie to go and play with Bobby – they're great pals – and I'm laying the law down and saying that she can't go. To be honest, I must have seemed like a monster to Charlie and Suzie. My marriage is heading for the rocks, but I'm trapped.'

For a little while, there was silence. Linda could see the impossible situation John was in. But what could he do? Nothing. She could see that. She said, 'I know it's breaking the rules, but have you been tempted to tell Charlie?'

'God, no. It's not that I don't trust her. It's just that... I dunno. She might let it out to somebody or try and explain things to Suzie; all well-intentioned, but if it got out it would be a terrible betrayal to Bobby, and it wouldn't do the branch any good. And if it did get out, I don't know what Bobby would do. She's terrified.'

'I'm really sorry, John. I don't know what to say.'

'It's okay. I'm glad you know. Sarah's been a terrific support, but in the end nobody can do anything. The real horror is knowing that poor Bobby continues to suffer at the hands of that monster. And frankly, I can't see any way of it stopping unless he falls under the bus or unless she says we can blow the whistle, and I'm sure she's never going to do that no matter how much he abuses her.'

'As far as I know, we haven't heard from Bobby for several days. I wonder if she's okay.'

'Her step-father was away for a week, but that was over a week ago. He's probably back now,' said John.

'I'd like to think that no news is good news, but that's probably wishful thinking.'

John pondered upon her remark in silence. He himself had been wondering about Bobby. The week had gone well with Suzie and Charlotte. Suzie had gone to play with Bobby two or three times, and John hadn't had to worry, and everything had gone much better at home. He and Suzie were friends again, and because he had been so much more relaxed, he and Charlie had enjoyed each other's company in the same old way as before. But he knew that Simon had been home now for three or four days, and he'd begun to get anxious again. Bobby hadn't rung the centre since before Simon went away, and whilst he hoped that Simon was not up to his vile tricks again (a hope which he knew was pie in the sky), he wanted to hear from Bobby to know how she was. She was of particular concern to the whole branch.

'Do you ever think about leaving the Sams, John?' asked Linda.

'One day, I suppose, but I'm not thinking about that at the moment. As long as people like Bobby and the kind who you've just spoken to keep ringing up, I'll keep slogging it out. Why do you ask?'

'They say that burn out happens after about three years. I've been here at least three times that length of time, and you've been at it even longer.'

'Ah well, perhaps we've both got a screw loose,' he said, and then the phone interrupted. 'I'll take it. You need to log your call,' he said as he went into the booth and lifted the phone to his ear.

'Samaritans. Can I help you?'

'It's Bobby,' said the timid voice.

'Hallo, Bobby,' said John and pulled himself into the phone. Linda heard the name Bobby and looked up. 'This is John speaking. I'm really glad you rang, Bobby,' he continued in a gentle voice. For a little while, there was silence, and he waited patiently. Then he heard her crying. 'I'm sorry you're so upset. Has something happened?' Again there was silence and John waited. 'You know we're on your side and want to help you through this.'

'I'm scared,' she managed in a little voice.

'I know. You've been having a terrible time, and you've been so brave.'

'Something happened, and I was scared,' she said in a whisper, and he could feel the pain in her voice.

'Can you tell me about it?' said John, and immediately wondered if he should have asked.

'I can't tell you,' she said, and he heard her whimpering again.

'That's all right, Bobby. You don't have to say if you don't want to. Just say anything you're comfortable with.'

'But I do want to say, though.'

John realised something had happened that had really upset her that she wanted to tell him but found it too difficult. He suddenly wished he was better at this.

'If it's too difficult for you, just say one or two words at a time. I'll understand, Bobby. Just say what comes into your mind,' said John and saw that Linda had turned the other phone off, not wanting the noise of it to suddenly blare out and disrupt his call. What she did was unusual and not really allowed in case another caller with a serious problem was trying to get through, but as far as she was concerned this call with Bobby was too important. She moved her chair and sat down just outside John's booth.

'Mummy went out tonight. I was on my own, and I knew he would come.'

'Had you gone to bed?'

'He came up later and said he wanted to kiss me goodnight. I didn't want him to,' said Bobby in a trembling voice. John squeezed his fingers around the phone as he listened to her words.

'Just take your time, Bobby; you're being so brave.'

'He did something different. It's the first time he's done that. I didn't know what was happening,' she broke off with the tears flowing again.

'It's all right, Bobby. I know this is terribly hard for you. I wish I could be there with you.'

'I want Daddy. I do so want Daddy,' she whimpered, each word stumbling out of her.

'I know you do. I wish he was there for you too,' said John, at the same time inwardly cursing at his pathetic gestures of help.

'He hurt me. He hurt me so much, and I was so confused when he pushed my legs apart. His thing was so painful, he hurt me so much, he hurt me,' she cried, and John knew that she was now truly howling uncontrollably. He held the phone away from him and looked down at it. As he looked and heard her crying, he felt his own tears welling up behind his tightly screwed up lids. He suddenly felt Linda's hand with a reassuring touch, and he put the phone back to his ear.

'He should not have done that to you, Bobby. He did a very bad thing, and you're the most wonderful little girl to have told me about it. I've never known anybody so brave,' whispered John, as he struggled to try and find some words that would ease her pain. But there were none and he knew it. He just listened to her crying now. He did not speak and neither did she. He knew she was there and she knew he was there and that was enough.

He knew she wouldn't go and she knew he wouldn't go. And for several minutes, he just sat quietly and listened to her weeping until gradually her sobs petered out.

'I'm still here, Bobby,' John whispered into the phone.

'I'm sorry,' her words were so faint.

'Don't be sorry. You've nothing to be sorry for.'

'I have to go now.'

'Bobby, would you like us to help you? To tell somebody so that we can stop Simon?'

'No! No one must know. No. Please, you promised.'

'No, we promise not to unless you say. But we only want to stop Simon.' Christ, he didn't want to pressure her.

'Please. No one must know. If anyone finds out about me I'll kill myself.'

'Oh Bobby, where are you now?'

'I'm in my bedroom.'

'Is Mummy home?'

'Yes, she's gone to bed and Simon too.'

'I know Simon hurt you but...' John felt himself biting on his words, 'but are you all right? Are you damaged, I mean, has he injured you...? Do you know what I mean...?' Christ, what words could he use? All his training and experience seemed to be deserting him.

'There was blood but it's gone. And I still hurt.'

'You should you see a doctor, Bobby. I'm very worried about you' said John, as he groped around for the right thing to say.

'I'm not going to a doctor. I don't want anyone to know. You won't tell, will you?' she said with a sudden urgency.

'No, we won't tell unless you say we can, Bobby. But we are worried about you. Are you sure you're all right?' pressed John. *Christ*, he thought, *this is getting ridiculous. The poor girl simply couldn't go on like this.*

'I'm all right. Please don't tell. If anyone found out it would be awful living'

'Bobby, we love you. Lots of people love you. We were going with you to see your teacher. Do you want to try again?'

'No, it was a mistake. I'm glad it went wrong now because of what he...' She suddenly stopped speaking, before going on, 'Please don't tell. Please,' she implored.

'We won't tell. I promise,' said John and as he spoke he felt a deep, terrible, grinding regret. This was the most dreadful and wicked outrage. Simon was a monster, and she was completely at his mercy. Unless something happened, this outrage could go on indefinitely.

'We all love you, Bobby, and we wish we could do more for you.' John tried again, knowing his words were pathetic. Then there was another long silence, and John could tell that she was probably sitting on her bed just holding herself and despairing.

'Do you think you could try telling your Mummy about what happened?' John suggested.

'Mummy won't listen. She would get cross the moment I said anything about Simon. Whenever I've tried before, she just brushed me aside before I had a chance to say,' said Bobby so emphatically that John realised it must be true.

'She doesn't understand, Bobby, but she loves you.'

'She only loves Simon. Daddy's the only one who loved me, and now he's gone.'

'I'm sorry. This is so hard for you.'

'I have to go. My battery is nearly gone,' she said.

'Call us again, Bobby. Whenever you like. We're always here,' said John, not wanting to lose her.

'Bye,' said Bobby, and then the phone went dead.

John replaced his receiver and let out a long, deep sigh. 'God almighty! That poor girl. What he's done to her. Now she's had to endure rape. She's fucking nine, Linda. Nine! And he's raped her.' His anger, frustration, distress, concern, all rolled into one erupted out of him as he spoke.

'Surely we should have involved safeguarding by now. What does Sarah say?

'I know it looks that way. But it's not so simple. I honestly think she could take her life the moment her secret is exposed. And don't forget, as far as she is concerned she doesn't know that we know who she is. She hasn't given us her surname and address. I know that by chance.'

'Do you really think she might take her life, John? It's not an easy thing to do. And even harder for a child.'

'Oh Christ, Linda, I don't know what to think. Okay, it may be wrong but I think we have to hold tight until she says we can blow the whistle.' He shook his head in total despair.

Linda laid her arms round him, 'She talked to you, John. She felt able to do that. That meant such a lot to her,' she said.

'Doesn't change anything though, does it. That bastard is still at it.'

'But we are here for her and we are the only ones. If she didn't have us to talk to, she'd have nobody. That's all we can do. You were there for her and knowing that we all believe her means so much to her,' encouraged Linda, even though she knew that in his heart John knew all that himself, and that it was so little. If she had taken the call instead of him, he would have said the same things to her. That's how it worked, and they all knew the score.

John sat back in his seat nodding and quietly getting himself back on track.

'It's twenty to twelve. You'd better ring in and off-load. The night shift will be here any second,' said Linda kindly.

'Okay,' said John and stood up to go to the phone in the admin room.

'And John,' said Linda, 'Leave it… Call me if…' she looked at him with a gentle smile.

He nodded and walked out.

****

John pulled into his drive at nearly half past twelve. He got out of his car quietly and didn't slam the door so as not to wake the whole neighbourhood or at least not set off the dog next door. When he got into the house, he noted that Charlie had left a couple of small lamps on so that he could see his way without crashing into things. She'd always joked that he was a clumsy ox and that if there was something to knock over he would do it. He quietly made his way into the living room which was in darkness, but he switched on a dim standard lamp and then slumped down in an arm chair. He felt lousy; not sick but lousy just the same. The call he had taken with Bobby had really got to him. Of course, he had taken many difficult calls over the years, and in so many of them, it was difficult not to be affected. This was to be expected and was why the Samaritan Organisation had developed its own support system for its volunteers. It was never frowned upon if a volunteer was emotionally moved, even brought to tears, when listening to the misery and pain of some callers. Rather the reverse. For a volunteer to have any value or help for a caller, he should be able to express empathy and compassion, which was not really possible to fake. But John also knew, like all the other volunteers, they had to offer their service professionally. Without professionalism, the organisation would be doomed to failure.

He pondered upon Linda's remark about telling him to leave it all behind when he left the centre. All volunteers followed that policy – in theory at any rate. That was why they had the support of their colleague with whom they were on duty and then followed up by ringing to the duty leader for their shift so that they could unload before leaving the centre. It was a good system, and ninety percent of the time it worked. Apart from anything else, it reduced the temptation for any volunteer to reveal to anyone else what must remain confidential.

Rarely had John left a shift without being able to dump what he had listened to on the phone. A few times, calls had been exceptionally horrific or so moving that he had worried about them for a day or two, but they had never got him down. But tonight was different. He simply couldn't shake off the depth of horror and distress he felt that seemed to ooze out of Bobby. He had felt her physical presence as if she was standing right next to him. He could almost touch the tears on her face and feel her breath. The fact that he knew who she was and that she was his own daughter's friend had compounded the whole ghastly experience. He felt the anger because he also knew who her abuser was, and this made his heart pound.

Everything about Simon was wicked. He should have been looking after her and protecting her, more especially because she had lost her real father, but he had connived his way into her life so that he could abuse her.

And all the while he had smooth-talked her mother so that she thought he was wonderful and a loving support for her daughter.

John knew he wouldn't be able to sleep. He got up and went to a cabinet and took out the bottle of Glenmorangie. He poured a good two inches into a glass and went back to his chair carrying the glass and the bottle. He took a large gulp of the whisky pulling a face as he swallowed it. He continued to sit in the chair, brooding and mulling over the situation with Bobby, Charlie and Suzie and wondering where the hell it was all going to end. He finished the whisky in his glass and poured himself another one which he sipped for a little while. Eventually, he put the glass down and tried to calm himself before going up to bed.

It was three o'clock when he suddenly woke to see Charlie in her dressing gown standing in the doorway.

'John, are you all right?' she whispered.

He didn't move and Charlotte moved closer and touched his arm, 'John, wake up. What are you doing down here?'

He gradually stirred out of his sleep and looked up at her, 'Sorry,' said John in a befuddled voice as he tried to become alert.

'What are you doing down here? It's about three.'

'Oh Christ… sorry… I dropped off.'

'Are you drunk?' she said as she spotted the bottle of whisky.

'No, of course not. I just wanted a drink. I must have sat down and fallen asleep.'

'I didn't hear you come in from the centre. I was fast asleep.'

'Oh yes…yes. I'm glad.'

'It gave me quite a fright when I woke and saw you weren't in bed.'

'Sorry. As I say, I just dropped off.'

'You look terrible. Is everything all right?'

'I'll be fine. You go on up. I'll be along soon.'

'Was it a bad duty?'

'Sort of.'

'You know I worry about you when I know something is wrong.'

'Don't start, Charlie. I'll be fine.'

'I'm not trying to nag. Come on, luv...' she said tenderly.

John waved his hand dismissively, 'It's all right. Some calls are...well...difficult... It's to be expected. If we weren't human, we couldn't do it,' he said and yawned.

'I've not seen you like this before. What's happened?'

'Nothing. The caller was distressed, that's all. You know that some calls are obviously difficult to deal with,' he said with a touch of impatience.

'Of course, I understand that, but you're obviously upset, and I don't like to see that.'

'Stop fussing, Charlie. It's difficult when you know the caller is in real trouble, and you know you can't do anything to help,' John tried to explain which he thought shouldn't be necessary; she knew perfectly well how the Samaritans operated, and it was obvious, anyway.

'So they're in really serious trouble...' persisted Charlotte, now with a frown on her face.

'Of course they're in serious trouble. Most of our callers have got serious problems. That's why they call us. Please go on back to bed. I'll be up directly.'

'But there must be something about this caller that's got you so stressed,' persisted Charlotte.

'For goodness sake, Charlie. It just so happens that I know them. That's all. It happens rarely, but it does happen.' Shit! Why did he say that? Why doesn't she go to bed and drop it?

'My God. What are you going to do?' said Charlotte feeling quite alarmed.

'I'm not going to do anything,' replied John beginning to feel uncomfortable about her unrelenting questioning.

'But you know who it is!'

'It makes no difference. They don't know that I know who it is, and they don't want anyone to know of their trouble.' Right, that should be an end of it. 'Now do go off to bed, Charlie. I'll follow you directly.'

Charlie sat down determinedly on the sofa opposite him.

'I've never interfered in the past, John. I've always respected the fact that you can't tell me things, and I've never wanted to know,' she said in a voice that told John something else was on the way.

'I know that, Charlie. It's never been a problem.'

'But I can see this is different. You've never been so upset like this before. Three o'clock in the morning. Almost drunk. It's got to be something. Surely it's something you can talk to me about if it will help you,' said Charlotte, and her voice became even more determined and concerned.

'You know I can't break the rule of confidentiality to anyone, not even you,' John protested.

'I don't want to know who the person is, silly. Surely there's no harm in telling me what the problem is,' she said, with a genuine belief that it didn't compromise any confidentiality.

'I can't do that, Charlie. I wish I could, but I can't. It just wouldn't help and probably make matters worse,' said John, who was now beginning to feel really irritated by Charlotte's persistence.

'Worse? I can't see how telling me that small thing can make any difference,' she said, dismissing his objections as being ridiculous. But then she had an afterthought. 'Unless I know them too, of course. My God, it's someone I know as well, isn't it?'

John stood up from his chair with growing annoyance. Why the hell was she going on at him like this? She knew damn well he couldn't tell her anything. 'Go back to bed. It's got nothing to do with you!' he snapped and immediately bit his tongue. If he acted too aggressively, she would become suspicious he was hiding something.

'Yes, well that's just about the sum total of it, isn't it? I'm just an inconvenience in your life. It's all about you and your Samaritans, and I can go to pot,' railed Charlie in a sudden outburst.

'You know that isn't true, Charlie. And it's not going to help if you know who it is,' he said, trying to placate her.

'Of course it will help. I can see you're upset. If I know who it is, I can help share the burden with you.'

'But you know I'm bound by confidentiality. I can't tell anyone. You've always understood that.'

'I'm not anyone. I'm your wife. If one of us is upset, that's exactly when we must confide in each other. It's what marriage is all about,' she retorted, nearly choking on her words.

'You're being totally unreasonable. I'm tired and I want to go to bed,' he retorted vehemently.

'Oh, I knew it wouldn't last. This is the same old selfish you. Just cut me out of your life. What do I matter?'

'All right. All right! It's Bobby.' It was almost a scream. John never did really understand how it was he blurted out Bobby's name. He thought about it scores of times, later on, simply wondering how he could have done it. Was it because he was tired? Was it because of the stress of the past few weeks that had suddenly become too much? Was it because Charlie had just kept on at him and made him feel he was being a brute again? He didn't want to blame Charlie. She had always played the game and never questioned him about his callers. On the other hand, he could understand, from her point of view, that she was concerned because she could see he was worried, looked ill even, and as his wife she wanted to help. But he knew that that really made no difference. He had told her and broken confidentiality. There was no excuse. He knew that many people would take the view that it was no big deal; it was only his wife, after all. What was the harm in that? But as far as John was concerned, they were all excuses; mealy-mouthed reasons for breaking a code in which he passionately believed.

'Bobby!' said Charlotte, and she could only gawp at him.

'Yes, Bobby! So now you know,' he spat out the words.

Charlotte suddenly dropped her shoulders with a scoff, 'You must be out of your mind,' she said, still glaring at him.

'If you're not going to believe me, why do you ask?' John replied with indignation.

'But Bobby's just a child.'

'Do you think children don't ring us?'

For a little while Charlotte made no reply. She stood, shaking her head and trying to take in what John had told her. To her it seemed too fantastic. Bobby was such a lovely and happy little child. Why on earth would she want to ring the Samaritans?

'Why on earth does she ring you?' she asked, her expression changing to bafflement.

'I can't tell you anymore,' he said and made as if to move.

'Wait! You have to tell me, now that I know it's Bobby.'

'No way! Especially as it's Bobby. Now forget that I told you anything.'

'What's the good of telling me half of it? If you didn't want me to know, you shouldn't have told me anything.'

'For Christ's sake! You made me tell you. You went on and on and on,' he railed at her now.

She suddenly became calmer and assumed what she thought was an authoritative stance. There was no point in rowing; it would get them nowhere. But she had to have all the facts. Until she knew what the problem was she would feel uncomfortable every time she saw Bobby. And it would worry the life out of her.

'Look John, let's not row. The point is I now know that Bobby calls the Samaritans. Suzie goes to play with her, for God's sake. Every time I see her, what am I expected to think? I know you've never met Bobby, but if you had you would see what a lovely little girl she is. Of course I'd want to know. Am I expected to question her?'

'No! You must never, ever ask Bobby what's wrong. You must promise me faithfully,' said John in a sudden panic.

'All right, I won't. But I have to know, John. Can't you see that not knowing will be a terrible worry for me? I won't feel comfortable being with her. I'll keep looking at her and wondering what's wrong.' She was almost pleading now.

Jesus Christ, thought John, he'd dug himself a hole which was getting deeper and deeper. Why had he opened his mouth? If only he had been firm and put his foot down, none of this shit would have happened. If! What a laugh that was. No good saying that now. He'd opened his trap like an idiot and now he had to pay. There was nothing for it. If there was the remotest chance of Charlie questioning Bobby, which would be a complete disaster, he'd have to head her off by telling her what was happening.

'All right. What I'm going to tell you is absolutely confidential. Is that clear?' he said in the sternest voice he could manage.

'I understand,' she replied.

'No. I mean it is absolutely and completely confidential.'

'Okay. I hear what you're saying.'

'Give me your word then that you won't reveal this to anybody.'

'Really John, is this necessary?'

He paused for a moment and then made a move as if it was the end of the conversation and he was going up to bed.

'All right. I promise.'

'It's a secret, and that's how it must remain.'

'Fine,' said Charlie and held up her hands in submission.

John paused for a few moments and then took a deep breath, 'Right, you want to know? I'll tell you. Your wonderful Simon is sexually abusing her,' he said, virtually spitting out the words.

Charlie stared back at him in stunned silence, totally shocked at what he had just told her. For a few moments, she seemed to be in shock, her thoughts seemingly scattered, unable to put together a response. Then,

213

suddenly, as if coming out of her stupor she burst out laughing. 'You must be mad,' she said, stumbling through her words with laughter, 'Simon?' she blurted his name with more peals of laughter.

John simply stood and watched her with disdain. In spite of himself, now he felt angry and wanted to make her see how stupid she was. He waited until her laughter had subsided, and then he said with as much venom as he could muster, 'Unthinkable? Disgusting? A respectable magistrate and pillar of respectability in the community?' He paused and glared at her before going on, 'Yes, well now you know what he's really like: Scum!' he spat out the final word.

Charlotte stared back at him, but faltering in her disbelief, 'I don't believe you,' she said, unable to conceal her tone of doubt.

'Do we disbelieve a child who can hardly speak because she's choked with fear? Who sobs her heart out because of the dread of what he does to her? Who stutters and weeps as she pours out her anguish and awful pain in her heart?'

Charlotte suddenly felt her knees go weak and the colour drained from her face. 'My God, you really mean it,' she choked. 'It's really happening.' She eased herself down into the chair in stunned shock.

'Yes, and it's been happening for ages.'

He stood and watched in silence as she held her head in her hands, the horror of what she had learnt overcoming her. She stood up and reached out to him, 'We must go to the police. We must tell Pauline,' she exclaimed in excitement.

'Don't be such a fool. That's out of question,' said John dismissively.

'We can't do nothing, John,' she said in a shrill voice.

'Bobby's already tried to tell her mother, but she just dismissed her, and she's still terrified that she won't believe her.'

'She won't believe her own daughter? Don't be so silly,' said Charlotte, scoffing.

'It's not silly. If Suzie accused me of messing about with her, would you believe her?'

'That's ridiculous. I know you, John.'

'Exactly. And if I was a paedophile, I'd manipulate your disbelief and use it to get a stronger hold over Suzie. Pauline's mad about Simon. She thinks the sun shines out of his backside. She can't help herself. She thinks that Bobby doesn't like Simon and tries to say bad things about him because she misses her own father,' he said, trying to explain.

'But Pauline would believe you, John,' said Charlotte, thinking she had come up with the obvious answer.

'Are you crazy? You know I can't say anything. Bobby has told us this in confidence,' said John in exasperation.

'But she's only a child, John. She can't possibly be expected to know what's in her best interest.'

'She absolutely knows what she wants. She's emphatic that no one knows what's been happening. It doesn't matter whether we agree or not. Whatever her reasons, we have to respect that. We have given our word that we will tell no one, and I've already broken it by telling you.'

Charlotte started looking around the room in bewilderment and frustration. This was crazy. Bobby was being sexually abused which she and John could put to an end. Yet he was saying they should do nothing; nothing because that's what Bobby had said she wanted. It beggared belief. How could the poor child not want it to stop? They would be party to the abuse if they did nothing. She didn't want that on her conscience. Okay, confidentiality was all very well as far as it went, but this was beyond the pale. John had to see reason.

'We simply can't stand by and do nothing, John. We have to do something. We have to!' she implored him.

'Do you think I don't want to? Do you think any one of us down at the Centre who take her calls doesn't want to? Of course we do. We agonise over it. We'd like nothing better than to get her away from that filthy swine. But we can't until she agrees. That's why I've been so unbearable lately. I couldn't tell you. I desperately wanted to but I couldn't. That's why I've been so hard on Suzie. I was so worried about her,' he explained at last.

'Suzie?' said Charlotte with a mystified frown. 'What's all this got to do with Suzie?'

'Well, because she...' his voice faltered as he realised that she hadn't yet realised the implication of Suzie's friendship, but then he saw the penny had dropped.

'Oh my God, John!' exclaimed Charlotte as understanding dawned on her. 'Suzie. She hasn't... you don't think...?' Her voice broke off in horror of what she was thinking.

'No. I feel certain nothing has happened to Suzie. But I've been so worried that it could have happened. That's why I didn't want her sleeping there.'

'But it could in the future if she went over there again.'

'Exactly. That's why we can't let her go there any more, at least unless we're sure he's not going to be around.'

'That's not enough, John. We've got to tell Pauline. You don't have to be involved so you don't have to break your confidentiality.'

'But you'll be breaking it because I've told you. There's no difference,' he said flatly.

'That's pathetic tinkering with silly manoeuvres to save face while this dreadful thing is going on and our own daughter could be at risk. Our own Suzie's safety is the most important thing in the world to me. We are her parents. We have to protect her,' shouted Charlie with a tone that had the ring of finality.

'I know that as well as you. And we will protect her, but we can't say anything about this to anyone. Do you understand?' He shouted back with as much force as he could.

'Why are you two quarrelling? I hate it…'

They both turned in shock and saw Suzie standing in the doorway in her nightdress.

Chapter Fourteen

Simon pulled up in the kerb outside St Catherine's Primary School and got out of his car. Already there were lots of mothers standing around waiting to collect their children after school. He wandered up the path and started to mingle with them, stopping to have a word with one or two and smiling at others who always smiled back. He was feeling good. All these mothers with their lovely children liked him and looked at him with respect. He was a magistrate, a person who administered the law and yet was not too high and mighty to chat with them. And they could see he was such a good father to that poor child who had tragically lost her own father. What a blessing it was that he had come into her life.

He saw Charlotte pull up on the other side of the road and make her way towards the playground gates. He weaved his way through the mothers and came up to her.

'Hallo Charlotte,' he said, displaying his charming smile.

Charlotte stiffened instinctively but concealed it with a gesture of the hand, 'Hallo Simon,' she replied and quickly turned back towards the school as if she was looking to see if the children were out yet.

'How are you today?' he asked.

'I'm fine. How's Pauline?' she said and kept her voice even.

'She's in fine fettle, thank you. Just giving her a day off from the school run duties,' he smiled again.

Charlotte made no reply but turned and looked up as she heard the bell and a moment later, saw the children pouring out of the main school entrance. Surprisingly, she saw Suzie and Bobby coming out early though both of them were dawdling across the playground.

'There they are,' said Simon, waving to catch their attention.

The girls gradually made their way over, and Charlotte wondered if it was her imagination that Bobby seemed to be moving awkwardly and hanging back.

'Hallo, Mummy,' said Suzie brightly.

'Hallo, darling.'

'Would Suzie like to come and play, Charlotte?' asked Simon.

'Oh yes please, Mummy,' said Suzie excitedly.

'Not tonight,' snapped Charlotte and bit her tongue for being so abrupt.

'Why not?' retorted Suzie.

'Um, because I'm sure Simon and Pauline have had enough of you recently,' said Charlotte, and knew immediately it was such a lame excuse.

'Not at all, Charlotte,' said Simon, 'It's a pleasure to have her.'

'You see, Mummy,' added Suzie.

'Nevertheless, not tonight. We want you at home. It's not convenient,' Charlotte persisted.

'Oh, that's a shame,' said Simon and winked at Suzie.

'We have to go, Suzie,' said Charlotte, moving away and inwardly wincing at her abruptness.

Simon laughed, 'Slow down, Charlotte; whatever it is, I'm sure it'll wait.'

Charlotte momentarily paused, 'Err, yes, I'm sorry. But I'm in a bit of a rush today,' she said, but continued to walk off towards her car.

'Bye. See you soon,' he called as she moved away. He looked down at Bobby and smiled, 'And how are you, princess? Let's go home.' He walked back to his car and Bobby followed.

Bobby only picked at her tea, and her mother could see that she was not herself. She didn't pressure her to eat if she didn't feel up to it and thought it a good idea if she went to her room to rest as she had asked. As soon as she got to her room, she lay down on her bed and closed her eyes for a little while. She began to think about her father and the things they used to do. They were always good things, happy times. They would go on holiday to the seaside; to Alton Towers and the safari at Longleat. Other times, the three of them, Daddy, Mummy and she, had gone to the Forest of Dean and had picnics.

They often went to the swimming pool as well and Daddy was a good swimmer. He had promised her that when she was ten they would buy her a puppy. She so wanted that to happen but wondered if it ever would, now. But the things she loved most of all were the little things. The times when Daddy would pull funny faces at the meal table or let her chase him in the garden with the hose pipe. Once when he was digging in the garden, he chased her with a worm, but it all ended in screams of laughter. But Daddy was gone now. She would never see him again until she was dead. The only thing in her life now was horrible Simon and Mummy who didn't seem to care about her as she used to. She had nothing to look forward to, and she would never be happy again.

She gently swung her legs off the bed and winced. She was sore down below and had a constant, dull ache. Simon had said he was so sorry if he hurt her, but she knew he didn't really care. Every time he touched her or pushed his thing into her mouth or what he did last night, he always did it with sweet phrases saying how wonderful she was and what a lovely girl, and how much he loved her. But it was all lies. He was really only thinking about himself.

She put her hand down between her legs and touched herself, and when she retrieved her hand and looked at it, she saw there was a smear of blood. The sight of it didn't frighten her. She knew she was hurt but was determined not to care. Her anger at what Simon had done would be a device to help her survive.

But as she stared at the smear on her fingers, her thoughts suddenly calmed her and a strange sensation swept over her. She looked at the blood more intently and saw that it seemed to offer a release of all that was bad in her and that was happening to her. It suddenly seemed the means to shed her feelings of dirtiness, shame and guilt that Simon had swamped on her. Why this should be or how it could be was beyond her understanding, yet the sensation was overpowering.

She moved slowly out of her bedroom onto the landing and stood quietly until she was satisfied that Simon and her mother were preoccupied in conversation downstairs. She moved along to the bathroom and opened a wall cabinet where Simon kept his razor for shaving. On the shelf next to his shaving foam was a pack of new razor blades. She slipped one out and went to a large cabinet on the other side of the room. She rummaged inside until she found the first aid box and took out a bandage and then went quietly back to her room.

She sat down on her bed and folded her hands in her lap, thinking about what she was going to do. Deep down, she felt that cutting herself was something she shouldn't do; that it was something awful and that her mother would be cross if she found out. She also felt scared because she didn't know how painful it would be. Yet beyond all this, she wanted to put the blade into her flesh and see the blood flow.

She pulled back the sleeve of her blouse to above the elbow of her left arm. She studied the inside of her arm and knew that any cut there would be less likely to be seen, but because the skin was so tender she thought it would be too painful. She turned her arm over and gently rubbed her fingers over the skin. The skin here was almost as soft, and she decided that this would be the place. She took the blade between her index finger and thumb and slowly drew it across the flesh. She didn't need to push down hard as it was so sharp, and she didn't want to cut too deeply as this was her first time. She ran the blade down her arm and made a cut about two inches long and immediately, the blood ran freely. So fascinated was she as she watched it run down her arm that she was unaware of any pain the wound was causing her. She reached for her box of tissues, and as the blood dripped when it reached her wrist, she stopped it from dropping on to her clothes or bedding. Her eyes remained riveted to it, bright red and glistening as it weaved its way down her skin. But more than any sense of horror or pain, she felt uplifted by a feeling of wonder.

The more the blood seeped on to the tissues, the more she felt at ease and at peace with herself.

She sat for several minutes, staring at her arm until the blood thickened and finally stopped flowing. She felt slightly numb, unsettled at what she had done whilst at the same time aware that it had made her feel better. She wiped the blood from her arm, but didn't disturb the cut which was forming a soft scab. She took the bandage and gently bound up the wound and pulled down her sleeve. There was no reason that her mother or anyone else should know what she had done. She didn't think the wound would take long to heal, and then no one would be any wiser. She was undecided if she would do it again but would think about that another time.

She rolled the bloodied tissues into a small ball and wrapped it in a clean one and put it in her school bag. She would throw it in a litter bin in the playground while she was at school tomorrow. She hid the razor blade in her pencil box. As soon as she was satisfied she had covered all her tracks, she lay down on her bed with the picture of her father and talked to him.

****

It was ten thirty when Charlotte got to the till in the supermarket. She had been in there for well over an hour pushing her trolley around in a dream. She was aware that she had put things in her basket that she would never have bought in the past and didn't want now, but she simply wasn't functioning properly. She unloaded her trolley on to the belt and automatically moved forward when the customer in front had finished. Normally, she would have packed her purchases with care, putting soft items and perishables separate from tins, jars and bottles. But this time, she put it all in together, either unaware or not caring that the softer, more delicate items were being squashed. She paid her bill and went out to her car in the car park, unloaded into the boot and then got into the car. Her mind was in a daze. After the shock and upset at what John had told her the night before last, she had gone back to bed but had hardly slept for the rest of the night. It had been difficult at breakfast too. She was aware that Suzie had been upset by what she interpreted as a row between her parents in the middle of the night. But Suzie had not referred to it when Charlotte had taken her to school. During the whole of yesterday, the revelation of what John had told her went round and round in her mind. When he had come home from work, neither had mentioned it, and the atmosphere had been strained. Even last night, she had slept badly again and knew that John himself had been tossing and turning most of the night.

As she sat in the car and watched people walking about, chatting, doing their shopping and going about their lives, she couldn't get her mind around the horror of what was happening to Bobby. She could not have imagined that someone as courteous, charming and friendly as Simon could, at the same time, be the dreadful monster that she now knew him to be. Unless, of course, it wasn't true. Could it be a fantasy made up by Bobby because she was missing her father so much? If she had been calling the centre for so long in such a dreadful state of distress as John had described, it had to be true.

Was she simply naïve or had her life been so sheltered that she didn't realise that such people existed in normal communities? The fact that she had unwittingly been duped into putting her own child, Suzie, in harm's way filled her with anger. Should anything have happened to Suzie, she would have felt greatly to blame and never forgiven herself. As for what Suzie might have suffered was too unbearable even to contemplate, but thinking about all this, worrying, fretting and agonising was not going to do any good. If nothing was done, the situation was going to drag on and probably get worse. She would make sure that Suzie didn't go over to play at Bobby's any more, but that wasn't going to be easy. And she realised now how hard it had been for John. Of course, he must have been upset, and her hard attitude would have been so hurtful to him. If he had only told her about the situation, she would have been more understanding. She knew he had insisted they could do nothing because of his confidentiality, but was that more important than getting poor Bobby out of her hellish situation? How could they stand by and do nothing while they knew what was going on? Surely they would be complicit in the crime. She had always stood by John and respected his judgement, but he could be wrong, like anyone else. And it was all very well, the Samaritans holding these high and mighty principles. It seemed to her that they were almost playing at being God.

She was a mother, and a mother's basic instinct was to fight for her child whatever the cost. And the same sort of principle stood when it was the child of another mother. The only thing that mattered was the protection of the child; any child, because they were innocent victims. She knew what she must do. She turned the ignition and drove away.

The drive to Pauline's was not more than a few minutes, but it gave her a little time to think what she would say. It wouldn't be easy, but they had become good friends, and she felt sure that Pauline would listen to her. It would be a terrible shock for her, but she would be there to support her. Apart from the horror of discovering what had been happening to Bobby, it would also be heart-breaking to accept that the man who she adored was responsible for it. She'd lost her first husband in tragic circumstances, and now she was going to lose her second one for being a monster. What a ghastly tragedy for any woman to have to go through.

Charlotte suddenly realised she had turned into the road where Pauline lived and a sense of panic began to creep over her. She eased the car into the kerb a few yards short of Pauline's house and switched off the engine. She closed her eyes for a few moments to try and calm herself. This was going to be a lot harder than she had thought. It seemed the obvious thing to do when she first decided to do it, but now she was not so sure. All the words she had rehearsed in her mind had suddenly deserted her. But there was no turning back now. With her growing sense of panic, she got out of the car and made her way the short distance to Pauline's house and rang the bell. It was only a few seconds before Pauline answered the door.

'Charlie! What a lovely surprise.'

'Hallo Pauline,' replied Charlotte, trying to relax.

'Come on in. I'm just about to make a pot of tea,' went on Pauline, as she turned away and began walking back into the house.

'Thank you.'

'We'll go in the kitchen. The kettle's just boiled,' said Pauline and took down a couple of mugs from the dresser.

'I can't stop long, Pauline.'

'You'll have a cup of tea before you go, won't you?'

'Well, I won't, thank you Pauline, if you don't mind,' said Charlotte, and could feel the nervousness in her speech.

Pauline turned around and stared at Charlotte. 'My word, you look so serious. Is everything all right?'

Charlotte began to shuffle on her feet. 'Well I…' she began but was interrupted by Pauline, 'Is something the matter, Charlie?'

'I just wanted a quick word… and… oh dear… there's not an easy way to say this,' stammered Charlotte.

'Goodness me, Charlie, this sounds dreadful. What on earth is it?'

'Well... it's Bobby.'

'Bobby? Oh dear, what has she done now?' Pauline shook her head.

'Nothing, she... this is so difficult to tell you.'

'Please, Charlie, you must. Has she done something terribly wrong?'

'No, no, of course not.'

Pauline suddenly became alarmed. 'Oh my God; she's all right, is she? She's not had an accident?'

'No, she's fine... I mean,' said Charlotte stumbling over her words. 'It's... it's...'

'Tell me!' Pauline was now frantic.

'It's Simon. He's, oh God, he's been abusing her,' suddenly Charlotte had blurted it out.

For a few seconds Pauline was struck dumb. And then she stared at Charlotte in horror. 'What?'

'I know this must be a terrible shock for you, but I had to tell you,' said Charlotte, blundering on.

'Simon? Abusing Bobby?' Pauline retorted, almost choking on her words.

'Please, Pauline,' said Charlotte, beginning to feel unnerved by Pauline's threatening tone.

'How dare you! How dare you!' Pauline began to rail as her eyes began to bulge, and her cheeks turn red.

Charlotte took a couple of steps backwards, fearful of what Pauline might do. 'It's true, Pauline. I'm so sorry, but Bobby has been saying what's...'

Her words were cut short by Pauline's outrage. 'What Bobby's been saying! For goodness sake, Charlie, she makes these stories up about Simon all the time because she misses her daddy. It's been hard for her. What do you expect?'

'But, Pauline…' Charlotte tried pathetically but was cut short again.

'Don't "but" me,' Pauline raged on. 'Kids pick up all these sorts of things at school. In her child's mind, she can't allow Simon to be a replacement for Roger. She sees him as the enemy, but she's a very naughty girl to tell such lies about Simon, who would rather die than let anything bad happen to her. Do you think I would have married him if he wasn't a wonderful person?'

'Of course not, but…' Charlotte attempted lamely.

'There are no buts. I'm utterly appalled that you should even think such a dreadful thing about Simon. You know him yourself,' Pauline scoffed, spreading her hands in disbelief at Charlotte's naivety.

Charlotte was beginning to feel that her cause was lost but was determined that she must make Pauline see the truth. 'Yes, Pauline, I have liked Simon, and I realise that it must be terrible for you to accept, but do let me try to explain.'

Pauline took a deep breath, 'Stop it! I won't hear another word. Simon will be devastated when I tell him what you've said.'

'Of course this is a dreadful shock for you, Pauline but John has told me that…'

'John! Well that explains it. Your husband is a misfit. That was obvious to Simon and me when you joined us the other evening. It wouldn't surprise me with anything he came out with.'

'I know John was rude when we visited, and it was unforgiveable, but this has nothing to do with Bobby.'

'Don't say any more. I'm going to have to have a serious talk with Bobby. She could start spreading these lies about Simon anywhere.'

Charlotte saw the anger in Pauline's face and felt alarm flooding through her body. 'It's not Bobby's fault,

Pauline. Please don't blame her,' she said, and suddenly realised she was now pleading.

As if ignoring anything further Charlotte might want to say, Pauline said coldly, 'I think it better if you keep Suzie away in the future. Please go now.'

Charlotte felt completely demolished. This wasn't supposed to happen. She had come to warn Pauline. She had come as a friend to warn her of the danger that Bobby was in. Why couldn't she believe her? Why did she have to get so angry? And how could she possibly blame poor Bobby? She was the one who needed rescuing, who needed her mother's love and protection from that monster living in their house. Christ almighty, Bobby was now going to be in bigger trouble.

Charlotte could only helplessly stand in silence. Her mouth had gone dry, and she was feeling weak with unbearable distress from Pauline's contemptuous dismissal. 'Please, Pauline, don't let us fall out. I'm really very fond of you. I'm simply trying to help.' Her tone was increasingly weak and pathetic.

'Just go!' This was not a request. This was an order; the words were hard and icy and full of venom.

Charlotte looked about her as if searching for some mysterious force that would suddenly appear and make everything better, some quirk of fate that would shine a light over this awful cloak of darkness that laid heavily over her and her friend. What friend? Now she was no longer a friend. Now there was only bitterness and anger between them. She had come in friendship and was leaving now with such bad feeling. She swallowed again and licked her dry lips. There was nothing more she could say. It was over. 'I'm sorry,' she said in a whisper and silently turned away and then stood aside as Pauline walked past her and led her out to the front door. It was opened without further words passing between them.

Charlotte stepped outside, and as she walked down the front path, she heard the door click shut behind her. As if in a daze, she wandered up the sidewalk and fumbled for her key, sprang the lock and slipped into the driver's seat. She felt numb. In no more than a matter of a few minutes, the dreadful situation she had come to solve had turned into a bigger nightmare. Was it her fault? Should she have stayed away and kept her mouth shut? Surely, that couldn't be right. Surely, it was right to do something to try and get poor Bobby out of that dreadful horror in which she was trapped. To have simply sat on the side lines and done nothing would be an unthinkable. But what was the good of all these arguments now? No use at all. She'd lost her friend; Bobby would be in bigger trouble and the plight of the poor girl would simply go on. Unless she went to the police. My God, perhaps that was the way out. Perhaps she should have done that in the first place. But wait a minute, was that plausible? She could hardly go waltzing into a police station and start blabbing about Simon abusing his step-daughter when she had no evidence. Simon, who was a magistrate – she mustn't forget – and well respected, would certainly deny it, and Pauline would definitely back him up, claiming it to be spiteful gossip, or she may even repeat that it was the fantasy of a child who missed her father. That explanation sounded really plausible, and Bobby would probably be too frightened to stand up against Simon and she already knew she wasn't being believed by her mother.

There was no way John would back her up because he could never admit that he had told her anything. She already knew that he was agonising over the fact that she had weaselled out of him what he had told her. Anyway, Charlotte suddenly realised that the police would probably laugh at her as a crank, or even worse, consider charging her with defamation of character. God, her thoughts were going off the Richter scale. This was all crazy. She'd have to calm down, pull herself together and accept the fact that she had done her best and could do no more. Damn it; she wouldn't tell John what she had done. At least Suzie shouldn't be in any more danger. She'd just have to carry on as normal but pray for poor little Bobby. She fired up the engine and drove off.

Pauline stood at the window and watched Charlotte's car disappear down the road. She felt quite sick. She wasn't sure if it was from anger, hurt or simply shock. How could Charlie, of all people, believe such cruel things about Simon? If only she knew how much he adored Bobby and wanted to look after her. He had been so patient with her too, never criticising her when she was rude to him or said unkind things about him. He had been the greatest thing that had come into both their lives since Roger had died. That was what was so galling about Charlotte's attitude: the fact that she couldn't see that Simon was just about the most unlikely person in the world to do anything bad to Bobby, or any other child for that matter. Not only did he love children, but he was passionate about protecting society in general from wrongdoers. Ask anyone who knew him: teachers from the school; parents; friends, not to mention those he knew well in the police; they would all look in horror at the ridiculous accusation that Charlie was making. Of course, it had all come from that rude, oddball of a husband of hers. He must be at the root of it. It beggared her belief that Charlie, her own friend, could be so stupid as to be taken in by the silly fantasy of a nine-year-old child. And in God's name, how did Charlie imagine that Simon ever had the opportunity to abuse Bobby? They all lived in the same house together. Did she really think anything could possibly happen to Bobby under her own nose? The more she thought about it, the angrier she became, pushing aside any feelings of hurt. And as for Bobby: she would have to have a very straight talk to her about the seriousness of what she was saying. She obviously didn't understand the implications of what she was spreading about; she was just a child, but she had to be told quite firmly that she couldn't go around saying such terrible things about Simon. Also she had to be sensible enough to know that she must be more attentive to Bobby; spend more time with her and show her that she understood how much Bobby missed Roger.

It also dawned on Pauline that kids of nine today were a lot more streetwise than they were in her days. They saw all sorts of images on TV and in magazines and gossiped amongst themselves about sexual scandals of celebrities – which she didn't, for a moment, think they understood, but which nevertheless filtered into their psyche. Children today probably realised that anything of that nature was just the sort of stuff that could be used against someone if they wanted to hurt them. And that's what Bobby was trying to do. She wanted to hurt Simon because he wasn't her daddy. Poor Simon, it wasn't his fault.

Pauline went back into the kitchen and stared at the two tea cups that hadn't been used. Feeling drained, she picked up the tea pot and filled one of the cups. She added a drop of milk and took a sip. It was only lukewarm and she sighed. She went over to the sink, poured out the remains of the cup and emptied the tea pot. She wanted to cry. She hated any kind of upset, and if it involved Simon or Bobby, it would always bring her to tears. What was she going to do? She would have to tell Simon, of course. He would be shocked and hurt that Charlotte could have believed such rubbish, but he would put his arm around her and tell her not to worry. He was so kind and such a strength. This sort of thing never upset him. He just took in his stride. But that didn't mean he wouldn't be upset that Bobby had tried to spread such lies about him, especially as he loved her as if she were his own daughter. She knew what he would do: he would take Bobby on one side, sit her down and quietly tell her that he understood how difficult it was for her to see him as Roger's replacement. He wouldn't be angry, and he wouldn't criticise. He would tell her that he would try even harder to be good to her and do everything in his power for her to see that he only wanted her to be happy. How many people would be as understanding and kind as that, she wondered; very few. He was a saint. No, she would have to be the one to administer any kind of punishment, if that was appropriate, but everything else she would leave to Simon.

She rinsed the cup and teapot and then got out the ironing board. She still had three more of Simon's shirts to iron.

Chapter Fifteen

Bobby turned over and looked at the digital clock on her bedside table. It was 2.15. She had been awake for at least an hour and had managed to stop crying only ten minutes ago. She was calmer now, and her breathing had settled down. She turned again and laid on her back. She could see from the far window that there was nearly a full moon. She stared at it for a little while, thinking that Daddy would be up there somewhere in heaven, perhaps close to the moon, and that he might now be looking down on her and saying how much he loved her. He would understand how she was feeling; how upset she had been when her mother had collected her from school and was not very nice to her. She hadn't had a chance to speak to Suzie who had to walk much further down the road to where her mother was waiting. That was odd because she and her mother always waited together. As soon as she had got into the car, she knew she was in trouble. It was the expression on her mother's face; it was unsmiling and tight, and as soon as they pulled away, her mother had started scolding her for saying nasty things about Simon. She said it had to stop because it was all lies, and it was so unkind. She had said that she wouldn't like it if other people went around saying nasty things about her. Her mother had gone on about it all the way home and hadn't even once asked her if Simon had ever done anything bad to her. She simply believed that everything she had been accused of saying about him was completely made up. She would tell Simon everything Suzie's mother had said and that tomorrow she would have to apologise to Simon. She couldn't do it today because he would be home after she had gone to bed. And she had to promise that from now on all these wicked stories must stop.

Bobby stared up at the moon again and smiled weakly. 'I love you, Daddy,' she whispered. She vacantly turned her head from side to side on the pillow hanging on to thoughts as they came and went. How did Suzie's mother know what Simon had been doing to her? Mummy hadn't believed it but Suzie's mother had. Otherwise, she wouldn't have tried to tell Mummy. Or did she? Mummy would have told her that it was all untrue, and then Suzie's mother as well would think she was a liar and a horrible, wicked girl. And then Suzie wouldn't like her either and not want to be her friend any more. That must have been the reason Suzie's mother had parked a long way up the road after school, just so that Suzie wouldn't have to speak to her. She was going to be even more on her own now. Tomorrow, Simon would take her on one side so that they were alone, and her mother would agree to it. It's what she wanted. She wanted her to apologise to Simon and that was the way to do it. But what would he do to her? She screwed up her eyes and tried not to think.

'Who told Suzie's mummy, Daddy?' she asked, staring up at the moon. Nobody knew except the people she spoke to on the telephone. They said it would be secret; that they wouldn't tell anyone and she had believed them. But they were the only people who knew what was happening and had said they believed her. But they must have broken their promise; they must have tricked her all along and finally decided that they were no longer going to put up with listening to what she was saying without telling somebody else. Somehow, they must have tracked down Suzie's mother and told her everything. They were clever and could do these things, and they had laid a trap for her. So now she couldn't trust them anymore. She would have no one. Suzie would be told, if she hadn't already been, and then Suzie would tell other children at school, and then the teachers would know, and then the whole world would know and everyone would stare at her and laugh at her or turn away from her, and there would be nowhere for her to hide. The only person who would pretend to be nice to her would be Simon who would take her away to some secret place and hurt her again. And if she cried out no one would come to help her.

Only Daddy could help her. Only Daddy understood. She looked up at the moon again and saw him waving and smiling down at her, and she reached out with her hand. 'I will, Daddy. I'm coming,' she cried out in silence as tears of happiness ran down her face.

She threw back the bedclothes and got out of bed. Very quietly, in the darkness, she fumbled for her clothes and got dressed. She moved over to the door and after opening it a little, she listened. Everything was quiet. Holding her shoes, she silently tiptoed along the landing, and then made her way downstairs where she waited and listened again. There was still no sound. She went through to the kitchen, unlocked the back door and slipped outside. She put on her shoes and looked up at the moon and smiled. 'It's all right Daddy. I'm coming,' she whispered, and silently went down the garden path and through the gate that led to the tack room on the edge of the paddock.

The tack room was not much more than a shed and there was no light, but she knew exactly where to find Pansy's headcollar. She lifted it off the hook and went across the paddock where she could easily see Pansy grazing in the moonlight. Pansy lifted her head, and she slipped on the headcollar. 'Hallo Pansy. We're going to see Daddy. Those people I've been talking to, they've broken their promise and told what Simon's been doing. They said they would never tell, but they have. I have no one now. There's just you and me. You mustn't be afraid. Mummy said that when Daddy died, he felt nothing. It was all over instantly. So we shall be the same,' she whispered into Pansy's ear.

When she turned away and gave a gentle tug on the lead rope, Pansy followed meekly as she was led out of the paddock and on to the short dirt track that ran down to the road. The pavement was wide enough for them to walk side by side, and on the inside, there was a slight verge with boundary hedging. This stretch of road was used by Bobby every day on her way to school, and she knew that the slip road down to the 417 led to the M5 motorway and was only about three or four hundred metres away. A single cloud drifted across the moon and they were swallowed up in darkness for a little while. Occasionally, Pansy dropped her head and tried to nibble the grass on the verge. The road ahead and behind them was deserted, but Bobby could hear the occasional rumble of a lorry engine drifting up from the fast 417.

It only took them a few minutes to reach the roundabout and slip road. 'Nearly there, Pansy,' said Bobby and walked on down towards the three-lane highway. Occasionally, a single car or lorry sped past, but being the middle of the night, even this stretch of highway remained almost deserted. Bobby began to wonder whether or not she had made a mistake because she had imagined there would be many more vehicles speeding along. Never mind, she thought, it would only take one lorry, and because there were so few vehicles, it would probably be going much faster.

At the bottom of the slip road, she hesitated and let Pansy nibble the grass at the side of the hard shoulder at the foot of the embankment. She looked back down the highway but it was in darkness with no headlights in sight. She tugged on the lead rope and began to walk along what was a very narrow, hard shoulder on this stretch of the road with Pansy reluctantly following behind. She had only gone a little way when a motor car streaked past at high speed. Pansy momentarily jerked her head in fright, 'It's all right, Pansy. We're going to be all right,' soothed Bobby.

As they walked on, the occasional car and lorry flashed past at high speed, and after they had gone another 100 metres, Bobby stopped. 'This is far enough, Pansy. This is where we will do it,' she said and looked back up the road and saw the tiny lights of the next far off approaching vehicle. She reached down and ran her hand over Pansy's thick mane and scratched her the way she knew she liked it. 'When I shout, you come with me, Pansy. We will do it together, and then we'll be with Daddy, and we'll be so happy,' she whispered in a voice that was calm and firm. She stared down at the pony with a smile and then turned and looked back up the road again.

In the distance, she could see the lights of a lorry approaching on the inside lane. At first, she couldn't quite make out what kind of vehicle it was because the lights were unusual. But as the vehicle drew nearer, she could see that in addition to its headlights there was a line of small, decorative lights right the way across the top of the cab, and she knew instinctively that the lorry was a very big one. And then she could hear the deep throaty groan of the engine and feeling her body tense

238

she pulled on the lead rope and moved to the edge of the hard shoulder. Soon the lights began to dazzle, and the engine deafened and she could feel a rush of air sweep over her as the lorry stampeded towards them. Her fingers tightened round the lead rope, and she breathed in a deep breath in readiness to shout for Pansy. And then, in a matter of split seconds, she felt engulfed in a blaze of light and deafening blare from the lorry's horn. She felt the lead rope snap tight as she leapt forward as if into an erupting cauldron. She sensed a streak of lightning explode in her face and then there was nothing.

Inside the lorry, the driver wrenched the steering wheel to force a swerve as his foot shot down like a piston on the brake pedal even as the impact of flesh and bone slammed into the front of his cab. He had been given no time, no warning. And as burning rubber scorched off the tarmac, the giant lorry slewed to a halt, and the driver dropped his head into his hands across the steering wheel. Great God in heaven. What had happened?

****

Simon came out of the shower at a quarter to seven and dried himself off. Pauline wouldn't get up until seven so he was able to take his time. He had a busy day ahead of him in court, and he wondered when it would be the best time to take Bobby on one side and deal with that young lady. He had to admit to himself that he was surprised that she had actually found the courage to tell Charlotte what he had been doing. In fact, when Pauline had told him what Charlotte had called to tell her, he could hardly believe it. He had been fairly confident that Bobby wouldn't have dared challenge the hold he had over her and grudgingly conceded that she was more gutsy than he had imagined. Exactly how much she had told Charlotte, he didn't know and Pauline didn't know either because she hadn't given Charlotte the chance to go into detail. That was good in one way because Pauline had dismissed the accusation with contempt. Good old Pauline, she would stand by him to the bitter end. He had taken her in his arms and kissed her and assured her he would never harm her or Bobby, and she had responded with complete faith in him. It was a clever move too, to say he quite understood that Bobby missed her father and that she shouldn't be blamed. Pauline had been quite overwhelmed by his patience and understanding. But whatever Bobby had said to Charlotte, it must have been convincing enough for her to believe it and feel that Pauline should be told. Would Charlotte take it any further, he wondered? Probably not. She had no evidence except the fantasy story of a young child who was not even believed by her own mother.

It was a pity that Pauline and Charlotte had fallen out though. That may have been a bit hasty. He would have to try and persuade Pauline to make up with Charlotte again, and he would think of the best line to take when he himself bumped into Charlotte. If he could win Charlotte's confidence again, it would make his position more secure than if there was animosity between the two families. He liked Charlotte, and he felt that she really liked him. He'd pull her around in time and make her see she had misjudged him. There was only one other source that might strengthen Bobby's story and that would depend on how much she had confided in Suzie. If she had told Suzie everything and Suzie had believed her, there was just the remote possibility that Suzie might start blabbing it around to the other children at the school who might, in turn, go home and start gossiping to their parents. That scenario would probably die a death as soon as it took life. And in any case, if Bobby had told Suzie everything, she would have told her in confidence, and Suzie would just as likely have respected that.

He stared into the mirror and frowned. He would have to make sure he had not overlooked any loopholes. It would be best if he just made light of Bobby's accusations. If he acted outraged or angry (which he was), it might look as if he were acting too defensively and by implication appear guilty. Bobby would be a different matter. He felt certain she wouldn't risk trying to tell anyone again, having been totally disbelieved already. She would be frightened that people would look at her as a liar and a bad girl, and she would hate that. He would reinforce that thought in her mind so that she gave up the idea of ever trying to tell anyone again. He would show her that he was angry and disappointed in her, especially disappointed, and would expect her to be friendlier to him in the future. If people could see her smiling and joking with him, there would be no possibility of them having any suspicions that anything was amiss. On further reflection, he thought he might refrain from touching her for a little while. He would have to restrain himself sometimes, fight the temptation, but in the long run it would probably prove to be the wisest plan. If Bobby thought that he was going to leave her alone, that what had been going on between them was a thing of the past, she would relax and feel more at ease with him and genuinely want to get closer to him. When he considered the time was right, they could pick up where they had left off. The more he thought about it, the more it felt right. It was clever thinking and he felt good.

He collected his things and went back to the bedroom where Pauline was already in the other en-suite

241

shower. He called out that he was going down stairs and left the bedroom. He walked along the landing, and as he got to Bobby's bedroom, he banged on the door and shouted that it was time for her to wake up and get ready for school. He went on downstairs and into the kitchen where he filled the kettle and switched it on, and then put a saucepan of water on the cooker for his boiled eggs. He hummed quietly to himself as he laid the table and then turned on the radio. He listened for a few moments to the interview between John Humphrys and the Chief Secretary to the Treasury, and then as the saucepan of water came to the boil, Pauline came into the kitchen.

'Did you call Bobby, darling?' she said and took a loaf from the bread bin and cut two slices to toast.

'I banged on her door and called out. I'm sure she'll be down shortly,' Simon replied.

'Can you drop her off at school this morning or are you too busy?' she asked.

'No, that'll be fine. I'll have a chat with her on the way about you know what,' he said, smiling at her. But underneath he was wondering what the little brat had said. Thank Christ, at least Pauline had obviously disbelieved her.

'I'm so sorry you've had to deal with all this. She's becoming really difficult.'

'Nonsense. Storm in a teacup. I'll sort it out with her, and we'll get along fine,' he assured her.

'Thank you, darling. I'd better shake her up, otherwise it'll be a mad panic to get ready for school.' She went to the open kitchen door and called out,

'Bobby! Hurry up, your breakfast will be ready.' She waited for a reply, which didn't come and then came back into the kitchen with a frown. 'Likes her bed too much.'

'There's still plenty of time,' said Simon, as he popped two eggs into the saucepan of boiling water. 'I was thinking it might be a good idea if you were to call Charlotte today and try to patch up things. What do you think?'

'Oh dear, are you sure? I was very angry with her yesterday,' said Pauline hesitantly.

'Of course you were, and that's only natural, but she was only doing what she thought was for the best. It was an instinctive response. She doesn't know Bobby as we do and how much she misses Roger,' said Simon.

'You're right, of course. You're so good, Simon. I'll call her later and apologise,' said Pauline and took out the toast from the toaster.

For a few minutes, they were distracted by the interview on the radio, but then Pauline looked at the clock on the wall. 'It's getting late. I'm going up to rouse madam out of bed,' she said and went out of the kitchen and made her way upstairs.

When she opened Bobby's bedroom door, she was immediately surprised to see that she was not in bed, neither was she in the room. A frown creased her face as she looked from left to right, as if she would suddenly see her appear, and then went back along to the landing to look in the bathroom. Still no sign. With a touch of frustration, she returned downstairs to the kitchen.

'She's not up there, Simon.'

'What do you mean?'

'She's not in her bedroom or the bathroom. I didn't hear her get up earlier, did you?'

'No,' said Simon bunching up his mouth in thought. 'She's probably gone down to Pansy. She's done that before,' he continued.

'Well, she's a naughty girl to do that. Playing about down there when she should be having her breakfast and getting ready for school,' said Pauline, feeling peeved.

'Not to worry,' said Simon, and he put the last piece of toast in his mouth and washed it down with the remains of his tea. 'I'll go down and fetch her.'

'Are you sure? Thank you,' said Pauline, and sat down feeling relieved.

Simon slipped on his jacket and went out. He walked down the garden, made his way to the paddock, and scanned the field to see if he could see Pansy. As there was no sign of Pansy or Bobby, he walked over to the tack room and looked inside. Still no sign of Bobby.

At first, he wasn't quite sure why he felt a sense of alarm. There had to be a perfectly reasonable explanation, but he was nagged by doubt. An unease at the back of his mind began to unsettle him as he made his way back to the house.

'What was she doing?' asked Pauline as he came back into the kitchen.

'She's not down there,' he said with a mystified expression on his face, which immediately alarmed Pauline.

'Well, she has to be. Where else could she be?' she said, expecting Simon to know, of course, where that would be.

'I don't know. I couldn't find Pansy either.'

'Pansy? She's not in the paddock? She couldn't have got out, could she? And Bobby gone to look for her?' said Pauline unconvincingly.

'I couldn't see any broken fence,' said Simon, his thoughts beginning to quicken.

'Simon, I'm worried,' said Pauline with real concern in her voice.

'Let's keep calm, Pauline. I'm sure there's a perfectly reasonable explanation,' replied Simon, trying to conceal his own growing anxiety. Something was going wrong. He could sense it. Something deep down was worrying him and whatever it was, it was not going to be good for him.

'We've got to find her, darling. We can't just sit here. Should we call the police?' suggested Pauline, and her heart was beginning to race.

'I think that's a bit premature,' said Simon. 'I'll take a drive around the local roads to see if I can find her. She may well have decided to take Pansy for a walk,' he went on, knowing that such an idea was so unlikely.

'Surely, she would never do that. I'll come with you.'

'No. You wait here. She might turn up suddenly. I don't know: she could have gone around to the neighbours or something,' he said and gave her a reassuring kiss as he grabbed his car keys and went out.

As soon as he got into the car, he pulled away and drove down the road and around the corner where he pulled into the kerb and turned off the engine. His thoughts were racing. He told himself there was no reason for that, but he couldn't help it. He didn't, for a moment, kid himself that she hadn't gone off somewhere, but he couldn't yet work out the full implication. Coming so soon after Charlotte's visit, Pauline's disbelief in what she had to say could easily have unhinged Bobby so that she felt she must run away. If that were the case, what explanation would she give when they caught up with her? She surely wouldn't start making the same accusations about him again. She knew that would make bigger trouble for her. There was no way they could keep the fact of her running away – if that's what she had done – a secret. It would spread like wildfire around the school, and people would ask questions. Could the finger be pointed at him? Damn it, he'd always felt so confident. He would have to keep his wits about him. The one plausible ace he kept in his hand was the suggestion that she desperately missed her father. Everyone knew that and felt enormous sympathy for her. He would play on that to divert any other theory. Where the hell was she? That was the more pressing issue.

As he pulled out, he wracked his brains to guess which way she might have gone. And then he remembered Pansy. He'd forgotten all about her. She obviously hadn't gone for a ride because she wasn't that confident. She had only ever sat on her going around the paddock. That really bugged him. Had she taken her with her? Whatever for? Having Pansy with her would make getting away without being discovered much harder for her. He pulled out into the A46 and drove up to the roundabout that provided the slip road down to the 417. He decided that she wouldn't have gone down there; far too exposed. He moved along the A46 turning off at every turning before doubling back and driving on.

In spite of himself, he was beginning to get anxious in a way that was out of character for him. Where was she? He had assumed he would have found her quite quickly, but now he was beginning to accept that he was not going to find her. Pauline would be going mental with worry. She would be imagining that Bobby had been abducted and hidden away somewhere. He knew that was out of the question. No one could have broken in during the night and grabbed her, and she wouldn't be a valuable target anyway. Shit! Where had the stupid girl gone? He thumped his hand down on to the steering wheel in both frustration and a gnawing anxiety that was growing deep inside him. He looked at the clock on the dashboard and realised he had been out now for over an hour and had better get back. Perhaps she had turned up and given a perfectly innocent explanation.

As he pulled into the drive, Pauline ran from the house looking frantic. 'Have you found her?' she cried and on the verge of hysteria.

'I'm sorry, darling. I've been everywhere. No sign anywhere,' he replied as he got out of the car and held her in his arms. 'But we mustn't panic. She's a sensible girl. I'm sure she'll turn up,' he offered, but he knew it had a hollow ring.

'I've rung the police and given them details. They're going to send somebody around to get some more. They tried to fob me off by saying that we hadn't missed her for very long.'

'They get a lot of calls reporting missing children, but they reckon there isn't usually a reason for concern for 24 hours. Most of them turn up.'

'I don't care about other cases. Bobby's gone off in the middle of the night. I can't see her ever doing anything like that. Don't tell me she's running away.'

'Of course she's not, darling. But children behave in extraordinary ways sometimes. Even Bobby: I think perhaps I'm to blame,' said Simon shaking his head.

'No, Simon. How could it possibly be your fault?' Pauline protested.

'We both know she misses her father. We've been over this before. He's gone, and I've come along. It might be terrible for her in a way we can't fully understand,' he suggested, showing concern.

'But you've been so kind to her; and patient. What more could you have done?'

'I'm not her Daddy though, am I? We have to realise it's going to take a long time,' he said and held her closely to him.

'I would die if anything happened to her, Simon,' she said, fighting back tears.

'Nothing's happened. Come on. We must be patient, and let the police do their work,' he said and eased her into a chair. 'I'll get you a cup of tea.'

Chapter Sixteen

Nick Jarvis sat on the hospital bed and held his head in his hands. He was feeling like he'd never felt before. His breathing was heavy, and he kept slowly shaking his head in despair. Next to him stood PC Bates and PC Hall from traffic. They were patient and prepared to wait. Nick looked up, 'I've got to get my lorry,' he said wearily.

'It's quite safe, Nick,' said PC Bates. 'It's parked up and there's an officer on guard.'

'But my delivery. The drop will be waiting and my job will be on the line.'

'We've been in touch. You're not to worry. You're still in shock and not fit to drive,' said PC Bates.

'Jesus, that poor kid,' said Nick, and there were tears in his eyes.

PC Bates and PC Hall looked at each other and silently nodded in agreement to proceed slowly. 'Take it easy, Nick. Do you feel okay to answer some questions?' said PC Hall.

'I'll tell you what I can. I'm not sure about anything,' said Nick with a bewildered shake of his head.

'Just tell us as much as you can remember,' said PC Bates.

'My drop is in Bristol. I've done this trip hundreds of times. I was in good time. Visibility was okay and as usual at this time of night, there wasn't much traffic,' he said, still shaking his head. 'Jesus, I still can't believe it,' he broke off and was buried in his thoughts.

PC Bates waited a little while and then said, 'Go on, Nick. What happened?'

'I was doing just under 60 on the inside lane. She's comfortable at that speed. I suddenly caught sight of, well I didn't know what it was at first, a strange sort of shape on the hard shoulder. Actually it's not a real hard shoulder on that stretch of road.'

'How close were you when you first saw this whatever?' asked PC Bates.

'I dunno. About 100 metres. As it wasn't on the highway so I wasn't bothered. As I drew near though, I was sort of struggling to see what it was. I could see what looked like a child with an animal. But I couldn't make out what it was. It was too big for a dog and too small for a cow. I mean, for Chrissake, you don't expect to see a kid with an animal twice her size walking along that stretch of road in the middle of the night.'

'It's okay Nick; take it easy,' said PC Hall.

'Christ. What the hell was she doing there anyway? Anyway, I got to within about 20 metres, and I blew the horn. I don't know why. I just had a sort of gut feeling to blast my horn. Christ, I saw this animal jump 20 feet in the air, and the kid leapt out into the road straight in front of me. I mean I was on her. I couldn't do anything,' said Nick, and again he dropped his head in his hands.

'Are you sure the pony, we know now it was a pony, didn't knock her into the road or something like that?' asked PC Bates.

'Well, I dunno. It all happened so quickly. That could easily have happened. My first reaction was that she had jumped. Well it looked that way. I could be wrong. When I blasted the horn, the pony made a violent move. I mean I saw everything okay, but at the same time it was a bit of a blur, I s'pose. I think the pony sort of jumped or shied away from the road. Bloody good job, otherwise I'd have had her as well.'

'Could you be more specific about whether you think she jumped or not?' persisted PC Bates.

'It seemed like it at the time, but I couldn't swear to it. The more I think about it, the more I think she was knocked into the road as it happened at the same time as the pony spooked. And that was because I blew the horn. It's pretty loud and would have scared her. It all happened so fast. On my mother's life, I couldn't do anything about it. Mind you, travelling at 60 in the dark and coming across something completely unexpected like this, your eyes can play you tricks. Poor little sod,' said Nick, and his face creased in genuine anguish. 'I think she jumped...but then again... Oh, I dunno. I think maybe it was the pony that completely knocked her into the road. It seems more likely.'

'It's okay, Nick. You've told us a lot.'

'You know what was worse was that I hit her so hard, I knocked her clean into the airway in front of me and before I could stop I actually drove over her. I mean, it was terrible. I couldn't do anything about it.'

'We're not here to blame you, Nick. We're just trying to find out what happened.'

'What about the poor parents? They'll go crazy. I couldn't help it. I swear it wasn't my fault.'

'Nobody is saying that, Nick. We have to ask all these questions, you know that,' said PC Bates, and then she stared at Nick for a few moments. 'This is very important, Nick. I believe what you're saying, but as you say, you were travelling quite fast, and whatever it was you thought you were looking at there would have been shadows in your headlights. Is it possible that the girl could have tripped or be pushed by the pony if it was startled by your horn?'

'I've already said. Oh, I dunno. Could be, I s'pose. I don't know what to think now.' He looked down wearily, rubbing his face. 'All I know is I shall never forget it. I've been driving these lorries for over 25 years and nothing like this has ever happened to me before.'

'Okay, Nick. That'll do for now. You need to get some rest,' said PC Hall.

'How long are they going to keep me here?' asked Nick anxiously.

'You'll have to ask the doctor. You're still in shock. If you get some sleep, you should be able to drive soon,' said PC Hall, and he and PC Bates left.

Nick laid back on the bed and tried to get to sleep.

****

It was shortly after ten-thirty when a police car pulled up outside Simon and Pauline's house. Pauline saw them through the front window and rushed round to the front door. She opened it before they had a chance to push the bell. She saw they were both uniformed, and she noticed one was a sergeant. 'Have you got any news?' Pauline immediately blurted out.

'Good morning, madam. May we come in?' said DS Phillips.

'Yes, of course,' said Pauline, and led them through to the living room where Simon was waiting. 'This is my husband.' She indicated Simon with her hand.

'Good morning, sir. We have met before,' said DS Phillips.

'Indeed we have, Sergeant,' said Simon.

'This is my colleague DC Hughes,' said DS Phillips indicating the constable with him.

'Please, have you any news?' asked Pauline impatiently.

DS Phillips cleared his throat nervously, 'We think your daughter may have been in an accident,' he said.

'An accident! What do you mean? What kind of an accident? Is she all right? Where is she?' Pauline poured out the questions as the blood began to rush through her veins.

'Does she... do you own a Shetland pony?'

'Yes. Pansy,' said Simon. 'She's also gone missing. Have you found her?'

'Yes, sir. She was picked up grazing on the embankment on the 417, just down the road from here.'

'My God. On the 417,' said Simon, suddenly off balance.

'She's quite safe, sir. She's presently being kept in a nearby field by a farmer.'

'What about Bobby? Is my daughter all right?' said Pauline frantically.

'There was an accident last night on the 417 a couple of 100 metres before the slip road up to the M5 to Bristol. It involved a lorry and a pedestrian. It was a child, I'm afraid,' said DS Phillips, thinking how much he hated this part of his job.

'Oh my God, no,' said Pauline, and she began to crumble.

DS Phillips took a small photograph out of his pocket and handed it to Pauline. 'Do you recognise this photo, madam?' he asked quietly and handed the photo to Pauline.

It only took Pauline a moment to register. 'It's Roger. Bobby always carried it,' she said and her whole body began to tremble.

'Roger?' enquired DS Phillips.

'It's my wife's first husband. Bobby's father. He was killed in a motor accident,' said Simon.

'How did you get this?' asked Pauline.

'We found this photo in the pocket of the child who was involved in the accident, I'm afraid.'

'Is she all right? Is she in hospital? Where is she?' Pauline was becoming hysterical.

DS Phillips paused for a moment and then glanced at his colleague and then at Simon who understood and reached across to Pauline and put his arm around her to support her.

'I'm sorry,' said DS Phillips, but his voice was barely audible.

Pauline wanted to scream but her throat was so constricted that she couldn't make a sound. She began to sway and sink to her knees so that Simon had to take her full weight. Keeping a firm hold, he lowered her to the sofa.

'I can only say that death would have been instantaneous,' said DS Phillips and then remained silent.

Pauline haltingly found her voice, 'How? Why was she there? What was she doing, Simon?' she sobbed in total bewilderment.

'I don't know, my darling. We may never know,' comforted Simon.

'I'm sorry to be the bearer of such tragic news, madam,' said DS Phillips.

'The driver. Was he speeding? Was he drunk? Did he lose control? How could this have happened?' Pauline was almost screaming in utter disbelief and confusion.

'The driver is presently in shock. His breath test proved negative, and from his account he had no chance to avoid the accident,' said DS Phillips. 'There will be a more detailed investigation as to what happened.'

'I want to know everything,' said Pauline, choking on her words and knowing full well that it wouldn't change anything. Her lovely, dear Bobby was dead. And having faced it before, she knew what agony she would have to struggle with again.

'We'll leave now, if that's all right, sir,' said DS Phillips.

'Of course; I'll see you out,' said Simon, as he gently released Pauline.

'Madam,' DS Phillips nodded his goodbye.

'Thank you, Sergeant,' Pauline whispered and struggled without success to form a smile.

'I won't be a moment,' said Simon, as he led the two policemen out to the front door and then outside.

'A terrible shock, sir. I'm so sorry for you and your wife,' said DS Phillips.

'Thank you, Sergeant. It'll be especially hard for my wife, having lost her first husband in a motor accident.'

'Of course. I understand. One of you will be required to make a formal identification, and I should warn you, there will be an inquest.'

'An inquest? Yes, of course. I understand that,' said Simon with a touch of anxiety.

'There's a suggestion that the child deliberately jumped in front of the vehicle. If that were true, her death would be due to suicide. I thought it insensitive to mention this to your wife. I shouldn't have mentioned it to you sir but…'

'My God, yes of course. Thank you. But surely that can't be so. Where has such a suggestion come from?' said Simon in sudden shock.

'I can't say anything more at the moment sir, as I'm sure you understand. We'll be in touch,' said DS Phillips and quickly turned away to go and cut off the possibility of any further questions.

'Yes, yes, I see. Thank you,' replied Simon rather limply and then watched them get into their car and drive off. Already the thoughts in his mind were beginning to stampede. Inquest? Shit! Suicide? Shit! That's the last thing he wanted. An inquest would ask all sorts of questions. Damn it, that was the purpose of them: to ask questions. Had she committed suicide? Surely the stupid girl wouldn't have done that? Thank Christ DS Phillips had told him about that possibility on the quiet.

Running away was bad enough, but the thought of suicide would destroy Pauline completely. And yes, people would gossip about Bobby's death when they heard about it. Most of them would think she was running away. What else could they think: middle of the night; wandering down the 417 with Pansy? Jesus, she would hardly have been going on a picnic. People would look at him and Pauline and wonder why two and two were making five, but they would be crest-fallen and most of them would be sympathetic. Everyone they knew regarded them as model parents so they'd pull through in the end without people thinking they were guilty or responsible of anything bad. But suicide: that was a different kettle of fish altogether. That idea had to be squashed from day one. If someone was going to kill themselves, it would be assumed it was because of something really serious.

The bloody inquest would want to know everything. He would have to immediately cut off any wild suggestion of abuse – which he had to believe was the last possibility that people would even consider – by distracting them to another reason for Bobby's misery. The death of her father was still the ace in his pack.

Everyone knew about that and would quickly nod their heads in understanding. He might even suggest, just as a second back up reason, that Bobby had recently mentioned in confidence to him that she was being bullied at school. He could be vague about any details and let that thought grow in other people's minds. He'd hold back on that idea in reserve until he could see which way the ball was going to bounce. But an inquest, in itself, was making him jumpy. An inquest could open a can of worms and when the deceased was a child, people's imagination usually went into overdrive.

The fact that an inquest was normal with road fatalities shouldn't be a problem. But supposing some bright spark thought there should be a post-mortem. Oh God, no, please not that. That wasn't necessary. For what possible reason would they want that. No, his imagination was beginning to get the better of him now. He had to stay calm and think rationally. Just suppose there was a call for a post-mortem. Okay; what would that show. Nothing. There would be no incentive for them to look at her genitalia. He couldn't change the fact that he had had full sex with her. It was the first time, yes, and he knew he'd hurt her, but would any damage in that area raise suspicions or prove anything – assuming of course, that they examined that area? After all, she had been in a terrible collision with a lorry. All sorts of terrible injuries would have been inflicted on her body so any damage down below could be a result of that.

Anyway, the idea of a detailed post-mortem was ridiculous. He was just getting into a silly panic. What he needed to do was go back into the house and comfort Pauline and prove to the world that they were two devoted and broken-hearted parents. He turned and went back into the house.

As the two policemen drove back to the station, DC Hughes said, 'Terrible thing that, Sarge. Poor kid.'

'Yeah. Double whammy for the mother. Doesn't seem right,' replied DS Phillips.

'You didn't ask 'em if they could think of any reason why the kid would go off like that in the middle of the night,' said DC Hughes.

'Not a good time. They're in shock.'

'There's got to be something wrong there somewhere, though,' pondered DC Hughes.

'What are you saying?'

'Well, bit odd, isn't it for a child to be out like that with a pony in the middle of the night? Why would she do that?'

'Kids. Could be any number of reasons.'

'Not good ones.'

'Doesn't have to be anything suspicious.'

'Maybe not. Just a feeling, that's all.'

'Proper little detective, are we?' said DS Phillips with a smile.

'Maybe Sarge, but there's no smoke without fire.'

'You're right, but the parents are pretty solid on all accounts. I've partly known Hargreaves since he's been on the bench. Likeable guy if you ask me, and she's obviously a devoted mum.'

'If she was running away or even killing herself, either way she must have been a pretty miserable kid,' persisted DC Hughes.

'Lost her own dad, didn't she? How bad can that be for a kid of her age?' offered DS Phillips.

'I guess you're right,' conceded DC Hughes.

'Still, there may be other things. Bullying is a favourite. Have a sniff around at school. You may dig up something smelly.'

'Will do,' said DC Hughes and sat back with a smile.

****

John was stuck in traffic. It always seemed to happen when he was in a hurry. And he was in a hurry now because Charlie had been trying to get hold of him for the last two or three hours. His mobile phone was flat, and he'd been away with a customer all morning. When he got back to the office, he had picked up her message that he must contact her or get home as soon as possible. What on earth could be so urgent he had no idea, but in any case, he had a bad feeling. As soon as he was out of town, he made good progress and, at last, he pulled into his drive. He was somewhat alarmed to see Charlie already at the open front door waiting for him. She must have been looking out for him, he thought, and realised that whatever it was she wanted to tell him it must be serious. He got out of the car and walked up the garden path to her. 'What's happened?' he asked with a serious look on his face.

'I've been trying to get you all afternoon. Where have you been?' said Charlie impatiently.

'Sorry. I've been tied up away from the office, and my mobile battery was down. What's going on?'

Charlie furtively looked up and down the street as if they were being watched, and then tugged John by the arm and pulled him in the house and shut the door.

'For goodness sake, Charlie, what is it?' said John.

'There's been a terrible accident,' she said urgently.

'Oh no! Not Suzie, please,' said John spitting out the words.

'No, not Suzie, she's upstairs. She's been crying.'

'For God's sake, what's happened?'

'It's Bobby. She's dead,' said Charlie, and her voice was shaking.

'Dead?' said John, and then stared at her in stunned silence.

'Yes dead. Do you think I'd make up something like that?' Charlie replied irritably.

'But how? I mean how do you know? How can she be dead?'

'Suzie came home with the news from school. She's in a dreadful state. It was announced. She was killed on the road. Knocked down by a lorry, I think. We haven't got all the details.'

'My God. Not poor Bobby. When did this happen? Did they say?' said John holding up his arms in complete bewilderment.

'I've only got what Suzie has told me. She says it was in the middle of the night. She was on the 417 just down the road from here and something about Pansy, her pony, was with her,' said Charlie, herself looking confused.

'This is crazy, Charlie. Are you sure it's true?'

'Of course it's true. I've already rung around one or two other parents and they've got the same information as us.'

'How can this be? Middle of the night? With Pansy? This can't be true.'

'Of course it's true. Nobody would make up a story like that.'

'But what was she doing there?'

'I don't know. Nobody knows. We've just got to wait for more information. There's also a rumour about her having jumped in front of the lorry.'

'Jumped? What do you mean: she deliberately tried to kill herself?' he said and felt the mystery was getting more confusing.

'How do I know, John? I don't believe it. It's all so crazy. What was she doing on the 417 with Pansy in the middle of the night?'

John's mind began to race. Something was going on here. It was staring him in the face, but the news was such a shock that it wasn't immediately registering. Bobby was dead; she'd been killed on the 417 in the middle of the night while taking Pansy with her. What was she thinking? Running away? Not likely if she'd got Pansy with her. And the rumour about suicide; surely that was some wild, irresponsible gossip. Surely, she hadn't really jumped. Could she have really done that? She had always given him the impression that she would only do that if someone found out what was happening to her. He didn't doubt that was a possibility if her secret was out but nobody knew. So he didn't believe she would have done it.

'I only spoke to her the night before. I don't know what she was doing, but I can't believe she deliberately took her own life. She said she'd only try that if anyone found out about her. It was the one thing she dreaded; even more than what she was suffering with her step-father and there was no way anyone else knew what was going on,' said John feeling despair engulf him.

Charlie didn't say anything but began to fidget nervously.

'Maybe you should ring Pauline and ask if we can do anything to help her. She must be in terrible shock,' suggested John.

For a little while, Charlie continued to say nothing, and John stared at her wondering if she had heard what he said, 'Charlie, do you think you should ring Pauline? It's a gesture,' he repeated.

Charlie began wringing her hands, 'John, I'm frightened. I think I may have done something I shouldn't have done,' she stammered.

'What do you mean?'

'I went to see Pauline yesterday. I was going to tell you, but you were out until late, and you went off so early this morning,' went on Charlie, determined to get it off her chest.

'What's this all about, Charlie?' said John.

'I told Pauline everything.'

'Everything? What are you talking about?' said John with a frown.

'I told her that Simon was abusing Bobby. I simply thought she had to know,' went on Charlie, and there was now pleading in her voice.

'You did what?' exploded John.

'I'm sorry. I thought I was acting for the best.'

'For Christ's sake, do you know what you've done?'

'I couldn't just stand by, John. That poor child…' said Charlie who was now getting upset.

'And now she's dead. Does that make you feel any better?' snapped John with venom.

'Pauline didn't believe me. She hit the roof and said that Bobby was making it all up. She more or less threw me out and ended our friendship.'

'You had no right to tell her. You promised me. It was the one thing Bobby dreaded. I told you that. She trusted us, and she's been betrayed.'

'Pauline thinks that Bobby told us, and I got the impression she was going to be punished for it,' went on Charlie in misery.

'Oh Christ,' said John, and hung his head in his hands.

For a few moments, there was total silence between them, each trying to deal with an onslaught of mixed emotions. A terrible thing had happened, had been happening, and the outcome was unbearable. Feelings of guilt, stupidity, uselessness, confusion; they all swirled round in their heads.

'What was happening to her was so wrong, John,' Charlie pleaded again.

'Of course it was bloody wrong. It's always wrong when people call us; that's why they call us,' he snapped, not hiding his anger, but he knew it was as much anger at himself as for her.

'Not that it will do poor Bobby any good, but I shall have to resign the Sams. Shit!' he choked out the words.

'Oh no. Surely not, John,' said Charlie in shock.

'Of course I will. I broke the rule. It's the rock on which the Samaritans is built,' he said despairingly.

'But nobody else will know.'

'*I* will know!' he snapped, glaring at her. 'Don't you understand? I could never again say to a caller what they tell me is confidential. It would be false. I've put a stain on the organisation, and the only way to remove that stain and restore its integrity is to resign.'

'But it's such a big part of your life. To resign will be devastating for you.'

'No more than I deserve. It's not about me. I don't matter. What matters is what's happened to poor Bobby. It doesn't matter a damn about me. Who the fuck cares? It's poor Bobby that matters and now her mother,' said John with a deprecating snarl.

'It's all my fault,' said Charlie, feeling sick with guilt. John hung his head but didn't reply. 'Is that what you think? Is it my fault?'

'I don't know whose fault it is. My God, how she must have suffered. She must have somehow believed that we had told Pauline what she had been telling us. She must have thought – God knows how – that we had turned against her, and she would have felt absolutely desperate.' He put his hands up to his face in agonising guilt.

'It might have been an accident. Could it have been that, John?'

'I s'pose. I don't know. I can't get my head around her being out in the middle of the night on the 417 with Pansy. What on earth was she thinking of?'

'I've got to ask you, John. Do you think she really might have killed herself because of what I did?'

'I don't know. She'd said all along that she would kill herself if it got out.'

'But why? She was a victim. She had done nothing wrong.'

'We know that, but she didn't see it that way. She was terrified that nobody would believe her; that her mother wouldn't believe her because she's so besotted with Simon. She was terrified she'd lose all her friends, and then she'd have to face Simon again and wonder what he would do. She was completely alone. We were the only crumb of comfort she had. She trusted us, and I blew it by telling you.'

'Maybe it wasn't that. You said she grieved so much for her father. Perhaps it was because of that.'

'Maybe. I don't suppose we'll ever know. We don't even know if it might have been an accident. I hope to God that will be the accepted verdict.'

'I'm so sorry, John. I've let you down.'

'Never mind that. It's poor Bobby and Pauline we should be thinking about,' said John.

'Of course, John. Will there have to be an inquest?' asked Charlie, not knowing why she asked the question.

'Of course there will. Fat lot of good that will achieve. Confirm how she died, but they'll never know why.'

'You could tell them,' said Charlie with a touch of urgency.

'For God's sake, Charlie, when will you understand? I can't say anything. I've already done it once and betrayed her; and you have too!' shouted John.

'But if you say nothing, Simon will get away with it, and he's free out there to maybe abuse another child.'

'I've already told you. It's not just because of the rule of confidentiality – even after death. I've got no evidence. To simply say the child was telling us she was being abused is not evidence. Pauline will say she makes up these stories because she misses her father so much. It's logical, isn't it? A lot of what our callers say is sometimes fantasy. We have no evidence, and you can bet that Simon – snake in the grass that he is – would be putting his two penn'orth in. We've no chance. He's done what he's done, and he'll get away with it.'

'And in the end, she's died because it's my fault. I should have said nothing,' said Charlotte. 'At least, it was probably my fault if it wasn't an accident.'

'You shouldn't have said anything, no. And I shouldn't have told you. But,' he paused before going on, 'I don't know the answer. It's all our faults, Charlie. Mine for betraying her trust and telling you. Yours for telling Pauline; Pauline's for not believing Bobby but most of all, of course, the biggest villain is that monster Simon. And he's going to get away with it,' said John with a tone of finality and sank down on to the sofa overcome with utter despair and guilt.

****

In spite of the fact that Pauline went to bed that night having taken a powerful sedative prescribed by her doctor she hardly slept. Every muscle in her body ached

265

and her emotions were on the rack. Her thoughts swung from not being able to fully grasp or believe that Bobby was actually dead to the horror of visualising the dreadful manner of how it happened. The inescapable fact that Bobby must have been so unhappy and that she was either too busy or insensitive to realise this was filling her with guilt.

When Roger had died, she and Bobby had tightly bound themselves together to bear their grief. But it had been only just over a year before Simon had come into their lives. She had fallen madly in love with this wonderful man who opened a brand new world of safety and happiness that should have been for both of them, but Bobby had found herself alone. A year was not long enough to grieve and Pauline now felt an added torture herself for not keeping her daughter close when that closeness was needed most.

As the night hours bore on, she slipped into bouts of shallow sleep, waking only to gently weep before drifting back again. In her waking moments, she pulled closely into Simon who, she knew, was doing his best to help her with her anguish as well as coping with his own feelings of loss for the child he had come to love and think of as his own daughter. She could not have known that his restless tosses and turns were prompted by emotions and fears that were different to her own. She could not know that his feelings of guilt were utterly justified for reasons opposite to her own. She could not have known that he was dealing with feelings of panic at what he had done to Bobby and which might be exposed. She could not have known that his mind was in turmoil for fear of what might come out at an inquest, and if that were to happen, a dreadful future awaited him.

When morning finally came, she groped her way out of bed and shuffled into the shower with a vain hope that the warm water washing over her would, in some mysterious way, diminish the harshness in her suffering. At breakfast neither she nor Simon could find words enough to express their feelings. Grunts and stares and tears went back and forth across the table, and in that primitive communication, they found enough understanding. They both knew that arrangements had been made for them to visit the hospital where Bobby was presently rested so that a formal identification could be made. Such an undertaking was a task from which Simon dearly wanted to be excused, but Pauline had insisted the need for her to see her daughter for the last time, and his rightful place would therefore be at her side.

'Are you sure that seeing Bobby will not be too distressing for you, my dear?' said Simon.

'I have to see her, Simon. It will help me feel close to her,' Pauline replied.

'She was hit by a lorry, darling. She may be...' he paused before going on. 'She may be disfigured. You will want to remember her as the lovely child that she was.'

'No. I want to kiss her goodbye. And I want her to know that I am close,' said Pauline and looked into Simon's eyes as if to say she was sure he would understand. He nodded in return and reached across the table and held her hand.

'Then we will say goodbye together,' he said and looked at his watch. 'I'll clear this up, and when you're ready, we'll go,' he continued and then began to clear the table. She nodded with a smile and went upstairs to get ready.

For several minutes, she sat at her dressing table and stared at herself in the mirror. She looked at her face and thought she had aged 20 years in a single night but was past caring. She combed her hair and barely touched her lips with pink lipstick and then went downstairs where Simon was already waiting. He took her in his arms and held her close to give her strength, but the gesture, as with all his other gestures of support and loving care, ripped a hole in his soul for he knew that it was he who was responsible for Bobby's death and Pauline's misery. For a moment, a thought pierced his mind, a stabbing thought; a thought he had never experienced before; a thought that made him feel he'd been cursed because of his overwhelming lust for children. He'd not chosen to be this way. The devil had planted it there while he was still in his mother's womb. He was helpless to fight it, and such was the lot of his life. It was wrong. It was wicked, and he couldn't pretend to think otherwise even though he had so often convinced himself that children were willing to participate. That was false, twisted thinking, and he was guilty of a dreadful crime against an innocent child.

He held Pauline for a few moments and then he led her out to the car. They drove slowly but their journey to the hospital still only took 20 minutes. When they arrived, for a little while they sat in the car holding hands, each in their respective ways to gather strength.

'I'm ready,' said Pauline suddenly and turned to smile at him. He nodded in response and helped her out of the car and, taking her arm, led her to the reception where they were met by DS Phillips. They explained their visit, and then the receptionist spoke quietly and briefly into the phone and a few moments later, they were approached by a doctor who introduced himself and asked them to follow him to the private room where Bobby had been prepared and presently rested. As they stood outside the door, the doctor gently told them that they could take as long as they liked and then excused himself.

'Whenever you're ready. Just take your time,' said DS Phillips.

Pauline breathed in deeply, and then Simon held her arm as they both moved towards the door. Pauline hesitated as she suddenly and acutely sensed that behind her back in the rest of the building, people were scurrying about to and fro, going about their business in the land of living, speaking into telephones, doing jobs of work, discussing TV programmes they had watched the night before, gossiping about children and schools, despairing at the weather or bewailing the government for the state of the country. In front of her, on the other side of the door, lay the body of her dead child. For Pauline, the contrast could not have been more extreme nor the separation so profound, yet in a strange way that she couldn't understand, she experienced a calm recognition that this was the way of life. Her young and lovely daughter had been the greatest joy in her life. All she could do now was kiss her goodbye forever and then, holding them close to her heart, return with nothing more than sweet and happy memories.

She nodded she was ready, and then holding on to Simon, they entered the room.

****

DC Hughes sat alone in an empty classroom at St Catherine's Primary school. She had been at the school most of the morning mingling with and talking to the pupils during their breaks. The headmistress had introduced DC Hughes at assembly, explaining that she was there to try and find out if any child knew of any reason why Bobby might have been unhappy. She had explained there was nothing to fear from DC Hughes and that the children could speak freely without thinking they might be in trouble. Apart from anything else, DC Hughes considered the exercise in general terms, an opportunity to show the good face of the police and a worthwhile PR job.

Before the assembly had taken place, DC Hughes had managed to have a talk with the headmistress in her office. She had been very open and friendly and had explained that they had never had any incidents of bullying – at least none that had been brought to her attention. She insisted that all the staff were alert to anything like that. Of course, she couldn't know what went on outside the school gates, but as far as she knew all the children were happy. DC Hughes liked her and felt confidence in her and inwardly wished that she herself had had such a happy schooling.

DC Hughes had enjoyed herself with the children. They had all been so different. Some of them on the far side of the playground had pointed in her direction and then giggled. Others had asked a host of questions about what she did and many made cheeky comparisons with TV cops. When she had managed the opportunity to ask her own questions about Bobby, all the children had replied that they knew of no particular reason that would have made her unhappy except that many of them knew that she had lost her father some time ago. It seemed that the school was indeed a happy place, just as the headmistress had claimed.

DC Hughes would be going shortly, unless any particular child turned up to talk to her privately. But apart from that the headmistress had suggested that Suzie Elliot should come and have a chat because she had been, as everyone knew in the school, Bobby's best friend.

When Suzie arrived, DC Hughes chatted about the school and said how much she liked the school to put her at ease, and then told her how sorry she was that Suzie had lost her friend. Suzie responded by saying how sad it made her feel and how much she missed her.

'Everyone says that she was a happy girl with no worries. Did you think the same, Suzie?' asked DC Hughes.

'Yes, she was my best friend. She did cry sometimes, though.'

'Why was that?'

'Because she missed her father. He died in an accident. I don't know when.'

'Did she talk about him then?'

'Not really. But she hated it if I called Simon her father.'

'Didn't she like her step-father?'

'I don't think so. She said he was not the same; not like her own father. I know what she meant.'

'Do you think Simon was unkind to her?' asked DC Hughes.

'Golly, no. I think he's lovely. He was always kind to her and wanted to be friends. I don't know why she disliked him so much although I think it's because she missed her father so much.' said Suzie.

'Was she ever teased by any of the other children?'

'I don't know what you mean.'

'Well, sometimes children can be unkind. Perhaps they might have made a hurtful remark because she had a different father now, to her own.'

'No. I think most of them knew that her own father had been killed in an accident.'

'Okay,' said DC Hughes, thinking that there was not much mileage in continuing questions. There didn't appear to be any obvious reason why Bobby should be unhappy, except that she missed her father, which was pretty natural. She obviously wasn't neglected in any way. She had apparently been popular at school, and her step-father was obviously a caring person who was doing his best. 'Unless you can think of anything else that might have made Bobby unhappy, we'll leave it there and you can go back to class.'

Suzie stood up to go but then she hesitated,

'What is it?' asked DC Hughes. 'Is there something?'

'It's probably nothing.'

'Tell me anyway. You never know.'

'Well. Oh, I don't know. Sometimes, well a couple of times, she asked me some funny questions. Not exactly questions.'

'What sort of questions?'

'It's sort of difficult to say. They were just odd, that's all. She asked me if I would still be her friend if she was bad.'

'Bad?'

'I didn't understand. I mean, she said if she'd done something bad. I didn't know what she meant. Of course, she wasn't bad.'

'And she said nothing more?'

'Not really. There was one thing. She asked me if they put children in prison.'

'That is a strange question. And you have no idea what she meant?'

'Not really. She asked me if I thought they put children in prison for lying.'

'For lying?' For a few moments DC Hughes tried to make sense of what Suzie was telling her. 'And as far as you know had she ever lied?'

'Of course she hadn't. She'd never lie.' Suzie frowned in indignation.

'Sorry. I'm sure you're right. It's just that it was an odd question, that's all. Can you think of anything else?'

'No. Sorry.'

'That's fine. You've been very helpful. You'd better get off back to your class now.'

Suzie said thank you and left leaving DC Hughes thinking that she had not been able to throw any light on to why Bobby would want to kill herself. The likelihood was that she hadn't taken her own life after all. Maybe they'd never know why she went out in the middle of the night with Pansy. It wouldn't be the first time that a child did something completely extraordinary. If she hadn't gone down the slip road on to the highway where the traffic was fast and carried heavy vehicles, the tragedy might never have happened. It was probably a freak accident.

DC Hughes got up and walked back to her car nodding to herself that in detective work, it was never easy.

Chapter Seventeen

Simon drove down the M5 until he came to junction 14 where he pulled off and headed for Thornbury on his way to meet Nick Jarvis. It hadn't been difficult to get his address because such information was not confidential. Nick Jarvis was not going to be charged with any motoring offence, and an insurance claim was not involved. Simon was planning to tell Nick that the purpose of his visit was to express his and Pauline's sorrow for Nick's own distress at having run over their child. They were not attaching any blame to him and did not want him to nurse any sense of guilt. Simon hadn't told anyone of his visit, including Pauline, because, for his own reasons, he wanted to keep it to himself.

The real reason for his visit was to try and ascertain whether or not Bobby had really jumped. Simon felt it would be far better, especially for himself, if it could be shown that Bobby did not take her own life because it suggested she must have been desperate. Then there would be a lot more searching questions. On the other hand, if it seemed most likely that she was simply wandering down the highway with Pansy and had accidentally drifted into the road, the finger-pointing would go away. No one would know what she was doing down there at that time of night, but it wouldn't be impossible to dream up all sorts of reasons. She was, after all, just a child and children did all sorts of strange things from time to time, especially if they had an active imagination.

It wasn't long after he had pulled off the motorway before he reached Thornbury and quickly found Nick's address. The house was a semi in need of a lick of paint, and there was a Vauxhall Astra parked on the road outside. Simon pulled up behind it and, without hesitating, got out of the car, walked up the garden path and rang the bell. He hadn't made an arrangement to call, so he was relieved when he heard that someone was in and was coming to the door. When it opened, he saw a short, slightly overweight woman with poorly dyed blonde hair of about fifty. She stared at him and frowned.

'I'm so sorry to call on you unexpectedly; is it Mrs Jarvis?' said Simon, smiling pleasantly.

'Yes,' said Mrs Jarvis.

'My name is Simon Hargreaves,' began Simon and was then cut short by Nick Jarvis walking up the hall towards them.

'Who is it, Lily?' said Nick and came and stood by his wife.

'Ah Mr Jarvis. It's Simon Hargreaves. I'm sorry to drop in on you out of the blue. I wonder if I could have a word with you?' said Simon.

'What about?' said Nick warily.

'It was my step-daughter that was involved in your…' again Simon was cut short.

'I don't want any trouble,' snapped Nick.

'Oh no, no,' said Simon quickly, with an even broader smile. 'I've just come to say how really sorry my wife and I are about the whole thing and to assure you that we do not hold you to blame. Do you think I could come in? I won't stop,' Simon went on persuasively.

Nick and Lily both stared at each other questioningly. Nick suddenly nodded. 'Come in,' he said and led the way into the kitchen.

'I couldn't do anything. It all happened so quickly. I don't know what she was doing there,' Nick immediately started to unload.

'I quite understand, Nick. May I call you Nick?' said Simon. Nick nodded with a shrug. 'It's been a terrible tragedy for both my wife and me, and I'm sure the whole thing was a terrible experience for you too, and I'm really sorry about that,' Simon continued.

'Would you like a cup of tea?' asked Lily.

'That's very kind of you, Mrs Jarvis, but I won't, thank you. I won't stop long,' replied Simon.

'I'm sorry for your loss. Nick has been very upset by the accident,' said Lily and smiled at her husband.

'Of course. I quite understand. What I wanted to ask you, Nick, if you don't mind, is exactly what happened?'

'I've said it enough times. The road was clear. I saw her on the side of the road, it's not a proper hard shoulder, but she was well to the side. She had this pony, but I couldn't make out what it was at the time. I blew my horn instinctively as a warning, and the animal sort of shied, I suppose, and the next thing I know, I was a few feet from her, and she jumped in front of me. I slammed on the anchors, but I had no chance,' said Nick, in a way that sounded as if he had repeated the story many times before.

'Yes, I realise you had no chance to avoid her, but I was wondering if it was at all possible that she didn't deliberately actually jump but that the pony made her stumble forward or even kind of knocked her off balance, and what appeared to be a jump was, in fact, something entirely different?' said Simon, with a tone of confidence.

Nick suddenly frowned as a sense of doubt entered his mind, 'Well I err... yes, it could have easily been that. I said jumped because it was a sudden movement, but either way I had no chance of avoiding her,' said Nick, with a frown.

'The thing is, Nick, I'm sure you can see that if she jumped, it would be suicide which is a very distressing interpretation for my wife to deal with. On the other hand, if it was an accident – and I assure you I'm not trying to persuade you that it was – but if it was an accident, it would be such a comfort for my wife. At least of the two explanations. So if you have any doubt or if you think she might have tripped or even been knocked by the frightened pony when you blew your horn, then you may wish to express that view,' said Simon gently.

'That's true, luv,' said Lily. 'It would be awful for her poor mother to think her child had committed suicide if it was an accident.'

'Yeah, well I s'pose she could have been knocked off balance now that I think about it. I think actually that the pony spooked when I blew the horn. It's pretty loud and probably terrified the animal. In my mind it looked as if the child had sprung from nowhere, not nowhere, from the side of the road, but now as you mention it, I suppose it looked more likely she had been knocked or even kicked or pushed by the pony. It seems more likely,' said Nick, with a growing conviction.

'The point is, Nick, that if there's any doubt... think of the added distress for my wife. You wouldn't want to make a mistake, I'm sure,' said Simon, with a spread of his hands. 'Do you think that is the most likely thing that happened? We only want to get to the truth.'

'Well there is doubt, isn't there, Nick? You can see that now, what with that pony jumping or pulling or whatever it was she did. The child wouldn't want to jump in front of the lorry, would she, luv? Doesn't make sense,' said Lily encouragingly.

'Yeah, I think you're probably right,' added Nick.

'She was such a happy child, always smiling. The idea that she could have wanted to take her own life seems unimaginable to my wife and me. It would be so out of character.'

'Of course,' said Lily.

'The pony she was with, Pansy, is so strong. And, of course, any horse or pony that gets spooked is very often more than an adult can cope with, let alone a child. I can imagine Pansy giving an enormous jerk that could easily knock her off balance with such force that it could look like she was jumping.'

'D'you know, I think that's what must have happened. I blew the horn, the pony shied and sent the poor girl into the road as I drew level.'

'Well, as I say, you mustn't blame yourself, Nick. It was just a horrible accident.'

Simon felt he'd done enough. He didn't want to overdo it. He suddenly felt relaxed. 'Well, I won't keep you. As I say, the reason for my visit is to say how sorry my wife and I are that you had to face this. Nasty for everyone concerned,' said Simon and pushed out his hand. Nick stared at it and then limply took it.

'No problem. I'm sorry for your and your wife's loss,' said Nick.

'Thank you. It will take time. Goodbye, Mrs Jarvis,' said Simon and shook her hand also.

'Goodbye, Mr Hargreaves. Thank you for coming. Very kind of you. Give our best wishes to your wife,' said Lily.

'I will, thank you,' said Simon and turned and made his way to the front door. Nick followed and opened it and with a mere nod Simon strode down the path, got into his car and drove off.

As soon as he got to the end of the road, he took a deep breath, 'Yes!' he shouted and punched the air and then sped off for the motorway and headed for home.

****

DC Hughes wriggled her shoulders as she felt a slight shiver. She'd been to the mortuary on a few other occasions, and it wasn't her favourite place. She was still uncertain about whether or not she should have even come. Okay, she had this idea that this was the kind of dogged pursuit she should adopt if she wanted to be a real detective, but in her mind she knew that what she was thinking was pure conjecture. Even so, she couldn't shake off a nagging feeling about poor Bobby's death. She admitted that suicide was the least likely explanation, but if it had been, could there have been some other explanation than that she was grieving so much for her father? What that reason might be she didn't know. And she didn't want her imagination to go wild. She'd simply ask Dr Mathews a couple of simple questions, and if he couldn't shed any more light on his findings, then she would leave it at that.

The door opened a moment later, and the pathologist, Dr Mathews, came in. He was a big, jovial man in his fifties. He had a big, broad, friendly face, and he enjoyed his work, which he had done for many years. He didn't live locally and was one of the three pathologists accredited by the Home Office to carry out post mortems on behalf of the police in cases of a suspicious death or suicide. He'd met DC Hughes on two other occasions and liked her.

'Ah, DC Hughes. How nice to see you again,' he said with a broad smile.

'Hallo, Dr Mathews. Thank you for seeing me.'

'No problem. I'm heading home in about an hour. And as far as I know, there's only a little more here for me to do. How can I help?'

DC Hughes hesitated before speaking, 'Well, I just wanted to ask you a couple of questions about your findings with Bobby.'

'That poor child, yes. Poor might. Absolutely tragic. I've got my report almost together. Pretty straightforward accident. Horribly violent, but death would have been instantaneous.'

'Yes. That does seem to be what happened.'

'And?' Dr Mathews looked at DC Hughes with an arched eyebrow.

'Well... if, and I'm only saying "if" but if it wasn't an accident but suicide would there be any way of telling from your examination of her body that that was the case?'

'Your bosses have already asked me to consider if there is anything that may suggest that possibility. I didn't think they thought I'd find anything. Have you any strong reason for thinking that it wasn't a straightforward accident?'

'To be honest, no. At least, I have no evidence. It's been suggested that as she was grieving so much over the death of her father that it might have given her a motive, but there could be some other reason.'

'Like what?'

'Well, she could have been bullied at school. I've explored that, and it doesn't look as if that was the case, but I just have a gut feeling that as she went out secretly in the middle of the night it wasn't to have an accident but more likely to take her own life. And if it wasn't because of bullying and it wasn't because she missed her father so much, then it had to be for some other reason.'

'You're asking me to speculate about her body which suffered massive trauma pretty much to all her organs. Because she was a child I did consider the possibility of self-harm or even sexual abuse. If that's what you're thinking about.'

'Do you think that so far-fetched?

Not necessarily. I've tried to take swabs from the anus and vagina for analysis for semen, but her lower body was seriously damaged. It was almost impossible. I couldn't produce anything that would stand up in court.'

'Okay. It was just a thought. Were there any marks anywhere that simply seemed out of place or inconsistent with her other injuries?'

'You've been watching too many detective dramas.'

DC Hughes shrugged her shoulders, 'Oh well, maybe. I had to ask.'

'That's fine. As a matter of fact, there was one very small wound that I noticed which made me wonder, now that you mention it. Very small. I shall out it in my report. Probably nothing. I'll show you.'

He moved over to the wall and drew out a cadaver. He pulled back the sheet to reveal Bobby's body which made DC Hughes bite her lip to control her emotion. 'Are you okay?' asked Dr Mathews kindly.

DC Hughes nodded but didn't speak.

'Here,' he pointed to Bobby's left forearm. 'There's a very tiny incision. See it? No more than two inches long and not very deep. Done not very long ago, I should think.'

DC Hughes peered at the incision. She said, 'What does it tell you?'

'I'm not sure. I am certain, however, that it wasn't caused by the impact of the lorry. This was done with something very thin. Sharp. Something like a razor blade, I would have thought.'

'So it might have been self-inflicted?'

'That's possible.'

'Self-harm, in other words?'

Dr Mathews made no reply.

'I know this is making a big jump, but can you tell if she might have been interfered with sexually?'

'A very big jump. In any case, I couldn't answer that. As I've already said, the whole of her genitalia was completely crushed. I understand that when the lorry hit her – which would have killed her – she was thrown forward, and then he drove over her. Thirty or forty tons, I believe. It would be impossible to make even a guess.'

There was a silence for several moments.

'You have suspicions?'

'Not really. Just a gut feeling. I'm almost certainly wrong. Unless there was anything else.'

'I'm afraid that's all. I think that an accident will be the correct decision for the coroner,' said Dr Mathews. DC Hughes nodded.

'It was worth asking. Thanks for giving me your time.'

'Not at all. It's good to see our young police are on their toes. I wish you luck.' Dr Mathews put out his hand, and DC Hughes took it. 'Thank you.' She turned and went out. As soon as she got back in the car, she flopped back in her seat. 'Shit. I got it wrong or someone's very lucky.'

****

It was just before 11 o'clock on the day before the inquest when Pauline switched off the vacuum cleaner and put it away. It had become a kind of ritual every day

282

since Bobby had died. She went through the motions of doing housework, not really knowing what she was doing or even whether it needed doing. She moved around the house like a zombie, heavy-lidded and with a drooping head.

Although she went through the motions of doing housework, she didn't care whether it was done or not. She didn't care about anything anymore. She had Simon in her life of course, and she cried in his arms every night in bed, but the emptiness that seemed to fill her very being was always there. She wasn't living her life; she was simply existing. There was nothing for her now but dead time which dragged on day after day, night after night, that had no meaning. There was no school run; no making lunch sandwiches; no preparing tea at 4 o'clock; no clearing up a child's clothes strewn across her bedroom floor; no birthday parties; no nothing. She could be dead. Perhaps she was dead and didn't realise it, except that if she were dead she wouldn't be feeling such terrible pain.

She sat down at the kitchen table and rested her hands on the top and stared into space. Simon was coming home at 1 o'clock for lunch, as he had been doing for the last few days, so that she wouldn't be spending a whole day on her own. But she still had two hours to fill with the same emptiness. For a little while, she sat in silence with her eyes closed. She had been wanting to do something for several days but knew that the ordeal would have been beyond her. She had hardly entered Bobby's room. She had pushed the vacuum cleaner around, stripped the bed and washed the bedding, tidied up and then left it. But now she felt that by going in there she would find a special closeness.

Slowly, she made her way upstairs, then made her way along the landing and stopped outside Bobby's door. She put her hand on the door handle, but for a few moments she couldn't turn it. Then, with a supreme effort, she opened the door and went in. The room was filled with sunshine and Pauline felt a sense of welcoming. She stared around the room, registering all the bits and pieces that had always been there and which she knew so well. She wandered around, picking up knick-knacks, pieces of ribbon, brush and comb, a cheap jewellery box that had no jewellery in it, the framed photo of her first husband.

Inside the wardrobe, there was an assortment of shoes at the bottom and dresses hanging up. She fingered them, and lovingly touched the material to her face. On the chest of drawers, there was a small pile of books and some CDs which were beginning to gather dust. She opened the top drawer and smiled at the items of underwear and socks. The next one down contained T-shirts, blouses and cardigans, mostly pushed in together higgledy-piggledy. The bottom drawer contained jeans and shorts which she felt prompted to lift out and hold up. Two pairs had the knees threadbare, and she remembered how much Bobby loved them precisely because of that. It was when she went to put the jeans back that she spotted the notebook nearly concealed by the bottom pair. She lifted it out with a curious smile and went and sat down on the bed. For a moment or two, she idly flicked the pages from cover to cover, neither looking nor seeing what they displayed. Holding the book between her hands, she rested it down on her knees as if the effort of reading any of the contents was too much for her. She closed her eyes and tried to relax the muscles in her face. For so long, they had been screwed up either to hold back tears or allow them to flow freely. Moments passed; minutes passed; and then she idly picked up the exercise book again and began to turn the pages.

She had only scanned the first two pages before she felt a surge of goose pimples that scorched her skin at the same time as her heart took a leap. With trembling fingers, she started pulling back the pages, her eyes sweeping over the words that were written there. A grotesque expression of horror formed on her face. She let out a most terrible scream which went on and on and on. The screech was so wild and piercing it sounded as if some wild and unknown creature from the jungle was in the last throes of an agonising death. She began rolling around the room, clutching the notepad to her chest until the screaming subsided into uncontrollable moans, which in turn petered out to sobs as if a silent tidal wave swamped over her, stifling her breath. The room began to spin and her legs became lifeless. She fell back on to the bed and lay still for two or three minutes. She came around slowly, groping at empty space as if it would give her something to hang on to pull herself up.

As the room settled, and some strength returned to her legs, she rolled off the bed and steadied herself. She stood still and hunched, holding on to the footboard at the bottom of the bed to stop herself from collapsing on the floor. Her mouth was dry and her tears were dammed up behind her eyes, but in a little while, as if some primitive force had taken charge, she groped her way downstairs, clutching the notepad, and staggered out of the house. She scanned the road left and right as if she might see some monster, and shuffled her way to her car. With trembling fingers, she started up the engine, backed out and headed down the road.

It took her 15 minutes of erratic driving to get to the police station. She pulled off the main road into the car park without signalling, causing a following driver to honk his horn and swear at her out of the window. She switched off the engine and collapsed back into the seat. For a few minutes, she took deep breaths and exhaled slowly, but it did little to slow her pounding heart. Would she ever feel normal again? Would her world ever be normal again? She had never felt such emotions before. They were raw; burning, ripping her apart in different, erupting directions. Surely, this signalled the end of her nightmare, or maybe it indicated this was just the beginning. All she could think of now was Bobby; her beloved Bobby; her little girl who had come to her and whom she had failed. She herself, didn't matter anymore; only Bobby. Bobby was crying from the grave, and this time she would be heard.

****

At 1.15, Simon began to wonder where his wife was. He had been home for a quarter of an hour and had expected her to be there. Normally, the table was laid for lunch, and the cooker was turned on by the time he got home; but today the table was bare, and the cooker was cold. By half past one, he was starting to get anxious. Of course, he realised that Pauline was grieving so much about Bobby's awful death that her behaviour was likely to be erratic. She could have gone for a walk or seen one of her friends where she could simply sit down and talk. He was going to have to be exceptionally patient and comforting to her. Perhaps he should take her away for a holiday; a place that was quiet and in the countryside. It was going to take a long time for her to get over it and she probably never would.

On the other hand, he had his own sadness to think about. Bobby had meant so much to him and had given him so much pleasure. He had spent such a lot of time and effort on her to get what he wanted and know that he was safe. At least, he could feel fairly confident now about being safe. Her death would not be attributed to him in any way, and, in fact, he would continue to be seen as a man who had been caring and patient with her and full of understanding of her difficulties at having lost her real father. There was absolutely no way anyone could possibly suspect that he had been having sex with her. He felt confident that Richard Deakin wouldn't have blabbed about their connection outside of work, and the police wouldn't have found anything in Richard Deakin's house to incriminate him. The inquest would be just a formality. The coroner wouldn't be able to explain why Bobby would have been out on the A417 with Pansy in the middle of the night (nobody could) but he would almost certainly bring in a verdict of accidental death. Panic over.

All in all, once Bobby's funeral was out of the way, and things began to settle down, he would be able to turn his mind to his main concern which was finding a replacement for Bobby. He'd had high hopes of making progress with Suzie, Bobby's friend. She was such a beautiful child, and he had to admit he had often fantasised about her. He would have to tread carefully so as not to arouse any kind of suspicion, but he felt fairly confident that Charlotte's belief of Bobby's story of being abused by him would soon die a natural death, if it hadn't done so already. She was a sensible woman and would realise that Bobby's stories about being abused by him had been sheer fantasy. He would have to make sure that Pauline renewed their friendship. He would encourage her and it would all work out very nicely in the end. He would manage to get more access to Suzie, and he would have a chance to develop their friendship. Good. Things weren't so bad after all.

He looked at his watch and saw that it was now 1.45. He tut-tutted and pondered for a few moments. He thought it was better to give her a ring. He took out his mobile phone and touched her number. After a few rings, he got the recorded message that she was unavailable. May as well have a drink. Surely she wouldn't be much longer? If she intended to be really late, she would telephone him. He took a bottle of single malt whisky from the cabinet and poured himself nearly two inches. He took a large gulp and grimaced as the liquid scoured his throat. A moment later, the front door bell rang. He went through the hallway and opened it. Facing him were DS Phillips and three other police officers.

'Sergeant, what can I do for you?' said Simon in surprise.

'We have a search warrant to search your premises. May we come in, sir?' said DS Phillips and walked past Simon with the other officers in tow.

Simon felt the blood rushing to his cheeks. 'What's this all about, Sergeant?'

DS Phillips ignored his question. 'I understand you have a safe, sir. Could you give us the key, please?'

'That's all my private and confidential papers concerning work. I can't let you see that.' Simon's forehead began to get damp.

'The key, please, sir.' As he spoke another officer picked up Simon's laptop.

'Put that down. You can't have that.' The officer ignored him. 'I demand to speak to my solicitor. You can't just come barging in here like this.' His head jerked from side to side as he saw the other police officers opening drawers and pulling out books in the bookcase and generally turning things over as they went about their search.

'The key!' DS Phillips held out his hand and stared at Simon with a steely eye.

'What?'

'The safe. The key, please.'

'I'm not sure where I've put it. I mislaid it a few days ago.'

DS Phillips nodded at one of the officers, who moved to Simon's desk and began opening drawers. He didn't find the key in any of the drawers, but when he slipped his hand under the desktop, his fingers connected with a hook from which the key dangled. He immediately slipped the key into the lock of the safe that was built into the wall and opened the door. He pulled out a number of DVDs and photographs. He looked across at DS Phillips and nodded.

DS Phillips turned to Simon. 'Simon Hargreaves, I am arresting you on suspicion of possessing thousands of indecent images of children. You do not have to say anything, but it may harm your defence if you do not mention something when questioned which you may rely on in court. Anything you do say may be given in evidence.'

Simon stared back in horror. 'There must be some mistake, Sergeant.' Then he saw a police officer shut down his computer and placed it in a plastic bag.

'Hey, you can't have that,' Simon almost screamed.

'All your property will be returned in due course, sir,' said DS Phillips in a flat voice.

'This is absolutely outrageous. Do you realise I'm a magistrate?'

'Indeed, sir. Shall we go?' said DS Phillips, taking hold of Simon's hands and slipping on handcuffs.

'I'm expecting my wife, sergeant. I must wait for her. She'll be so worried.'

'Your wife will be all right, sir. We must go.'

'I need to call my lawyer,' Simon protested.

'All in good time, sir,' said DS Phillips, as he handed Simon to one of the other policemen whilst the other two continued their search.

Simon was led to a police car where he was pushed into a back seat. Simon's head began to spin, and he felt sick. This couldn't be happening. He had covered all the angles. Bobby was dead. There was no evidence, no proof, he'd swear blind his innocence and without her to contradict, the case would collapse.

Curse the search warrant because they would have found a huge amount of child pornography in his safe which would have to be opened, and the material on his computer would damn him. But even as these thoughts rushed through his mind, he knew he was doomed. He knew they must have evidence that he had abused Bobby. He'd missed something, and whatever it was, it would be his undoing. His lawyer would fight, but in the end, they would get him. There was no way out of it. He was headed for prison; a Vulnerable Prisoner wing to protect him from the other cons; cons who hated paedophiles. But they would get him; they always did, one way or another. Pain, horror, misery awaited him. As the car pulled away, he turned and looked back at his home which he would never see again.

Chapter Eighteen

It was almost 11 o'clock when Linda finished her third call of her shift which she had been doing with Sarah. She came out of the booth with a sigh. 'Husband's a compulsive gambler; been made redundant and spent the last of what small savings they had. She's at her wit's end,' she said and flopped into the seat at the table opposite Sarah.

'So everything is dandy in her life then,' said Sarah with a shrug.

'God, some people's lives: makes you realise how lucky you are,' said Linda. She and Sarah liked doing a shift together, although it didn't happen often. They had become good friends and saw each other socially sometimes.

It had been a fairly busy shift. Sarah had had two fairly long calls, both of over an hour each: one, talking to a woman who had just lost her husband after 50 years of marriage and was struggling with life on her own; the second one was from a 40-year-old woman who had tried to take her life on two or three occasions. As a child, she had been sexually abused from the age of ten to fifteen. When she was finally able to escape because her abuser, a close uncle, had died, she was able to gradually bury it at the back of her mind and get on with her life. But she had never told anybody about what had happened to her. In her late twenties, she got married and had two children and life had become fairly normal for her. But finally, the experiences of her abuse came back to the surface, and she had a nervous breakdown. In the end, she had revealed everything to her husband who tried to give her comfort. He had done his best to give her understanding, but it had not been enough, and her life had become misery. It was not an uncommon call.

Linda had had a face-to-face with a familiar caller: a schizophrenic who had become regular over a very long period of time. Having no friends and a family that rarely had time for him, he had found his occasional visits to the Centre a lifeline which had helped him ward off the thoughts of suicidal feelings which crept up on him when his mood began to go downhill. She had had a couple of sex calls and one from a man who said he had taken a massive dose of mixed pills in order to kill himself because he was in terrible debt. The phone had gone dead during their call, and she didn't know if he had passed out and would come around next day or if the cocktail of drugs was fatal. It was tough, but par for the course not to know what happened to their callers when the calls ended.

In between calls, Sarah and Linda had been able to snatch some chat and have a cup of coffee and would soon be going home. The next shift would be coming on to do the night duty, and the work would go on. Tomorrow, Linda would be back in her florist shop, and Sarah would be at the hospital doing her stint of nursing. They were two ordinary women; good women who had a sense of compassion for their fellow men. No pay, no medals, but they loved doing shifts just the same.

The phone rang in one of the booths. 'I'll get it,' said Sarah and went into the booth and lifted the receiver. 'Samaritans; can I help you?'

Down the phone came the sounds of weeping. Sarah waited for a little while. 'You sound so upset. It must have been hard for you to call,' she said in her gentlest of voices. 'There's no need for you to speak at the moment if it is too difficult. I won't go away. Just speak to me when you feel comfortable to do so.'

For a little while the weeping continued.

'I wish I was dead,' the words of the caller were slurred because of her weeping and Sarah sensed a deeply traumatised woman.

'You sound so unhappy.'

'I have to tell... I have to tell someone who will listen ...' said the woman.

'Just take your time. I will listen to everything you tell me. My name is Sarah. Anything you tell me is confidential. I'm so glad you rang,' Sarah whispered into the phone.

'I can't bear it... I can't... my child killed herself...'

'Oh, that's so terrible for you.'

'I should have known. I should have listened.'

'I'm sure you loved your child and did everything for her.'

'He abused her... my husband. She tried to tell me, but I wouldn't listen, and now she's dead,' the caller stumbled through her tears and then there was at least a minute of heart-rending crying. Eventually, 'My lovely Bobby. My lovely Bobby. Gone forever.'

Sarah felt the blood shoot through her veins as realisation overwhelmed her. She quickly got hold of herself. 'She must have been the dearest love for you,' she said as gently as she could.

'She was. She was. She was so lovely, and I didn't listen. My poor, poor Bobby.'

Sarah was stunned to realise that the caller must be Pauline, Bobby's mother. For a little while she said nothing. She knew it was right to be quiet and resist the urge to say something which could sound completely useless.

'I'm so sorry. Losing Bobby will be a terrible loss for you.'

'I found her book; a school book in her bedroom. She'd written it all down and hidden it from the world, but now I know, but it's all too late.'

'Stay and tell me all about Bobby. For as long as you like, let us talk. Tell me about your child and your lovely memories of her,' said Sarah gently.

'The man I loved I thought was wonderful... but he was a monster.' Again, she couldn't hold back uncontrollable tears.

'I won't go away. I'll stay with you all night if you need me to.'

Slowly the tears subsided into intermittent sobs. 'It all started just over a year ago. I had lost my first husband when Simon came into my life...'

The End

Author's Note

Samaritans was started in 1953 by Chad Varah, a clergyman, with a handful of volunteers. Since then, it has grown from its humble beginnings to over 200 branches in the UK with many thousands of listening volunteers.

More than ever today, callers from every age, race or religion and from every walk of life, who are suffering from emotional stress and anguish, sometimes to the point of considering suicide, call on them in their thousands, 24/7, 365 days a year.

The callers do so in the certain knowledge that they will not be judged and that everything that reveal will be held in absolute confidentiality unless they give their permission to do otherwise.

There is in place a small team of specialist professionals who can be called upon on very rare occasions to make decisions whether intervention is thought necessary on any caller of any age because of the need for safeguarding. But always as is the way of things, identity and location need to have been willingly offered.

NW